Shooting
Star

Sometimes you find what you didn't
even know you were looking for...

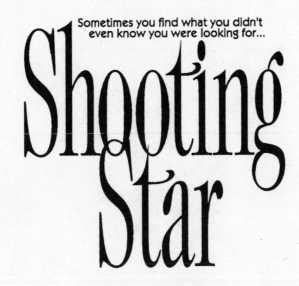

Shooting Star

ROSEY GRIER
AND
KATHI MILLS

THOMAS NELSON PUBLISHERS
Nashville

Published in Nashville, Tennessee, by Thomas Nelson, Inc., Publishers, and distributed in Canada by Word Communications, Ltd., Richmond, British Columbia, and in the United Kingdom by Word (UK), Ltd., Milton Keynes, England.

Library of Congress information

Grier, Rosey.
    Shooting star / Rosey Grier and Kathi Mills.
        p.   cm.
    ISBN 0-8407-7736-1 (pbk.)
    I. Mills, Kathi, 1948– . II. Title.
PS3557.R48838S48   1993
813'.54—dc20   93-18407
                                                                   CIP

Printed in the United States of America

2 3 4 5 6 7 - 98 97 96 95

To my friends Mike and Lori Milken—
We're with you in this struggle and we will win.

—Rosey Grier

To the one who is my source and inspiration
for everything.

—Kathi Mills

His chest heaved and his well-worn Nikes slapped the pavement as he pushed himself onward through the almost deserted streets of suburban Los Angeles. Squinting into the setting sun, Brett Holiday barely noticed the well-kept older homes along the tree-lined neighborhood where he jogged. It was much like the neighborhood where he had grown up in Colorado Springs, the neighborhood where he had first played—and fallen in love with—the game of football.

But that was twenty-five years ago, when Brett was still a kid in grammar school, a kid with a dream and a future. Everything seemed to be out there ahead of him then.

Now, the distant sound of a barking dog didn't even register on Brett's consciousness. The only sound he could hear was the roar of yesterday's crowds, cheering him on to another victory. Brett Holiday. Star quarterback for the Los Angeles Rams. Everybody's hero. The one they could count on to come up with that brilliant last-second play, that miraculous Hail-Mary pass that would bring his adoring fans to their feet, screaming and shouting in triumph and admiration.

And then, at the height of his career, Brett sustained a severe knee injury. Although he had worked his way back, the recovery had been a long one. In the interim, he was replaced as starting quarterback by Chuck Nelson, a younger, more agile player. The fact that Brett was now known as the Rams' "number-one backup quarterback" only added insult to injury.

With the back of his arm he wiped the sweat from his forehead before it could drip down into his eyes, then rounded the corner into an alley. His curly blond hair lay plastered to his head in damp ringlets. A baggy pair of blue and gold Rams shorts was all he wore besides some stretched-out, not-so-white socks, which had already slid down inside his shoes. His skin glistened in the dying rays of sunlight, and his breath came in gasps, irritating him.

I used to run twice this far without getting winded, he thought. *Not anymore. Besides, even if I could run like I did before the injury, I still probably wouldn't get my starting position back. Not with that Chuck Nelson kid around. He's quick and he's smart—and he's young. How do I compete with that? How do I—*

He saw it from the corner of his eye. The flash of movement behind the trash cans. Quick. So quick it almost didn't register in his mind. But Brett's vision was still sharp and clear, trained to catch even the slightest motion as his piercing blue eyes swept hawk-like across the entire expanse of a football field. Within the close proximity of the alley, even with his mind preoccupied as it had been, any sudden movement was bound to catch his attention.

Every instinct warned him to push on, to ignore whoever or whatever was hiding behind those cans, to escape while he still had the chance. But even as his heart hammered in his chest—from exhaustion or from fear, he wasn't sure which—he knew he would stop.

Offense. The word shot through his mind. A reminder? A warning? Either way, he understood its meaning. He wouldn't edge slowly, defensively toward the trash cans, allowing his fear to rule his actions. He would, instead, go on the offensive, take command of the situation, as he was trained to do. He was, after all, a quarterback—a leader, not a follower—and he knew from experience that points were scored by the offensive line. He squared his shoulders and strode purposefully toward the cans, trying to control his wild breathing.

"All right, come out from behind there!" he ordered, grabbing the handle of one can and jerking it away from the others.

The dark eyes that stared up at him from beneath the short-cropped ebony hair showed only a momentary hint of fear before going hard and cold. They were set in a lean face, mahogany in color, with hints of brown and gold shadows from the setting sun dancing across his skin, creating a vulnerable effect against his otherwise angry features. His lips parted slightly, as if he couldn't decide whether to curse at Brett or to spit on him. It was a face that made Brett's hammering heart stop cold in his chest. A face he knew he would never forget.

It was the face of a cynical old man, an old man who had seen too many of life's disappointments to expect anything but the worst of what the world had to offer. But Brett wasn't staring down at an old man. He was staring at a long, gangly boy of no more than thirteen or fourteen, crouched on his knees, looking for all the world like a wild panther, ready to pounce and fight for survival against anyone who threatened his territory. Brett knew immediately that included him.

Their eyes locked; neither of them spoke. Brett wondered which of them was more scared. He wondered why the boy was hiding behind a trash can. He wondered what the boy was thinking. He wondered what, if anything, he should say to the boy. Then Brett wondered why in the world he didn't just turn around and walk away—better yet, turn around and run away—and leave this kid to get on with whatever he had been doing before he was discovered. As Brett tried to convince himself that this would be the wisest course of action, the boy's mouth began to move. The words that came out were the words of a man, but the crack in his voice betrayed him for the unsure adolescent that he was.

"Hey, man, who you think you are!" he demanded, unfolding himself from his uncomfortable position and lifting himself upright, his bony shoulders thrown back as he raised his head and looked Brett right in the eye. "What you mean comin' 'round here botherin' people, dude? You think you own this alley or somethin'?"

Brett heard the boy's words, but couldn't think of a thing to say. After all, the kid was right, he didn't own the alley, and he supposed the kid had as much right to be there as he did. Still, there was something. . . .

"Hey, man, what's wrong with you, dude?" the boy asked. "Can't you talk, or what?"

Brett realized suddenly that he'd allowed himself to be taken off the offense and put on defense. The kid was sharp. He knew what he was doing. Brett cleared his throat.

"I can talk just fine," he answered, hoping his voice sounded more authoritative than he felt. "I just don't like people sneaking around, that's all. What are you doing back here hiding behind trash cans, anyway?"

"What's it to you?" the boy asked, defiantly jutting out his chin. "It's a free country, ain't it? Least that's what you white folks always tellin' us." He looked down briefly and nodded toward the trash cans. "This here trash got your name on it or somethin'?"

Brett shook his head. "No, it's not my trash. And it's not my alley." He paused a moment, their eyes meeting once again. "And I guess it's not my business, either, is it?" he asked, turning to walk away. He'd taken only a few steps when he heard the boy call out to him.

"Hey, man, wait a minute."

Brett turned back. The boy moved toward him slowly, his head cocked to one side as if he were studying him. He raised his hand and pointed a long, thin finger at Brett's face. "I know you, dude," the boy announced. "You used to be a football player or somethin', right?"

Brett winced. *Used to. Has-been. Number-one backup.* Everybody knew. Even black kids who hung out in alleys knew. They all knew.

"I play for the Rams," he said, his jaws tightening as, once again, he felt himself on the defensive. "I'm a quarterback."

The boy nodded slowly. "Yeah, now I remember. You used to be pretty good, huh? 'Fore you got hurt. Now they got that new dude. What's his name? Nelson? Man, he's great! And fast! Taller than you, too, ain't he?"

Brett winced again. This kid was beginning to get on his nerves.

The boy opened his mouth to go on, but before he could speak, Brett noticed for the first time how tight and dirty his thin T-shirt was. He glanced down at the boy's jeans. They were so baggy it was a wonder they didn't slide right off his straight, almost nonexistent hips. His worn-out tennis shoes looked several sizes too small.

"Hey, dude, don't let it bother you, man," the kid was saying. "I mean, as long as they let you sit on the bench and keep collectin' that fat salary, who cares, right?" He flashed a smile, and Brett was surprised to see it looked almost sincere. "I'll bet you make enough bread to go anywhere you want, huh?"

Brett shrugged. "I do all right," he answered, wondering where the conversation was headed.

"Yeah, well, I know where I'd go if I had all that bread," the boy announced. "To New York!"

Brett raised his eyebrows. "New York? Why New York?"

The boy laughed. "Why not? It's big and it's fast and I ain't never been there. 'Sides, I hear they got some great lookin' chicks in New York." He laughed again, and Brett couldn't help but smile.

"You don't have to go to New York to find great looking chicks," he told the boy. "There's plenty of them right here in L.A., you know."

"Oh yeah?" the boy asked, raising one eyebrow as a grin spread across his face. His dark eyes sparkled with mischief. "Show me one," he demanded. "I ain't seen none 'round here lately."

"No kidding," said Brett. "Just how many great looking chicks do you suppose are going to come strolling down this alley? And if they did, you think they'd be interested in somebody who hides behind trash cans?"

The boy's grin disappeared and his dancing eyes faded back to hard. "Hey, man, why don't you get outta here? Go on, get back where you came from! I got things to do 'sides stand 'round here all day and talk to some old used-to-be honky football star."

"Like what?" Brett challenged, ignoring the deliberate insult. "Just what is it you got to do, anyway? You never did tell me what you were doing hanging around those trash cans."

The boy's eyes narrowed and Brett shivered slightly as he felt the brisk evening breeze against his damp body. These early April days could be warm, but the temperatures dropped quickly when the sun set. As he stared at the skinny black kid standing in front of him, the truth suddenly ripped through Brett. The boy hung out in the alley because he had no place else to go. Could it be that he was rummaging through the trash looking for something to keep him warm? Worse yet, for something to eat? He didn't want to believe it, but the longer he stared into the ageless eyes of this defiant man-child, he knew he was right.

"Forget it," said Brett. "It's a free country, like you said. You want to hang around trash cans, it's your business." He shrugged and turned slightly, as if to go. "Me, I'm getting kinda hungry. Think I'll head on home and see if dinner's ready." He hesitated, trying his best to look indifferent. "You, uh, . . . you want to come along?"

The boy looked surprised. "Me? To your house? You gotta be kiddin', man. I ain't never been to no white man's house for dinner. 'Sides, I . . . I got other plans."

"Yeah?" Brett shrugged again. "Well, whatever you say. Of course, if you think you could change those plans, I wouldn't mind having some company on the way home. Gonna be dark soon. Cold, too."

The boy gazed into the distant skyline. The sun was gone. The sky had turned a faint purple in the ever-present L.A. smog. His thin face and oversized eyes mirrored the loneliness of the approaching night. Brett looked away. He didn't want to embarrass the boy by staring at him.

"Yeah, well, maybe I could," the boy conceded. "Just this once, dude."

Brett smiled. "By the way," he said, "my name's Brett. Brett Holiday."

The boy nodded. "I know," he said. "I heard it before."

Brett waited. The boy shifted his weight uneasily, as if trying to decide whether or not to identify himself. Brett could see the struggle going on within the boy. When he finally opened his mouth to announce his name, Brett felt as if he'd gained a victory. That's when he realized that the boy's name was all he had to give away.

"I'm Fox," the boy said. "Fox Richards."

"Fox, huh?" asked Brett, a smile teasing his lips. "Where'd you ever get a name like that?"

The boy's head jerked up defensively and his dark eyes blazed. "Somethin' wrong, dude?" he asked. "You don't like my name, or what?"

Brett tried to cover his amusement. "No, nothing's wrong," he said. "I think it's a great name. It's just . . . well, it doesn't sound like a name a mother would give a kid, that's all. Must be a nickname, right?"

The boy hesitated briefly. "Yeah," he admitted. "Yeah, it's a nickname. My real name is . . . Elmore. Like my . . . like somebody my mama used to know." He glared at Brett, daring him to respond.

Wisely, Brett didn't.

"Come on, Fox," said Brett, nodding toward the end of the alley. "Let's get home. I'm starved, aren't you?"

Fox shrugged. "I could eat," he admitted. "Say, dude, did I hear you say somethin' 'bout dinner bein' ready? That mean you got somebody at home fixin' it for you? A wife or somethin'?"

Brett groaned silently as, for the first time since meeting Elmore "Fox" Richards, he remembered Ariane. Beautiful Ariane. His loving—but not so patient—wife. His wife who was probably already annoyed with him for being late for dinner. As they turned their faces toward home, he swallowed a laugh, suddenly remembering a line from one of his favorite Sidney Poitier movies.

Maybe, he thought, *I could just walk in and announce, "Guess who's coming to dinner!" No,* he decided with a sigh, *it'll never work. If there's one thing my wife hates, it's surprises. And this particular dinner guest is definitely going to be a surprise!*

CHAPTER 2

Ariane slammed the oven door shut for the fourth time, threw her potholders down on the cream-colored linoleum floor and stomped out of the kitchen into the living room, where she plunked down in the plush white recliner, angrily chewing her fingernail.

Late again! she fumed silently. *How could he do this to me? He knows I only have a couple of nights every week when I don't have to go to school. You'd think he'd want to spend them here with me, not out jogging, trying to prove he's still young! I don't know who it is he's trying to impress. . . .*

She realized then what she was doing and jerked her hand away from her mouth. With all the money she spent having her nails done, she wasn't about to ruin them just because her husband couldn't make it home in time for dinner! So what if the tuna casserole was ruined. So what if she'd stopped at the bakery on the way home from work and picked up Brett's favorite dessert. So what if she'd planned a romantic evening alone, just the two of them. So what if her husband preferred to spend the evening running around who-knows-where by himself, finally dragging in late—not to mention hot, tired, and sweaty. So what! She jumped up from the chair and stormed back into the kitchen to turn off the oven.

"Let it get cold," she grumbled. "Why not? It's already burned. If he doesn't care, why should I?" She took one last peek inside the oven, then slammed the door shut again, and switched off the control.

I work at that law office all day long, she thought, glancing over at her neatly set table. *I run errands like some flunky for those stuffed-shirt bosses of mine, then come home and try to make a nice dinner for somebody who doesn't even appreciate it. All he worries about is the end of his precious career. He doesn't even think about how hard I'm working to get mine started.*

She sighed impatiently and absentmindedly began to chew on another nail. *You'd think he'd offer me a little more encouragement once in a while. It's a long hard pull to get a law degree, and sometimes I wonder if it's all worth it. I mean, it's not like we need the money or anything. Sometimes I think if I hadn't spent so many years dreaming about becoming a lawyer, I'd just forget the whole thing. Especially when he acts like this and doesn't even show up for—*

She heard the front door open and wheeled around, tossing her dark hair angrily, her eyes blazing as she stood, hands on hips, ready to confront her husband.

"It's about time!" she began. "Where in the world have you. . . ?"

Her voice trailed off as Brett stopped in the kitchen doorway. His blond curls were still wound tightly to his head, but they were no longer wet, as they usually were when he came in from running. In fact, he wasn't sweaty or out of breath at all. But the look on his face was one she had seen many times before. That sweet, little-boy look that she just couldn't resist, even in her angriest moments. She sensed right away, however, that this time

was different. No way—*no way*—was he going to be able
to come up with an acceptable explanation for the
scruffy, defiant-looking black kid standing in the doorway next to him.

"Hi, honey," he said, his voice a bit too cheery. "I'd
like you to meet Elmore . . . I mean, Fox Richards. Fox,
this is my wife, Ariane."

Fox nodded almost imperceptibly in Ariane's direction. The silence hung over the kitchen like a shroud, as
the three of them stood motionless, each waiting for the
other to speak. Finally, Brett cleared his throat.

"Uh, I invited Fox to stay for dinner," he explained,
as faint beads of perspiration began to show on his
forehead and upper lip. He smiled then, and when
Ariane saw how ridiculously uncomfortable he looked,
she almost burst out laughing.

Almost. But not quite.

"Well," she said, forcing a smile, "how nice. It's
always such a pleasure to have unexpected dinner
guests." She cut her eyes meaningfully toward Brett,
then back again to Fox. "Why don't you *both* go on into
the bathroom and wash up," she suggested, "while I set
an extra place for . . . Elmore, is it?"

The boy's eyes came to life for an instant. "Fox," he
said. "The name is Fox."

"Fox," she repeated, resisting the temptation to
turn and glare at her husband. "Yes, of course."

She heard the water running in the bathroom as she
retrieved the potholders from the floor, opened the
oven door, and stood staring at the blackened casserole.
Brett and Fox hardly spoke as they walked back into the
kitchen, but she could hear the chairs scrape behind her,
the soft clatter of silver bumping against china as they
sat down and pulled the chairs up to the table.

How could Brett do this to her? It was bad enough
that he'd been late and ruined their evening together,
but this! Where in the world had he picked up this
shabby looking kid? And why had he invited him into

their home? For all they knew, he could be a thief—or worse! What if he were on drugs? Or in a gang? She'd heard somewhere that gang members all had nick-names, and Fox certainly sounded like a gang name to her. Now that he knew where they lived, he could bring his entire gang back and steal everything they owned—after they shot up the place, that is, along with everyone in it. Oh no, this was the last straw. This time she would put her foot down. Maybe this was all part of her husband's early mid-life crisis, but she was not about to tolerate it.

She whirled around, casserole in hand, and was about to slam the dish down on the table and demand some answers, when she caught sight of Fox, his skinny shoulders straining against his too tight T-shirt, staring at his reflection in the gleaming, exquisite china dinner plate in front of him. In that brief instant, Ariane saw the vulnerable young boy peek out from behind the mask of the hardened old man. She looked quickly at Brett to see if he, too, had seen it, but he wasn't looking at Fox. He stared at her, his blue eyes pleading for understanding. She sighed and set the casserole down gently.

Maybe, she told herself, *maybe it will be all right. It is just dinner, after all. And it's just this once. . . .*

The incongruous sight of the dried, burned casse-role sitting in the middle of the elegantly set table turned her cheeks crimson. *Darn you, Brett Holiday,* she thought, flashing him a withering look that assured him the subject was far from closed—they would definitely get to the bottom of all this later, once their "guest" had gone. For now, however, she would agree to a temporary truce.

She sat down, bowed her head, and waited for Brett to say grace. He hesitated for an instant, then prayed. As Ariane looked up, she caught Fox studying Brett, his eyes narrowed thoughtfully. When Brett returned his gaze, Fox's jaw clenched self-consciously, and he quickly dropped his eyes toward the dehydrated casserole. That's when Ariane remembered the steak.

"Do you like steak?" she asked impulsively, wondering even as she said it what had come over her.

Fox jerked his head up in surprise. "What?"

"I said, do you like steak?"

He frowned, tilting his head to one side as if trying to decide whether or not she was joking.

Once again, Ariane flushed with embarrassment. "What I mean is, I have a steak in the refrigerator and I just wondered if . . . well, since the casserole is burned and all . . . would you like me to fix it for you? The steak, I mean? It'll only take a few minutes and . . ."

She stopped as the lines in his forehead smoothed out and his dark eyes grew wide. "You gonna fix me a steak?" he asked.

"I'd be happy to," she said, "if you just let me know how you like it."

He frowned again, seemingly confused. "What you talkin' 'bout? How am I s'posed to like it?"

Now Ariane was confused. Didn't this kid know anything? "What I meant was," she explained, "do you want it well done, medium, or rare?"

The boy studied her for a moment. "What's fastest?" he asked.

Ariane almost regretted even offering the steak. It seemed the kid answered her every question with one of his own. "Rare's the fastest," she said impatiently.

A grin spread across his face and Ariane felt her irritation melting. "Then that's how I like it," he said. "Rare."

Ariane ignored the grin on Brett's face and turned toward the refrigerator. She had planned to barbecue the steak over the weekend. Oh well, she could always go back to the store.

"What you gonna do with this here casserole?" asked Fox as Ariane took the steak out of the refrigerator. She turned back to the table, about to explain that she would throw it down the garbage disposal, but stopped when she saw the look in Fox's eyes.

Brett must have seen it, too, because he quickly dipped the serving spoon into the casserole and scooped a large helping onto his own plate. "I'm gonna eat it while we wait for the steak," he announced, offering the spoon to Fox. "How about you?"

Fox hesitated for an instant, then shrugged and grabbed the spoon from Brett. "Sure, dude, why not?"

By the time Ariane put the steak on the table, she was sure Fox would never be able to eat it. He had already downed three helpings of burned casserole and two large glasses of milk. But he didn't miss a beat. Any hesitancy he might have exhibited when he first sat down at the table had long since disappeared as he stabbed the largest cut of meat and plopped it down on his plate. Ariane watched in amazement as he devoured it without once looking up.

Ariane picked at her own food, then glanced over at Brett. He watched her again, with those baby blue eyes she had never been able to resist. In spite of herself, she gave him one of her I-love-you-anyway smiles, then turned back to Fox. He had just finished and laid his fork on his plate.

"That was real good," he said, not quite looking up. "But I gotta hit the road, man. It's late and I gotta get . . . goin'. . . ."

The last word trailed off as he slowly stood to leave. Ariane thought of asking him to stay for dessert, but her relief at seeing him go stopped her. Still, the nagging questions in the back of her mind confused her. She knew nothing about this boy, other than his name—which wasn't much of a name, as far as she was concerned. Where had Brett found him? Why in the world had he brought him here for dinner? And just where was it that Fox was so anxious to go? Home? If so, why hadn't he mentioned his family? Or asked to call them, for that matter. Ignoring the unanswered questions, she got up to walk Fox to the door. She was surprised when Brett didn't do the same.

"Hold on a minute," said Brett, smiling and winking at Fox. "I mean, what's your hurry? You got a hot date with one of those great looking chicks of yours in New York or something?"

Fox didn't return Brett's smile. "Maybe I do," he said, scowling. "Maybe I do and maybe I don't. Maybe that's where I'm goin' and maybe it ain't. What's it to you anyway?"

Brett shrugged. "Just curious," he said. "After all, it's dark and it's cold, and awfully late to be taking off for anywhere as far away as New York. If I were you, I'd wait until morning to start out on a trip like that. Unless, of course, you had somewhere closer in mind."

Fox's jaw clenched again, and suddenly Ariane realized what Brett had already known. Fox had nowhere to go. Not home, not New York, not anywhere.

Even so, she told herself, there were hundreds of homeless people—kids included—sleeping in the streets. What could she and Brett possibly do about it?

The police, she thought. *Of course. They'll find him a place to stay for the night. Maybe if I suggest it gently. . . .*

Suddenly, Brett scraped his chair back from the table and stood up. "I just thought that," he said, his eyes zeroing in on Fox, "since it's so late and all . . . and since we have an extra bed . . . what I mean is . . ."

Ariane's heart skipped a beat. What in the world was her husband doing? Surely he wasn't thinking of . . . ?

"Stay with us tonight," Brett blurted out, his words building in speed and intensity and running together into one breathless plea. "Just for tonight, you can sleep in the guest room, the bed's all made and it's no trouble or anything, and then you can leave in the morning, I'll even take you somewhere if you want, it's no problem, really." He took a deep breath as his eyes darted toward Ariane. "You don't mind, do you, honey?"

Ariane's mouth dropped open in amazement, but she said nothing. She knew that once she'd had time to recover from the shock she would have plenty to say, but for the moment, her husband's words silenced her. She was even more shocked when Fox finally answered.

"Yeah, why not, dude?" he said nonchalantly, shrugging his shoulders as if staying overnight with people he'd just met was something he did all the time. "I am kinda tired. And like you said, man, I can always leave in the mornin'."

*

It was going to be a long night, he could tell. And certainly not a pleasant one. With Fox bedded down in the next room, Brett had hoped to be able to talk to Ariane, to explain to her why he'd asked Fox to stay, why he'd *had* to ask him. But now that they were finally alone in their king-sized bed—the one place where they always seemed able to work through just about anything—he had no explanation to give her. And it was obvious from the two feet of empty bed between them that she was in no mood to listen to anything he had to say. Still, he knew he had to try.

"Ariane," he whispered. "Honey, we need to talk."

Silence. He tried again, slightly louder this time. "Ariane, please listen to me. Talk to me. I know you're upset, but—"

"Upset!" she cried, bolting up from her pillow to a sitting position, the outline of her body tense and rigid in the semidarkness. Brett could feel her anger piercing through him as surely as if she were shooting him full of poison darts. "You think I'm upset? Well, I'm not upset, Brett Holiday. I'm furious! Do you hear me? Furious! How dare you—"

"Shhh," he whispered. "Ariane, please, he's right in the next room."

"Of course he is," she went on, lowering her voice to an angry stage whisper. "Of course he's in the next room. Why do you think I'm furious? And just whose fault is it that we have someone we know nothing about sleeping in our guest room, someone who, for all we know, may be a rapist or a murderer?"

"Ariane, please," Brett begged. "Try to think about this rationally for a minute. We couldn't very well send him out into the street. He's only a kid, for Pete's sake, not some desperate criminal."

"How do you know?" she demanded. "You don't know anything about him, do you? Not anything. Admit it. You don't even know if Elmore 'Fox' Richards is his real name. I mean, really, can you imagine anyone giving their own child a name like that? I think it's a gang name, or else something he just made up when he met you, a fake—just like him. As a matter of fact, I think he's a juvenile delinquent con-artist and I think you got suckered."

"Hey, now wait just a minute," said Brett, sitting up to face her. "What about you? Whose idea was it to fix that steak, huh? Come on, admit it. The kid got to you, too, didn't he? A little bit, anyway, right? Right?"

Ariane hesitated for a moment. "All right," she whispered. "Maybe a little. But there's a lot of difference between fixing someone a decent meal and offering him the run of the house. I can't believe you did that. You didn't even ask me. I was going to suggest calling the police or something."

Brett took her gently by the arms. "Listen to me, sweetheart. Be reasonable. How could I ask you? There was no time. I had to decide right then and there, before he left. And if we'd even mentioned the police, he would have bolted, I'm sure of it. Try to understand, babe. Just calm down and think about it for a minute. Right now, you're overreacting. You know how emotional you get sometimes."

She shook his hands free and pulled her arms away, her voice rising once again. "Don't you start in on that again, Brett Holiday. You're always accusing me of overreacting and being too emotional, especially when you know you're wrong and I'm right. That's your way of trying to win an argument, but it's not going to work, do you hear me?"

Her voice shook by then, but she took a deep breath and returned to a whisper. "Brett, I want that boy out of this house first thing in the morning, understand?"

Brett tried once more to touch her, but she pulled away as if she'd been burned.

"Don't touch me," she ordered. "Don't even talk to me until you tell me that kid is gone. Out of our house and out of our lives. For good."

She flopped over onto her side and lay with her face to the wall, the straight line of her back shutting Brett out in a way she'd never done in all their six years of marriage.

*

By the time Fox had climbed out of the hot shower and into a pair of Brett's oversized pajamas, he was sure he'd fall asleep as soon as his head hit the pillow. It was, after all, the first pillow he'd laid his head on in a while. The cool, crisp feel of the white muslin sheets caressed his tired body like the hands of a loving mother he could scarcely remember. His stomach felt full—almost painfully so—for the first time in days, and he probably would have drifted right off if it hadn't been for the argument.

He tried not to listen at first, but each time Ariane's voice would rise, it was impossible not to hear her.

Furious. That's what she'd said. Furious because of him. Furious because somebody she didn't know was sleeping in her nice clean bed. Fox wondered if she'd have been as furious if he were white. He wondered if she'd take those nice clean sheets off her nice clean bed in the morning and wash them—or just throw them away.

They're all the same, he told himself. *Every one of 'em. Actin' all uppity one minute 'cause you're standin' there in their fancy house, then fixin' some big steak when you didn't even ask for it. She didn't fool me none. Him neither. Big fancy football dude, can't even stand up to his own wife. Not me, man. Never catch me takin' no lip from no woman! Don't care how good lookin' she is. Who needs it, dude. . . .*

He put the pillow over his head to drown out any further outbursts from Ariane. But the pillow wasn't enough to drown out the fragmented snatches of memories that haunted him, even though he'd tried to outrun them for years.

"He just like his no-good daddy," the boyfriend used to say. "You watch. He end up jus' like him. A bum and a wino. Maybe he even end up dyin' in jail, too. I'm tellin' you, woman, the boy's no-good."

In the beginning, his mother had tried to defend him—but not for long. Fox would lie awake in the darkness and listen to them, willing his mother to be strong, to fight for him, to believe in him, to say it wasn't true—that Fox wouldn't end up like his father. But in the end, she'd given in. She chose the boyfriend, and he'd never seen his mother again.

Fox pressed the soft pillow tighter against his ears, refusing to cry, and wondered what Brett and Ariane found to fight about when they didn't have some stranger staying in their extra room and eating their food. He'd bet they found something. He'd never known of one family—not one—that didn't fight and eventually break up. The football dude and his good-looking wife weren't any different. He gave them two years. Two years, at the outside. Then they could divide up their nice clean sheets and their shiny plates and silverware and hit the streets—like him. Like he planned to do, first thing in the morning.

Yeah, he told himself, *that's what I'm gonna do. Clear outta here 'fore that football dude and his so-called furious wife wake up. And then I'm headin' for New York. . . .*

CHAPTER 3

Brett watched as the first gray light of dawn filtered softly through the peach-colored drapes, a nagging reminder that he couldn't put things off much longer. He had tossed and turned most of the night, dozing only fitfully as conscious thoughts and dream-images blurred together, confusing and unnerving him, leaving him more tired than when he had first closed his eyes in a vain attempt to sleep.

He glanced over at Ariane. She slept peacefully, as she had throughout the night, her long dark hair a beautiful, tangled mess, fanning out on the pillow around her. He listened to her gentle, even breathing, and was amazed that he could feel such a sense of irritation and resentment, yet still feel irresistibly drawn to her at the same time.

She had always affected him that way. From the first time he had laid eyes on Ariane almost seven years earlier, he was overwhelmed by her graceful, sensuous beauty. He also was intrigued by her volatile personality, the myriad of intense emotions dancing just below the surface, waiting only for the slightest provocation to burst into flames like the fire that burned in her emerald eyes, consuming everything in its path. Including Brett.

From the moment he had realized that the love glowing in those captivating eyes was directed at him, he was never again in possession of his heart. There were even times in the beginning when she seemed to own his mind, too. His every thought was somehow linked to her. Where was she? What was she doing? What was she wearing? Was she thinking of him? He was a man tormented, and he knew he would never find peace until he had convinced her to marry him. Much to his relief and joy, she readily agreed. Peace, however, was not what he found in his marriage to this hot-blooded, passionate young woman.

It hadn't taken Brett long to learn that as quickly and easily as the heat of love could blaze in his wife's eyes, so could the heat of anger. She was a woman who did nothing halfway. Since she had committed herself to love him, he could rest assured that she always would—with every ounce of her being. But when she was angry enough to deliver an ultimatum, she wouldn't back down easily. The ultimatum she had given him the night before left no room for doubt as to what she expected from Brett regarding Elmore "Fox" Richards.

He sighed. Had he been wrong to invite this unknown boy—obviously hungry and alone—into their home? Had he gone too far in offering him one night's sleep with a roof over his head and a bed to lie down on? And what was Brett to do with the kid now? Order him out into the street once again, to sleep in alleys and forage through trash cans for his next meal?

Wait a minute, he told himself. *Now I'm the one who's overreacting here. After all, this kid is not my problem. I don't know anything about him—who he is, where he's from, where his family is, or why he's not with them. Ariane's right. I should have called the police. They must know some place he can go.*

He sighed again and lifted himself out of bed. Sliding into his robe, he padded quietly past his still-sleeping wife and out into the hall to the guest room. The door opened without a sound. Brett peeked in to find the bed empty, the pajamas he had loaned Fox lying in a crumpled heap on the floor, and the pillowcase missing from the pillow.

Strange, he thought, turning and slipping noiselessly out into the kitchen. The two discarded banana peels in the middle of the table confirmed Brett's suspicion that Fox had already eaten and hit the road for . . . where? New York? Or just another local alley?

Brett shook his head. *Oh well,* he reminded himself, *he's not my problem. And at least now I can tell Ariane that he's gone.*

He started toward the bedroom, then stopped. What was it that was different? Why did he have this vague sense that everything was not as it should be? What had his subconscious picked up on that hadn't yet registered in his mind?

He turned back toward the kitchen, his sharp eyes scanning the room inch by inch. And then he saw it. Some of the drawers weren't closed as they usually were. One, in fact, was open several inches. Ariane was a fanatic about order. No matter how busy she got with her job or school, she never went to work in the morning or to bed at night unless everything was in its place. Neat. Always neat. She would never have gone to bed and left those drawers open.

He moved like a condemned man toward the corner drawer, the one that was open so much more than the others. The one that contained Ariane's great-grandmother's silver. Remembering the coverless pillow in the guest room, the ever-increasing feeling of nausea in his stomach pushed itself up into his throat as he stopped and pulled the drawer open the rest of the way. He could almost hear its emptiness echoing in his ringing ears.

＊

Not wanting to risk awakening Ariane, he grabbed a pair of jeans out of the dirty clothes hamper in the bathroom, slipped on an old pair of tennis shoes he found in the hall closet, and ran out of the house without socks or a shirt. He ran faster than he had in a long time, up one deserted street, down the next, ducking into every alley with a silent prayer on his lips, hoping, hoping. . .

The early morning sunshine hadn't yet had time to warm the air, but Brett hardly noticed. By the time he'd gone several blocks, he was sweating profusely, his breath once again coming in gasps, as it had the night before. Oblivious to his mounting exhaustion, he ignored his heaving lungs, his hammering heart and the blisters that began to rise on his sockless feet, as he plunged ahead with little or no sense of time or direction. He knew only one thing. He had to find Fox and get that silver back in the drawer before Ariane discovered it missing.

My fault, he scolded himself, over and over again. *All my fault. Ariane was right. How could I have been so stupid? Smart aleck kid knew exactly what he was doing. Played me for the chump that I am, right from the start. Conned me, that's what he did. Conned me with those big sad eyes and that raggedy look of his.*

He rounded a corner, almost tripping over a tabby cat that streaked across his path. *I should have kept going. I should never have stopped. Should never have looked into his face. Should have let him run off to New York or who-knows-where last night instead of bringing him home. What good did it do to take him in for one night, anyway? Now he's right back on the streets again, only this time with Ariane's silver.*

What in the world does he plan to do with it? he wondered. *Hock it, no doubt. Maybe I should check the pawn shops. No, they won't be open for a couple of hours yet. Gotta find Fox and get that silver home long before that. Gotta find him. . . .*

On and on he ran until he thought his chest would burst. And still he ran. Aimlessly, relentlessly, until he realized he was backtracking, searching streets and alleys he'd already covered, running in circles with no idea of where to go or what to do next. He realized, too, that by this time Ariane was already awake and had undoubtedly discovered the open, empty silver drawer. That's when he finally gave up. Slowing his pace and turning regretfully toward home, he couldn't decide which felt heavier—his tired, aching feet or his pounding, bewildered heart.

*

She'd spotted the open silver drawer the minute she'd walked into the kitchen. Even before looking inside, she knew the drawer was empty. And she knew exactly what had happened.

Unlike the night before when her feelings of anger and betrayal had surfaced in the form of harsh, demanding threats and accusations, today her rage turned to tears, pouring forth from deep within, washing over her in waves of loss and despair. That silver had been her mother's wedding gift to her, handed down from her great-grandmother, whom Ariane had never known. It had been her link to her past, to her own family name, to the person she had been before she had become Mrs. Brett Holiday. It was a past that had been far from perfect, but at least it had been hers. And now the silver—and a part of her—was gone.

When she'd cried until she was sure there were no more tears left inside her, she laid her head on her hands and sat quietly at the kitchen table, eyes closed, waiting. She knew he'd be home soon—without the boy, she was sure. And, she was just as sure, without her silver.

What would he say to her? What excuse would he offer? And what could she possibly say to him in return? Would he ask her to forgive him? If so, would she? *Could* she?

In all fairness, however, she knew he must be feeling just awful. He was aware of how precious that silver was to her, that it had been her favorite wedding present. But could he even begin to imagine the depth of loss she felt, as if, at the age of twenty-nine, her own personhood had been stolen from her, only to be hocked in some pawn shop to the highest bidder?

And all because of that darn kid, she reminded herself. Why couldn't Brett have left him where he'd found him? Why hadn't her husband been able to sense, as she had, that bringing that boy into their home would affect their lives for a much longer time than the one night he spent there?

She should never have offered him that steak, she decided. Brett had read so much more into that offer than she had meant there to be. He had taken it as a sign that she was softening toward the boy. Oh, if only she hadn't made that offer, then Brett might not have offered Fox a bed, and she'd still have her great-grandmother's silver sitting in her kitchen drawer where it belonged.

Suddenly, she remembered a story her grandfather had told her years ago when she was a little girl. It was a story about a kindhearted woman who'd gone outside one cold, wintry evening, only to find a half-frozen snake on her doorstep. Every instinct warned her to leave it where it lay, but her heart went out to the poor creature, so she took it inside. Curling up next to it in bed, she freely shared her body heat with the snake, feeding life back into its motionless body. Before long, the snake began to wriggle, and the woman felt rewarded for her good deed. But before she could get out of bed, the snake struck her, sinking its venomous fangs into her soft flesh. As she cried out in shock and pain, she looked over at the snake and gasped, "Why? I saved your life! Why did you repay me this way?" As the snake slithered quickly away he hissed, "Why not? I'm a snake. What else would you expect me to do?"

It was the first time she'd thought of the story in years. She wished now that she'd remembered it last night, that she'd told it to Brett, that they'd called the police, that they'd done something differently so she wouldn't be sitting here at her kitchen table, alone and heartbroken, feeling as if someone had just run off with her only heritage.

She heard the front door then, and slowly, hesitantly, she raised her head. Brett stood framed in the kitchen doorway, looking more exhausted and dejected than she remembered ever having seen him before, even after losing a major game. He was dirty and sweaty and needed a shave. Any other time, she would have gone to him, reached out to him. But even as their eyes locked, the unspoken words that hung between them stood like an invisible barrier that Brett seemed unable, and Ariane unwilling, to cross.

"You know, don't you?" he said finally, running his hand through his damp, matted hair. "About the silver, I mean."

She nodded, but said nothing.

He sighed so deeply she could see him tremble, but still she could not bring herself to go to him. He waited, but she didn't move.

"Well?" he asked, raising his hands as if in surrender. "Aren't you going to say something? Tell me what a fool I am, how I was wrong and you were right? Aren't you even going to say 'I told you so'? Go ahead, I deserve it. There's nothing you can say that I haven't already said to myself a hundred times. Nothing that can make me feel any worse than I already do." He stepped toward her, leaned over and placed his hands on the table, then looked into her eyes.

"Please, Ariane," he whispered hoarsely. "Say something."

She swallowed, staring back at him, unblinking. It was the first time since they'd been married that she had ever regretted being his wife, even for a moment, and it terrified her.

"What's there to say?" she whispered, her throat aching with the pain. "Fox is gone. My great-grandmother's silver is gone. We'll never see either of them again. Maybe I should be thankful that's all he took. But somehow, I'm not so sure it is. . . ."

CHAPTER 4

By the time Ariane left for work an hour later, Brett felt about as low as he could remember ever having felt in his entire life. After extracting a promise from him to call the police, Ariane hadn't spoken another word to him—about Fox or the silver or anything—as she'd moved around the house, picking up newspapers, fluffing pillows, rearranging knickknacks. In an effort to make conversation, Brett had considered reminding her that the cleaning lady would come the next day so she really didn't need to do all that tidying up, but he knew it wouldn't do any good. Neatness was a fetish with Ariane, and housekeeper or no housekeeper, she would leave nothing out of place before leaving for work. Besides, it was obvious she had not been in the mood for conversation.

He wandered aimlessly from room to room, searching for reassurance in the sameness of things, the familiarity of each piece of furniture, the neat, uncluttered routine of their daily lives. Surely by the time Ariane came home, things would be the same between them once again. By then, she would have had time to think things through, to realize that he had done what he felt he had to do. She would understand. She would forgive him. Surely . . .

As he passed from the formal dining room (which he was thankful they seldom used), with its elaborate cherry wood table and china hutch, into the kitchen, the empty silver drawer seemed to mock him. *Fool! Chump! Sucker! Thief!* He was shocked. Thief? He hadn't taken the silver. It was the kid, not him. All he'd done was . . .

"All I did," he said aloud, turning back toward the living room in an attempt to escape the accusing voice that seemed to echo off the kitchen walls, "was invite some kid I'd never seen before into our home without even bothering to consult my wife. And what does the kid do? Takes off with her silver. Who am I kidding? He could never have stolen it if I hadn't brought him home in the first place. No wonder she's mad. I might just as well have taken that silver and hocked it myself. I *am* a thief. A has-been, used-to-be football star, and now a thief."

He stood motionless in the middle of the living room, surveying his elegant surroundings—the plush white couch and matching love seat and recliner, the spotless glass and chrome coffee table, the burnt-orange drapes and beige carpeting. Probably not the colors or style he would have chosen had he been the primary one to decorate their home, but definitely a style that reflected his modern-thinking, up-to-date wife with her passionate mood swings.

Beige rug, orange drapes, he mused. *Cool and calm one minute, on fire the next. That's Ariane. Right now, though, I'd be relieved to see her on fire again. I'm used to that, I know how to deal with her passion. But this . . .*

His eyes came to rest then on the huge marble fireplace directly across from the couch. The grate, the hearth, all of it, perfectly clean. How he longed at that very moment to be able to curl up on the couch next to Ariane, as they had done countless times throughout their marriage, and watch the flickering flames together, secure in their love for each other and their joint plans for the future.

Their wedding picture hung just above the fireplace. He stared at it, transfixed, remembering how lovely she had looked that day six years ago as she'd walked down the aisle toward him, her father, so cool and proper, at her side.

Ariane's father. James. Funny how seldom Brett thought of him. Undoubtedly because they'd had so little contact with him since their wedding, and also because Ariane seldom mentioned him; when she did, she matter-of-factly referred to him by his first name. But then, what was there to say about James? Other than the fact that he had provided for Ariane's material needs throughout her life, he really hadn't been any support to her—emotionally, anyway. It was Ariane's hot-blooded Italian mother, Rose, who had been the one to lavish affection and attention on her daughter. Rose's death when Ariane was sixteen had been a devastating blow to the young girl, but Ariane had assured Brett that it had only served to reinforce her determination to succeed— in whatever she set her mind to do.

Brett remembered Ariane telling him soon after they'd met that James had been terribly disappointed that his only child had been a girl. Although she insisted she had overcome her father's disappointment, Brett couldn't help but wonder if his wife's perfectionistic ways didn't somehow belie her words.

Brett sighed, pulling his eyes away from the wedding picture and reminding himself of his promise to Ariane. *The police,* he thought. *I promised to call them. And I will, but . . .*

Turning abruptly toward the hallway, he hurried past the closed bedroom doors and stepped into the comforting haven of the last room at the end of the hall—the room he thought of as his office or den, the room Ariane affectionately referred to as his "cave."

He didn't bother to flip on the light. It wasn't necessary. He knew and loved every piece of furniture, every sports magazine, every trophy and plaque, every record and cassette, every videotape in the room. This, after all, was his domain. The last vestige of his football days. A tribute to the glory that had once been his.

"Once," he said, as if speaking to the room itself. "Once, you were mine. No more. A has-been. A chump, a thief and a has-been, that's me, all right."

Flipping on the TV, he lowered himself into his favorite chair—a well-worn, brown Naugahyde recliner, which Ariane insisted belonged in a trash heap—and leaned back with his feet up. Canned laughter assaulted his ears as the screen came to life with an "I Love Lucy" rerun.

Why not? he thought. *Seems appropriate. Nothing new. Nothing to look forward to anymore. Just reruns.*

He chided himself for his self-pity and for lazing uselessly in front of the TV when he could be out in the backyard making use of the swimming pool he'd had installed two years earlier. As badly as he knew he needed the exercise, however, he just couldn't bring himself to move from his comfortable chair.

The phone rang then and he jumped, startled by the unexpected reminder of an outside world. For a few brief moments, everything had seemed compressed into the dark, limited space of this one room. Now, resenting the intrusion into his private territory, he hesitated to answer. But, he decided, it could be Ariane calling. Calling to say she understood, that she'd forgiven him and everything would be all right again.

He grabbed the phone on the lamp table beside his chair. The deep male voice that responded to his anxious "hello" was not at all what he had expected to hear.

"Brett, what's goin' on, man?"

Brett was silent for a moment, staring at the receiver as if it had betrayed him. He had been so sure.

"Hey, you still there?"

He cleared his throat. "Yeah," said Brett. "Yeah, I'm here. How ya doin', Ron?"

"Man, I'm doin' great. And you know why? There's a Laker game tonight, and I've got two tickets right down front. What do you think about that?"

Brett tried to force some enthusiasm into his voice. "That's great. It really is. So, who's the lucky girl?"

"Girl?" Ron laughed. "What makes you think I'm takin' some girl?"

Brett smiled. "We've been friends for a few years now, remember? In all that time, how often have I seen you without some new girl hanging on your arm?"

Ron laughed again. Brett knew his friend enjoyed his reputation as a ladies' man. He also knew that, deep down, there was nothing Ron would like better than to find the right girl and settle down.

"Like you two," he'd told Brett and Ariane on more than one occasion. "Trouble is," he'd tease, winking at Ariane playfully, "now that the only perfect woman is already taken, how am I ever gonna be satisfied with anybody else? Course, if you ever get tired of this old man here, you know I'm just a phone call away." Ariane would laugh and tell him that, if she ever decided to trade Brett in on a new model, it certainly wouldn't be for another football player.

The sound of Lucy and Ricky arguing brought Brett back to the present. He'd forgotten about the TV. He'd also forgotten he was on the phone.

"What about you?" Ron was saying. "You want to go? Ariane's got school tonight, right?"

School. Another thing he'd forgotten about. Ariane would rush in from work, grab something to eat and be off again before they'd have a chance to talk at all. The thought of the long, lonely day stretching into the late hours of the night was more than Brett wanted to face.

Maybe getting out to a Laker game with Ron was just what he needed.

"Sure," he answered. "What time?"

"Six-thirty. I'll pick you up."

"Sounds good. Thanks."

"No problem." Brett could hear the smile in Ron's voice. "See ya then, man."

Brett sat, unmoving, in the darkness of the room, the phone still clutched in his hand. The dial tone buzzed in his ear long after Ron had hung up.

Why couldn't it have been Ariane? he wondered. *Is she ever going to forgive me? Is she thinking about me right now? Or is she just thinking about her great-grandmother's silver and about how Fox . . .*

Fox. The haunting face that had stared up at him from behind the trash cans the night before now rose, unbidden, in his memory. The huge, frightened eyes. The innocence of youth, stolen before its time. The hard, cynical mask, his only protection against the harsh realities of life. How had he ended up in that alley in the first place? How was it possible that anyone—especially a child—should have to sleep on the street and dig through trash for something to wear or eat?

Brett hung up the phone and closed his eyes. He was aware of the tragic plight of the ever-increasing numbers of homeless people throughout the country, and his heart went out to them. But never before had the homeless seemed more than one of many pressing social issues. Now, suddenly, that social issue had a face. A face and a name.

The question he had tried to ignore all morning now called out to him for an answer. Too loud to ignore. Too heartrending even to try. His temples throbbed with the ache of it.

Where is he now? Worse yet, where will he be tonight?

He shook his head. "Sorry, Ariane," he whispered softly. "I'm really sorry about your silver. But I did what

I had to do. You'll just have to try to understand. You'll just have to, that's all."

＊

She knew the moment she opened the door from the garage to the kitchen and stepped inside that he wasn't home. The air was different. The quiet was different. Empty. Deserted. Not the palpable, suffocating tension she had expected to come home to. A curious mixture of relief and regret washed over her as she made her way to the table—purposely averting her eyes from the now-empty silver drawer—to look for the note she knew would be there.

Ariane: Gone to the Laker game with Ron.

About as basic as you can get, she thought. But then, under the circumstances, what else was there to say? Should he have called her "sweetheart" or "babe" or "honey" as he usually did? Signed it with love? No. Cold wars called for politeness. And brevity. The fewer words, the better.

Although it sure would have been nice if he'd at least mentioned what the police had to say, she thought, sighing as she crumpled the note and tossed it into the trash, then turned and opened the refrigerator to look for something to eat.

A sandwich? No. Not what she wanted. Some fruit? A bowl of cereal? She'd been too upset for breakfast, had only picked at her lunch. She knew she should eat something, but her stomach was still too tight, too knotted up to allow anything else inside. Maybe later, she decided. Maybe when she got home from school.

She went to the bedroom, slipping off her heels and lightweight gray suit. By the time she had taken off her pale pink blouse and slip, all she could think of was how good it felt to get back into her blue jeans and tennis shoes. She was thankful that she could dress casually for school. Ten hours in high heels was more penance than anyone deserved.

Digging her notes out of her binder, she sat down on the edge of the bed for a quick review. Her discarded clothes, however, lay in an accusing heap on the floor in front of her. She sighed and got up to put them away.

Just once, she thought, *just once, I'd like to go off somewhere and leave things in a mess. Why can't I do that? Other people can. Especially Brett. He says I'm a fanatic. I suppose he's right. He also says I'm too emotional and that I overreact to things. I suppose he's right about that, too. I know I lose my temper too easily. I don't mean to, I really don't. But sometimes he makes me so mad. And this time . . .*

She shook her head as if to clear it, then sat down once again to go over her notes, but the words seemed to run together on the page. Images of her lost silver danced in her mind, as they had throughout the day. As the memory of Brett's pleading, guilt-ridden face swam before her eyes, she jumped up, shoving her notes back into her book. She would not allow herself to think about her husband. Not right now, anyway. She had to concentrate on her studies. Her career was important to her, every bit as important as Brett's was to him. Sometimes she wondered if he really understood that.

She snatched up her books and purse and hurried toward the kitchen door. Not only was she determined to block out all thoughts of Brett, she was also determined to stay so busy that she would not be able to think about the sad-eyed boy who had come into their lives for a night, stared at himself in her sparkling china, then stolen her great-grandmother's silver, and returned to wherever it was that he had been spending his empty days and dark, lonely nights.

A child sleeping on the streets, she thought, as she stepped down into the garage and walked over to climb into her car. *How is that possible? Oh, I know it goes on, but . . . but a child! Doesn't he have a mother? A father? Friends, family, somebody?*

She buckled her seat belt and put the key into the ignition. *Surely he must have a mother somewhere! And surely she's looking for him! I mean, if he were my child, I certainly would be. . . .*

She caught herself, as the old familiar ache for a child of her own began to gnaw at her. *No!* she scolded herself. *I am not going to start thinking about that again. Brett and I have talked it over many times, and we've agreed to wait until my career is established and we're both ready. And one thing's for sure—right now, we're definitely not ready!*

*

The sun was down and the parking lot was already filling up when Brett and Ron arrived at the Great Western Forum. Ron was his usual talkative, outgoing self, checking out every woman who walked by and joking with Brett. Brett, however, had a hard time responding.

"What's the matter with you?" Ron asked, slapping Brett on the back as they made their way through the crowd toward one of the many stadium entrances. "You've hardly said a word since I picked you up, and you haven't laughed once. I thought we came here to have a good time. Man, you're about as much fun as goin' to a wake."

"Sorry," mumbled Brett, looking up at his friend. At 6'6", Ron Daniels towered over Brett by five inches. A wide receiver for the Rams, Ron was muscular and quick—and almost five years younger than Brett. There was a time when Brett could just about keep up with him, but no more. Although Brett often went to the gym to work out with Ron, he always found an excuse not to jog with him. His pride just couldn't handle it. "I'm really sorry," he repeated.

Ron laughed. "I know you're sorry, man," he said, his brown eyes sparkling. "I figured that out a long time ago."

Brett smiled. It was hard to stay depressed around Ron. Brett admired his good-natured, easygoing manner. That, combined with his dark good looks, accounted for Ron's popularity with his friends, as well as with the ladies.

There had been very few black families in Colorado Springs where Brett grew up, none at all in his immediate neighborhood. The few individuals he saw were usually servicemen stationed at one of the nearby military bases. It wasn't until he got involved in college and professional sports that Brett found himself spending much time with any black people at all. Even then, he hadn't thought much about it, one way or the other, until he met Ron. Becoming best friends with Ron Daniels had been the easiest and most natural thing—next to falling in love with Ariane—that Brett had ever done.

Suddenly, he found himself wondering if he should tell Ron about Fox. After all, they talked about all sorts of things—women, football, the world situation. But this? Would he understand? Would he tell him what to do about Ariane? How he should have handled things differently?

Ridiculous, he decided. Why would Ron understand any of this when he couldn't understand it himself? Did he suppose Ron would have some magical answers for him just because he and Fox were both black? Brett shook his head. A dumb idea, he told himself.

"So, what's the story?" Ron asked as they handed their tickets to an attractive young blonde at the entrance. Ron paused for a moment to glance back over his shoulder at her, then continued. "You gonna tell me about it, or you gonna mope through the whole game and try to ruin my fun, too?"

Brett took a deep breath and shook his head. "Hey, I'm fine," he said. "Really. Just a little tired, I guess. No sweat. I'll be all right once the game starts." But even as the closing notes to the National Anthem faded and the Lakers began to announce their starting lineup, all Brett could think of was Kareem Abdul-Jabbar, the team's former star center, who had recently retired after a glorious twenty-year career in the NBA.

Forty-two years old, he thought. *Not only was the guy still playing at forty-two, he was still in the starting lineup. And here I am, eight years younger than he is, and I'm lucky to get a chance to play at all, let alone start. At least Kareem retired in style, with honors and speeches and expensive presents. Me, I'll probably just get a last minute phone call, telling me I've been cut from the team. Then what? What am I supposed to do with the rest of my life? Sit around in my den watching old game videos while my successful lawyer-wife supports me?*

"Hey, did you see that?" asked Ron, elbowing him in the ribs. "Man, nobody runs that pick-and-roll better than Magic Johnson and Mychal Thompson."

Brett didn't answer. He hadn't seen them make the basket because he hadn't even realized the game had started. Straining to concentrate, he watched as A.C. Green snatched a defensive rebound out of the air and passed the ball to James Worthy, who ran the length of the court and slammed it through the hoop for an easy deuce. Instantly, the fans were on their feet.

Like they used to be for me, he thought, rising slowly to join them. He'd no sooner stood up than Byron Scott intercepted an inbound pass and sunk a perfect twenty-foot jumper for another two points. The crowd went wild.

"These guys are really hot tonight!" exclaimed Ron, glancing excitedly at Brett. "That A.C., he's got the heart of a lion, doesn't he? And with James and Byron shootin' like that—incredible, man! I know it's still early, but we're gonna win, I can feel it."

Brett nodded in agreement. "Yeah," he mumbled. "Yeah, sure. We're gonna win."

But in his heart, he found it hard to believe that he would ever win at anything again. In fact, for the first time in his life, he felt like the biggest loser in the world.

CHAPTER 5

Ron was right. The Lakers won. By the time he and Brett had squeezed their way through the crowd and climbed into the car, Ron was hungry. Brett, however, was exhausted. Too tired even to think of eating, he asked for a rain check. When Ron dropped him off in front of his house, Brett had to force himself to put one foot in front of the other as he made his way, slowly, across the yard. Halfway there he stopped, turning to watch the taillights of Ron's red Jaguar fade into the night.

He sighed, wishing he could be more like Ron, that he could take life a little less seriously some times. For a brief instant, he even envied Ron his single lifestyle. But only for an instant. He knew he would never trade his marriage for the so-called freedom and good times of bachelorhood. He could still remember the TV dinners and the loneliness of sleeping alone that he had so gladly left behind to marry Ariane.

An ugly fear suddenly gripped his heart as he realized how much worse it would be now to have to endure TV dinners and sleeping alone than it had been before, when he knew nothing else. To lose Ariane after sharing his life with her for six years would be more than he could bear.

A gust of wind made him shiver and he glanced up into the night sky. No moon tonight, only a slight hint of scattered stars, twinkling faintly behind the night haze.

Cold and dark, he thought. *Cold and dark here, probably cold and dark in New York and everywhere in between. Where is he? What's he doing? Did he hock the silver? Use the money to travel on, or just to eat and to buy something to keep warm?*

Stop it! he scolded himself. *He's not your problem, remember? Besides, if he wants to steal things and live on the streets, who are you to try and change his mind? You've got enough to worry about already. Your marriage, your career . . . He's just some stray kid . . . just a kid. . . .*

Out of the corner of his eye, he thought he caught a flash of light streaking through the blackness overhead. *A shooting star?* he wondered, but he couldn't be sure. The sky in L.A. just wasn't as clear as the sky he'd seen when he was a little boy growing up in Colorado. There, shooting stars were almost a nightly occurrence.

His mind drifted back to the many nights he and his father had spent camping together in the mountains near Colorado Springs. Unlike Ariane and James, Brett and his father had been close, so close. . . . Brett sighed. He had missed his father since his death two years earlier, but never more than he did right now.

"Make a wish, son," his father had told him the first time they spotted a shooting star. "Make a wish, but don't tell anybody—not even me—what it is." It had become a favorite game of theirs, seeing who could spot that first shooting star, then wishing through closed eyes for something very, very special. The wonderful part of it was that Brett had never doubted his wishes would someday come true.

"Now I know better," he mumbled, turning away from the heavens before he could do anything foolish, like acknowledge the wish hidden so deep within his heart that even he could not yet call it by name.

That's when he saw him. A dark shadow, huddled on the ground next to the front door, silhouetted against the white stucco wall. Brett approached slowly, stealthily, holding his breath as if he expected to be attacked at any time. He stood next to him, close enough to hear his even breathing, before he was positive that it was Fox. He was sound asleep. Brett's heart leaped in his chest as he saw the dirty white pillowcase clutched tightly in the boy's fist. He knew exactly what was inside.

*

She was floating somewhere between the hard reality of her empty bed and the filmy images of her dream when she heard the voices. Whose? Someone in her dream? Yes. Must be. Had to be. Brett wasn't home, but it was his voice. His voice and. . .

No. She turned on her side and pulled the covers up over her ears. *The boy was here last night. Gone now. Gone with my silver. Can't be him. Can't be him and Brett talking. Can't be. . . .*

She opened her eyes slowly and tried to focus them on the illuminated dial of the alarm clock on the bed stand. Eleven o'clock. She couldn't have been asleep for more than ten or fifteen minutes. What was happening? What was going on? She was sure she'd heard Brett's voice. Brett and someone else. Who? Ron? Of course. Must have been. Yes, Ron.

Wait. She sat up, her body tense, her ears straining to pick up the sounds, distinguish the words.

"It's okay, really," Brett was saying. "We can talk about it in the morning, get it all ironed out then."

"Just so you know I ain't no thief," said the other voice. "I just borrowed it, dude, that's all."

"It doesn't matter," said Brett. "The important thing is that you came back, and that you brought the silver with you."

Ariane had her robe on and was out the door, down the hallway and into the living room before either Brett or Fox could say another word. Green eyes blazing, she stopped, hands on hips, and glared at them.

"How could you!" she demanded. "How could you bring this thief back into our home after all that's happened? I can't believe this. . . ."

Her voice trailed off as the look of surprise on Fox's face hardened and he thrust the dirty pillowcase out in front of him.

"Here's your stuff, lady," he said, his eyes narrowing slightly. "Like I told the football dude, I ain't no thief like my . . . like some people. I just borrowed it, that's all."

Ariane fought for control. She glanced over at Brett. His eyes were fixed on the pillowcase, as if his entire life, rather than her great-grandmother's silver, hung in the balance. She knew she should reach out and take it, but then what? Would Brett misinterpret that as acceptance on her part, the way he had misinterpreted her offer of a steak the night before? If so, heaven only knew what he might suggest next. If she let down her guard for one moment, she was sure her husband would do something else crazy—like invite the kid to spend another night in their home.

I don't care if he did bring my silver back, she thought, still hesitating. *I just can't let that happen. There's no telling what we'd wake up and find missing tomorrow.*

When it became obvious that neither Fox nor Brett was going to make a move until she did, she grabbed the pillowcase from Fox. Turning on her heel and marching into the kitchen, she emptied the contents onto the table and counted each piece.

All there. Thank God! Maybe she should consider keeping it in a safety deposit box at the bank so she wouldn't have to worry about having it stolen again. Or maybe have a small vault installed in the house somewhere, or . . .

No, she told herself. *No, I will not lock my great-grandmother's silver away where it can't be seen and appreciated just because Brett invited some hoodlum into our home. I'm going to settle this once and for all, the way I should have done last night.*

She spun around, ready to charge back into the living room and confront them both, but was startled to find them standing, just a couple of feet behind her, watching anxiously. It was impossible to tell which of the two was the more apprehensive. She hesitated a moment, then took a deep breath, determined to take control of the situation.

"It's all here," she announced, summoning up her most authoritative voice. "So we'd better call the police right away and let them know the silver's been returned. And then we can ask them about some shelters in the area—"

At the mention of the police, Fox's eyes opened wide. Before Ariane could finish another sentence, he dashed back into the living room, leaving both Brett and Ariane rooted to the floor, speechless, staring at the spot between them where Fox had stood. It was the sound of the front door slamming that brought them back to life.

"I'm going after him," Brett announced, turning toward the living room.

"No!" cried Ariane, grabbing his arm and pulling him around to face her. "No, let him go!"

She was sure she saw tears glistening at the corners of his eyes as he stared at her, the obvious war of emotions within playing across his face. But as she watched the war come to an end, she knew from his expression that he had decided to go. And there was nothing she could do to stop him.

She let go of his arm and turned away from him, holding her breath until she heard the front door slam once again.

＊

I can't believe I'm doing this. A few minutes ago I was too tired to stand up, now I'm running around in the dark, trying to catch a kid who hides behind trash cans and returns "borrowed" silver. And what in the world am I going to do with him if I do catch him? Convince him to come back home with me? Fat chance! Even if I could, Ariane would probably never speak to me again—especially when she finds out I never got around to calling the police in the first place. I must be crazy. If I had one ounce of sense, I'd—

He stumbled, his teeth coming down hard on his tongue as he fell. Wincing, he tasted the warm, salty blood, then shook his head in disgust.

Forget it, he told himself. *Just forget it and go back home where you belong. You're never gonna find him. He's—*

Somewhere to his left, a dog began to bark. Then another. And then, the unmistakable sound of a trash can being overturned. Sucking his sore tongue, he jumped to his feet and ran off once again, turning left at the very next alley, confident that he was at least headed in the right direction.

He didn't even bother to stop as he hurried past the overturned trash can. Fox was too smart to be hiding anywhere in the alley. Besides, the dogs had quit barking, only to start up once again as Brett ran by.

Stopping to catch his breath at the end of the alley, he peered up and down the deserted side street, straining to catch a glimpse, to hear a faint footfall. But it wasn't his sharply tuned eyes or ears that told him Fox was nearby. It was his heart. Even above its thunderous pounding, he sensed its message, and he froze. Breathing as quietly as he could, he waited, unmoving, knowing it was just a matter of time.

How long? Ten minutes? Fifteen? Twenty? Brett's heart rate and breathing had returned to normal, and his muscles began to ache. Just when he had decided that the kid was going to outlast him, Fox darted into the street from between the two buildings on Brett's right. Brett was after him in a flash. Streaking down the middle of the road, Fox veered suddenly to the left, stumbling through a flower bed, cutting across two lawns and setting off another chain reaction of barking dogs.

Brett was gaining on him, he was sure of it. Just a little farther. . . .

A porch light switched on behind them, another across the street, but Brett hardly noticed as he threw himself into the air, landing on top of Fox and bringing them both crashing to the ground in a tangled heap. *Crazy.* The word echoed through his mind as he pinned the thrashing boy beneath him.

"Let me go!" the boy yelled, struggling to free himself. "You better get off me, dude, or—"

"Or what?" interrupted Brett. "What are you gonna do, anyway? Beat me up? Call the police? What?"

The boy's jaws clenched and he glared at Brett as more and more lights flicked on in houses up and down the street. But even Fox's anger and defiance couldn't mask his fear.

"I want you to come back home with me," said Brett, keeping his voice as low as possible. When Fox opened his mouth to protest, Brett gripped the boy's arms tighter. "Listen to me," he went on. "I don't know all the reasons, but I do know you don't want anything to do with the police. That's okay. They don't know anything about you or the silver. Ariane wanted me to call them, but I . . . never got around to it. But just how long do you think it's going to be before someone around here calls them? If they haven't already, that is."

The boy went wild with fright then, surprising Brett with his strength. "Let me go!" he screamed, pushing at

Brett and rolling from side to side in an effort to get free. "Let me go 'fore they lock me up like they did my daddy! I ain't never gonna be locked up like him, you hear? Let me go, I said!"

Front doors began to crack open as a few brave souls poked their heads outside to check on all the commotion. Brett began to wonder if maybe he and Fox would both be locked up before the night was over. He had to get the boy under control quickly. But how? What could he say or do to convince Fox that he wanted to help him? Before he could think of anything, the boy went limp beneath him, as he started to cry softly.

"Knew they'd find me," he whimpered. "Sooner or later, I knew they'd find me, just like my daddy. Didn't go far enough, man, didn't run fast enough. Shoulda gone to New York, like I said. Never find me there, dude. Never find me there."

Brett let go of the boy's arms. It was obvious that there was no fight left in him now. He stood slowly to his feet, then reached down for Fox. Pulling him up, Brett then draped his arm across the boy's thin shoulders and steered him quickly down the street, away from the curious spectators and probing porch lights.

"It's going to be all right, kid," he said. "Everything's going to be all right. I don't know anything about what happened to your dad, but nobody's going to lock you up, I promise. You just come on home with me tonight, and we'll figure things out in the morning."

Fox stopped, but didn't look up. "Your wife," he said softly. "What about her?"

Brett's throat went dry as he felt a tremble roll through the boy's body. "Don't worry about Ariane," he said hoarsely. "She'll understand. You'll see. By the time we get back home, everything will be fine, and she'll understand. Trust me."

CHAPTER 6

Brett, wake up, I heard something! I think it's Fox." Ariane's voice slowly penetrated Brett's fuzzy, sleep-heavy mind. He felt his wife's hand on his shoulder, shaking him impatiently, urgently. "Brett, I think he's leaving again, and you'd better get out there and see what he's taking with him this time."

Brett blinked his eyes as her words began to register, then jumped out of bed and hurried out of the room. As he raced toward the living room, he heard Ariane's accusing voice float down the hall after him.

"I can't believe I let you talk me into this," she called. "I just can't believe it! When are you ever going to listen to me?"

He didn't answer. He couldn't have even if he'd wanted to. And he certainly didn't want to. Instead, he pulled the front door open, wondering if, once again, he would have to throw his clothes on and go running out into the streets looking for Fox. He was relieved to find the boy standing perfectly still in the middle of the walkway, the proud, straight line of his back toward Brett, his hands on his hips, staring straight ahead.

Brett approached him slowly, afraid the boy would bolt and run at the slightest provocation.

"Thinking about buying some property in this neighborhood?" Brett joked, stepping up beside Fox. A clenched jawline was his only answer. Brett tried again.

"How'd you sleep?" he asked.

A shiny blue Corvette passed by in front of them, but Fox didn't seem to notice. "Okay, I guess," he mumbled, shrugging slightly.

Once again, Brett noticed the dirty, too-tight T-shirt stretched across the boy's thin shoulders. "Hey, I don't know about you," he said, his voice louder than he'd meant it to be, "but I'm hungry."

Fox blinked, but said nothing.

"So," Brett went on, "why don't you and I go out to breakfast somewhere? It'll give us a chance to discuss what you're going to do today, where you'll go and—"

Fox whirled toward Brett, his eyes blazing and his chin jutting out defiantly.

"What you talkin' 'bout, dude? I already told you where I'm goin'. I'm goin' to New York. So there ain't nothin' left to *discuss*."

Brett hesitated for a moment. "Whatever," he said, suppressing a sigh. "Anyway, I'm starved. Come on, you gotta eat somewhere. Might as well be with me."

The boy's eyes narrowed slightly as he studied Brett. "Yeah, okay," he said, shrugging his shoulders once again. "Why not? But then I gotta hit the road, man. I ain't got no time to be hangin' 'round, understand?"

Brett nodded, wondering if he truly understood anything at all about the belligerent yet vulnerable adolescent standing in front of him—wondering, briefly, if he even understood himself anymore.

"Just let me run in and throw some clothes on," he said, starting toward the house. As he reached the front door, he stopped and looked back. Fox's eyes were fixed on Brett, but he made no move to follow him.

"You want to come back inside?" Brett offered.

"I'll wait here."

"Suit yourself. I just thought maybe you'd like to come in and change. You know, borrow some of my clothes or something. I know they'd be kinda big on you, but . . ."

"But what?" Fox answered, his eyes flashing to life. "You don't like what I'm wearin'? Maybe you're embarrassed to be seen with me. Cuz if you are, man, we can just forget this whole thing. I mean, it was your idea, dude. I ain't even hungry."

Brett opened his mouth, then closed it again. Stepping inside, he shook his head and mumbled over his shoulder, "I'll be out in a couple of minutes."

Ariane was there to greet him.

"Fox is waiting out front," he said, forcing a smile. She did not smile back.

"For what?" she asked. "Our checkbook? Credit cards? Or does he only accept cash?"

"Ariane, please . . ."

"Please what, Brett? Please let him stay another day, another night? Why not a month? Or a year? Maybe we could just adopt him and he could stay here with us forever."

"Ariane, you're not being fair. I'm just going to take him out to breakfast. You can't begrudge the poor kid that much, can you?"

She hesitated, her green eyes softening slightly. "He wasn't trying to sneak off with anything?"

Brett shook his head. "Nothing."

Ariane sighed. "Well, I suppose you're right. One breakfast can't hurt. But then what? What are you going to do with him after that?"

Brett swallowed. He had been wondering the same thing. "I suppose I'll have to turn him over to the proper authorities, whoever that might be. . . ." His voice trailed off.

"That, Brett Holiday," she answered, nodding her head in agreement, "is the first sensible idea you've had in days. I'm so relieved to hear you say it." She fixed her eyes on him sternly. "But this time, make sure you 'get around to it.' Don't put it off the way you did about calling the police. I want to be able to go off to work in peace today, knowing that by the time I get home, Elmore 'Fox' Richards will finally be out of our lives— once and for all."

She turned on her heel and headed for the hallway. "I'm going to take a shower. I'll see you this evening."

Brett watched her walk away, then sighed and followed her down the hall to their bedroom. He dressed quickly, splashed some water on his face, brushed his teeth, and hurried back outside.

Half expecting to find Fox gone, he was surprised when he stepped outside and almost tripped over him. The boy sat cross-legged on the front step, eyes closed, his face tilted up toward the morning sun.

"Love sunshine," Fox murmured, his eyes still closed. "Ain't never gonna let nobody lock me up in no dark place where there ain't no sun. Never."

Brett had thought about running back into the house for a pair of sunglasses, but changed his mind. "You ready?" he asked.

The boy's eyes opened slowly. "Yeah," he said, standing up in one quick, fluid motion, his long legs unfolding beneath him. "Where we goin'?"

"I don't know yet," Brett answered, leading the way around to the side of the house to the three-car garage. Once inside, he was sure he caught a flicker of admiration cross Fox's face as he glanced from the sleek, silver Mercedes to the bright red Porsche. That look of approval was quickly replaced, however, by one of bored nonchalance, as if shiny new Mercedes and Porsches were an everyday part of Fox's life.

"Which one's yours?" Fox asked.

"This one," answered Brett, climbing inside the Porsche. Fox got in beside him. "The other one's Ariane's."

"I like your wife's better," said Fox.

Figures, thought Brett, gunning the engine before he backed out. *He would have said that no matter which car I said was mine.*

They rode in silence while Brett tried to decide where to take Fox to eat. He wanted the boy to be comfortable, but as touchy as Fox was, Brett was afraid a fast-food place might insult him, as if he weren't dressed well enough to go anyplace better.

How do I get myself into these things? he wondered. *If only Ariane understood, then we could talk about it. I hate trying to figure all this out by myself. I really do need somebody to talk to about this, like Ron or . . . yeah, that's it! I'll go by and see if I can talk Ron into coming with us. Maybe Fox will respond better to him. Even if he doesn't, at least I'll feel like I have an ally.*

He turned the car sharply to the right and headed toward his friend's condo. Now all he had to do was blast Ron out of bed and convince him to come to breakfast with them. Knowing that Ron had been out late the night before and that he ate breakfast only during football season, Brett figured he had his work cut out for him.

He was right. Brett rang the bell and pounded on the door for a full five minutes before he got any response at all. He was about to give up when the door opened a crack and Ron peeked out and down at him.

"What is it?" he asked. "What are you doin'? You know what time it is, man?"

"Sure, I know," said Brett. "Do you?"

Ron opened the door a few more inches and rubbed his hand over his face. "I don't have to know," he said. "If it's still mornin', it's too early!"

Brett grinned at his groggy friend, who stood leaning against the doorjamb, wearing nothing but a gold chain around his neck and a pair of red-on-white polka-dot boxer shorts.

"Nice shorts," said Brett, his grin widening. "You look real cute."

"Very funny," answered Ron. "I wasn't exactly expecting company, you know."

"Well, you've got it," Brett answered. "In fact, he's waiting out in the car. We came to take you to breakfast."

"Breakfast! What are you talkin' about? Are you crazy? And who's this 'we' stuff? Who's waitin' out in the car? Ariane?"

"No. Fox."

Ron blinked and stared at Brett.

"You on somethin', man?"

Brett laughed. "Put some clothes on and come see for yourself."

Ron shook his head. "Just because you got me curious, I'm gonna get dressed and come out to the car. But you can forget breakfast. Soon as I see who this so-called 'fox' is, I'm comin' back in and gettin' me some more sleep."

Brett smiled as he walked out to the car to wait for Ron. "My friend will be right out," he told Fox, who sat silently, staring straight ahead, seemingly less than enthused about meeting anyone at all. When Ron came out, however, Fox's eyes lit up in recognition.

The boy cares more about football than he lets on, Brett thought. *In fact, I'll bet he cares more about a lot of things than he lets on.*

Still barefoot, Ron had slipped into a pair of tight faded jeans and a dark blue cotton shirt open in the front. The morning sun glinted off the gold chain that rested against his bare chest. He sauntered down the walkway toward them, then stopped, shaking his head slowly and grinning sideways at Brett.

"When are you gonna get a real car, man?" he asked.

Brett grinned back, but didn't answer. Their long-standing disagreement over the superiority of Porsches or Jaguars was a constant source of good-natured bickering between them.

Ron leaned into the open window on the passenger side. "So this is the 'fox' you were tellin' me about, huh?"

"*Fox*," the boy said emphatically, looking him straight in the eye. "Not 'the fox' or 'a fox,' just *Fox*. It's my name."

"Oh, I see," said Ron, raising an eyebrow as he stuck his hand through the window. "Well, Mr. Fox, nice to make your acquaintance. I'm Ron Daniels."

"I know," said Fox, ignoring Ron's hand. "I seen you on TV."

"Oh yeah?" Ron withdrew his hand. "So, you like football, huh?"

Fox shrugged. "It's okay."

"You ever been to a game?" Ron asked.

"No," answered Fox, his jaw twitching slightly. "Could have. Lotsa times. Just didn't want to, that's all."

Ron nodded. "Yeah." He stood up and looked at Brett. "Well, listen, I don't want to hold you two up, so I'm gonna let you go, man. I got me some serious sleepin' to do."

"Sure you won't come with us?" Brett asked hopefully.

"No, thanks. I'm not hungry. Just tired."

Brett walked him back to his door. As soon as they were out of earshot of the car, Ron turned to him.

"Where in the world did you meet this kid, anyway? I mean, he doesn't exactly look like he's from around this neighborhood, you know?"

"He's not," answered Brett. "I mean, I guess he's not. To tell you the truth, I really don't know where he's from. I found him in an alley and . . . never mind, it's a long story. Anyway, all I can get out of him is where he's going—to New York. Supposedly to pick up some good-looking chicks."

Ron chuckled. "Yeah, right. Man, I don't know about you. What are you tryin' to do, get into social work or somethin'?"

"I just want to help the kid," Brett answered. "Trouble is, I don't know how."

Ron opened his front door. "Well, you're gonna have to do it without me. I'm goin' to bed." He started into the house, then turned around and looked back at Brett. "Does Ariane know about this kid?"

Brett nodded, but didn't answer.

"And just what does she think about it?" Ron asked.

When Brett still didn't answer, Ron nodded knowingly. "That's what I thought," he said. "Man, you better unload that kid as soon as you can, you hear? He's nothin' but trouble, believe me. Nothin' but trouble!"

Ron's words echoed in Brett's ears as he made his way back to the car.

"Ain't comin' with us, is he?" asked Fox as Brett climbed in and started the engine.

"He would have," said Brett. "He was just tired, that's all."

"Sure."

They drove the rest of the way in silence, while Brett tried to think of some way to get Fox to open up. He had to get him to talk about his past, to explore the possibilities of a place to stay, to consider going to the authorities—anything to keep him from hitting the streets again and heading for parts unknown, New York included.

Brett finally pulled into the parking lot of a family-style chain restaurant, hoping for a booth toward the back where they could talk—or at least, try to. He spotted one as soon as they walked in, and headed straight for it. Fox followed in silence.

"What are you hungry for?" Brett asked, taking the menus from the waitress and handing one to Fox.

"Never said I was hungry," Fox answered, ignoring the menu.

Nothin' but trouble, thought Brett. *You were right, Ron. So was Ariane.* He cleared his throat. "Yeah, well, I'm starved," he said. "I think I'm going to have one of those Denver omelettes. That okay with you?"

Fox shrugged. "Whatever."

Brett looked at the waitress. "Two Denver ome-lettes," said Brett. "And two large orange juices. Coffee for me." He looked over at Fox, but the boy didn't respond.

Fine. If he can't even ask for it, he can do without. Coffee's not good for him anyway.

The waitress brought Brett's coffee right away, and he sipped it while they waited for the rest of their order. The coffee was surprisingly good, so he drank it black. In some restaurants he had to doctor it up a bit before he could drink it. He was working on his second cup, still looking for a way to break the silence, when two middle-aged women suddenly appeared next to their booth.

"Excuse me," said one of the ladies, her jet black hair swept up on top of her head and obviously held in place with several cans of hair spray. "Aren't you Brett Holiday?"

She was smiling expectantly, and Brett couldn't help noticing the sparkle in her bright blue eyes. He returned her smile.

"Yes, I am," he answered.

The woman turned to her friend. "I knew it!" she exclaimed. "I just knew it. Didn't I tell you, Shirley? Didn't I say, 'That's Brett Holiday over there'? Didn't I?"

Shirley nodded self-consciously. "Yes, you did, Joan. That's what you said, all right." She looked at Brett. "I'm sorry," she said. "We shouldn't have interrupted you."

Brett waved away her apology. "No problem. Our food hasn't arrived yet, anyway."

Joan's smile broadened as she shoved a napkin and a pen in front of Brett's face. "I knew you wouldn't mind," she said. "I told Shirley, I said, 'Shirley, these guys are used to this sort of thing. They sign autographs all the time.' Why, you expect it, isn't that right, Brett?"

Brett was sure he heard Fox snicker, but when he glanced over at him, his eyes were glued to a faded water spot on the table in front of him. Scribbling a polite but brief note on the napkin, Brett handed it back to Joan, who immediately read it out loud to Shirley.

"'May your life be filled with love and blessings always,'" she read breathlessly. "Oh, how sweet!" she cried, turning to show the autograph to her friend. "Isn't that sweet, Shirley?"

Shirley nodded again. "Sweet," she agreed. "But I think we'd better get back to our table. We've bothered Mr. Holiday and his friend long enough. Besides," she added, stepping aside as the waitress arrived with Brett's and Fox's order, "here's their food." When Joan opened her mouth to protest, Shirley took her firmly by the arm and steered her away from the booth.

"Good-bye, Brett," Joan called, glancing back over her shoulder. "And thank you!"

The waitress set their plates down on the table, then turned and looked at the two departing women. "Some people," she mumbled, shaking her head and walking away.

Brett smiled and turned back to Fox, but the boy seemed oblivious to everything but the food in front of him. For someone who'd made such a point of not being hungry, he attacked his omelette with a vengeance. He was halfway through it before he looked up at Brett, who hadn't even started on his yet.

"What's wrong with you?" asked Fox. "You waitin' to pray 'fore you eat, like you do at home?"

Brett flushed slightly. "Well, no, uh . . . I was just . . ."

Fox narrowed his eyes as he studied Brett. "You mean you only do that prayin' stuff at home? Don't like people watchin' or what?"

Brett opened his mouth to say something in his own defense, then closed it again. The kid was right. He didn't like people watching him pray. He'd always considered his religious beliefs quite personal. But suddenly they seemed more hypocritical than personal.

Fox had gone back to his omelette. Brett shook his head and began to eat. Why did he even bother? It was hopeless. Maybe he should just finish his breakfast and say good-bye, let the kid head out for New York or anywhere else he was bound and determined to go. After all, Brett had his own life to worry about. Why knock himself out trying to help some kid who didn't even want or appreciate his help?

But the memory of that dark shadow huddled beside his front door, clutching the dirty pillowcase full of silver, wouldn't let him walk away without trying. Just as he was about to open his mouth to speak, Fox dropped his fork onto his now-empty plate with a clatter and downed the last of his orange juice.

"Never had eggs like that," he said. "What you call 'em again?"

"A Denver omelette," answered Brett. "Good, aren't they?"

Fox shook his head. "I didn't like it, dude. Too many onions and stuff. What I really wanted was pancakes." He paused and looked at Brett's coffee cup. "And coffee. I like coffee."

Brett clenched his teeth and tried to breathe slowly. The picture in his mind of the vulnerable, sleeping boy lying in front of his doorstep the night before was beginning to fade.

"We need another coffee over here, please," Brett called to the waitress as she hurried by with someone else's order.

Brett picked up a piece of toast and spread strawberry jam on it, then looked again at the young boy seated across from him. He was silently tracing circles around the rim of his orange juice glass, staring at it as if it held the answers to the universe.

"What are you thinking about?" Brett asked.

Fox looked up, startled. "What?"

Brett drained the last swallow from his coffee cup. "I asked what you were thinking about."

The boy's face went hard. "What's it to you, man? You writin' a book or somethin'?"

Brett pounded the table with his fist, and Fox jumped. Brett was glad. It was nice to know the kid wasn't "cool" all the time.

"No," he said, feeling a flush of anger creep up his neck and face. "I'm not writing a book. I'm just trying to make conversation, okay? That's what people usually do when they go out to eat, you know."

Fox glared at him. "I didn't ask for this, remember? Nobody said nothin' 'bout *conversation* bein' part of the deal, man." He started to get up.

"Wait!" Brett reached out and laid his hand on Fox's arm. The boy stiffened and glared at Brett.

"I'm sorry," said Brett, removing his hand. "You're right. If you don't feel like talking, that's okay."

The waitress brought Fox's coffee, then refilled Brett's cup again. He picked it up and took a sip, resigned to drinking one last cup of coffee and then letting the boy go his own way. There seemed to be nothing else he could do.

"It ain't that I don't feel like talkin'," said Fox suddenly, his eyes downcast as he hugged his coffee cup with both hands. "It's just that . . . I don't know what to talk about, man."

"Doesn't matter," Brett assured him. "We can talk about all sorts of things, like . . . like football. You like football, don't you? I mean, you knew who I was when you saw me the other day. And you recognized Ron this morning, I could tell. Do you want to talk about football?"

"No."

Brett sighed. He knew he wasn't handling things very well. Here he was, trying to get this kid to open up, and all he could think of to talk about was football. He'd always been that way, even as a little boy. He remembered his mother telling him. . . .

He cleared his throat. "I know what you mean . . . about not knowing what to talk about. I have the same problem. In fact, my mom used to tell me that I had to learn to talk from my heart. . . ."

Brett's voice faded as Fox looked up at him. It couldn't be! But it was. Tears. There were actually tears glistening in the corners of Fox's dark eyes. Brett felt his heart break within him, and he knew there was no way he was going to let this young boy walk out of the restaurant—or out of his life, for that matter—without doing everything he possibly could to help him.

"I can't remember her no more," Fox whispered. "I can't remember her face, or the way she smelled, or even how she sounded when she laughed. I never thought I'd forget. But I did." A tear worked its way down his cheek. "Just like she forgot me," he added. "Just like my mama went off and forgot me."

Brett swallowed and blinked back his own tears.

"How old are you, Fox?" he asked softly.

"Twelve. Be thirteen this summer."

Twelve years old, thought Brett. *I was going to Boy Scout meetings and camping with my dad and throwing a football in the street. I had a home to go to. A home . . . and a mother. Waiting for me. And I'll never forget how she smelled . . . how she laughed. . . .*

"How old were you when she left?" Brett asked.

"Four."

Brett swallowed again. "Your father?"

The boy froze. "Dead," he answered, his eyes hard once again. "Died in jail. Locked up in the dark. My mama said it was the alcohol killed him, but that ain't true. It was the dark. Bein' locked up in the dark kills people."

Brett wanted to ask him why he believed being locked up in the dark would kill people, but he didn't. He had a feeling the boy was closer to being right than his mother had been, so the why didn't really matter at all.

"What was he like?" asked Brett.

"How'd I know?" said Fox. "I sure never saw him. Died when I was a baby. Saw a picture of him once, though. My mama said I look like him, but it ain't true. Only thing I ever got from my daddy's his name." His lip curled slightly. "Elmore Richards, Sr.," he said. "Just a old drunk, died in the dark. Not me, dude. Not Fox. I ain't never gonna be like him."

Brett took a deep breath and changed the subject. "Any brothers or sisters?"

"A little sister," said Fox, his voice breaking. "LaToya. She didn't belong to my daddy, though. She belong to my mama and the boyfriend."

"What boyfriend is that?" asked Brett.

"The one moved in with us when my daddy went to jail," said Fox. "I hated him. And he hated me. Used to tell my mama I was bad, just like my daddy. Tol' her so many times she finally believed him. Now they gone—all three of 'em."

"You mean," said Brett, incredulous, "your mama and . . . the boyfriend . . . took your little sister and left you behind?"

Fox shrugged. "Why not? LaToya was little and cute. And Mama said she looked like the boyfriend. 'Sides, Mama always told me she wanted a girl. Didn't want me, though. That's for sure."

Brett swallowed hard. "Where have you been living since then?"

"Lotsa places. Foster homes, mostly. And the pit."

"The pit?"

"You know. The hall."

Brett frowned. "I thought that was just for kids that got in trouble."

"Sometimes," Fox said. "Or when they got nowhere else to send ya."

"So that's where you've been staying?"

"Up until about a week ago. That's when I split, man. Decided to head out for New York."

"But why?" Brett asked. "Is it really all that bad at the hall?"

Fox looked at him for a long moment, as once again Brett realized how far apart their worlds were. He realized, too, how ignorant and naive his question had sounded.

"They feed ya, if that's what ya mean," Fox answered. "And they give ya a place to sleep. Compared to some places I been, dude, it ain't bad. But New York sounded better."

Brett nodded. How could he tell Fox that living on the streets of New York wouldn't be better? It would be like telling him that eating nothing but turnips out of his own garden three times a day for the rest of his life wouldn't be better than living on welfare. How did he know? He'd never had to do either.

"You never heard from your mother again?" he asked.

Fox shook his head. "No. Used to think she'd come back. Now I know she won't. Not ever." He shrugged. "But who cares, man! I don't need her no more. I'm almost thirteen. I can take care of myself now." He started to get up once again, then turned back to Brett.

"Thanks for breakfast and . . . everything, dude," he said. "The omelette was okay. Really."

"Wait a minute!" ordered Brett, his mind searching frantically for a way to keep the boy with him a little longer. "Don't go, not yet. I mean, what's the rush? We can stay here a while."

"What for?" asked Fox. "Can't make it to New York sittin' in this here restaurant all day."

"True," admitted Brett. "But we could at least finish our coffee first, couldn't we?" He forced a smile. "I get real grumpy without my daily dose of caffeine, . . . *dude*."

Fox shrugged and sat back down. "Yeah, well, I guess a few more minutes won't hurt." A half-smile touched his lips briefly. "Wouldn't want ya to have no withdrawal-fit or nothin'." He reached for his cup, then stopped, tilting his head slightly to one side.

"You hear that?" he asked.

"Hear what?"

"That song," answered Fox. "That's Jacqueline St. James, man, don't you know nothin'?"

Brett heard it then, faintly. Soft background music that apparently had been playing all along. He could barely make out the words. Something about "love for a lifetime." He wasn't familiar with it.

"I've heard her," he said. "She's pretty good. I just don't know this song. Is it new?"

Fox's eyes opened wide. "Yeah, it's new, but I've heard it before—lotsa times. Where you been, dude? And what you mean, 'pretty good.' Man, Jacqueline St. James is the best." He grinned and sat up straight. "She lives 'round here, you know. And someday—after I get rich in New York, that is—I'm gonna come back here and meet her. You just watch me, dude!"

Brett was watching him, but all he could see was the dirty, tight T-shirt stretched across Fox's adolescent shoulders and chest, as if the promise of the man to come were straining to burst out of the youth's restrictive body. What would happen to this young boy whose childhood had been lost? Was there any hope for the man he would someday become, or was he destined to die, "locked up in the dark," as his father had?

"Don't go to New York," Brett said suddenly. "Not yet, anyway. You could go back to the hall, just for a little while, just until I figure out something else, just until—"

Fox was shaking his head. "No way, dude. I can't go back there, even if I wanted to. They wouldn't let me, they'd send me somewhere else, somewhere worse, somewhere dark and . . ." He squeezed his eyes shut. "I ran away, man. I can't go back, don't ya see? I can't! 'Sides, what you gonna do to help? You just some broken-down old football player, dude. What can you do? Nothin', man. Just like everybody else ever said they was gonna help. Nothin'. Just nothin'."

"I'll find a way," said Brett. "I don't know how, but if you'll let me take you back to the hall, I promise you, Fox, I *will* find a way."

Fox opened his eyes and stared at Brett, a piercing stare that both defied and challenged Brett's words. "You crazy, man," said Fox, his voice barely above a whisper. "You just plain crazy, you know that? Why should I go and believe anything some crazy white man be tellin' me, huh? What you take me for, anyway, some fool or somethin'?"

"Maybe," Brett answered, his eyes still locked into Fox's gaze. "Maybe we both are. But I'm going to tell you something. Fool or not, crazy or not, I always keep my word. I promised you I'd find a way to help you, and I will."

Fox's jaw muscles twitched, but still he didn't blink. "Why?" he asked finally.

"Because I think you're worth it," Brett answered. "Because I believe that underneath that I-don't-care, tough-guy attitude of yours, there's a kid who wants to care and who wants to do the right thing, a kid who wants to grow up into a man people will be proud of someday. You just need some help getting there, that's all. And I'm the guy who's going to give it to you."

CHAPTER 7

Steering the gleaming red Porsche into the crowded parking lot in front of the main entrance to the state-run hall, Brett could almost feel Fox's body tense on the seat beside him. He eased into an empty space, turned off the ignition, and sat, squinting against the late afternoon sunlight that glinted off the windows of a high-rise building across the street. Neither of them spoke.

It had been a long day. And a draining one. After leaving the restaurant, Brett had taken Fox home with him, then called his lawyer, Matthew Jacobson. Matthew had promised to check into the matter immediately and get back to Brett before the day was over. In the meantime, he had cautioned Brett against allowing Fox—who was obviously a ward of the court—to stay overnight again. Matthew advised Brett that the officials involved wouldn't look favorably on his continuing to "harbor a known runaway." Brett, however, wasn't nearly as concerned with the officials' reactions as he was with Ariane's. How he'd prayed that Matthew would be able to tap his sources, pull some strings and exert enough influence to resolve the matter of this unexpected houseguest—quickly.

While he waited for Matthew's call, Brett had spent most of the day lounging by the pool with Fox, tiptoeing around the unspoken boundaries of the fragile agreement he'd managed to reach with the boy. Although Brett had promised to do whatever was necessary to help, he knew trust was an alien concept to this oft-betrayed man-child. One wrong word from Brett, and Fox would be gone—destined to live out what was left of his predictably short and tragic life, lost in the dismal, dead-end alleys that stretched endlessly between Los Angeles and New York.

So what? Brett had asked himself more than once. *Why not let him go? There are hundreds like him out there on the streets—thousands! I can't help them all. Why not just turn him over to the authorities and be done with it? It's what Matthew thinks I should do—Ron, too. And Ariane, of course.*

He turned his head to the left and peered out from under his sun visor at Fox. Still fully dressed, Fox lay back in the webbed lounge chair next to the pool, his face turned upward toward the sun. Only the occasional twitch of his jawline and the tight grip on his sweating soft drink can belied his relaxed demeanor. Fox's eyes were closed, but Brett sensed that he was wide awake and alert to every sound or movement around him.

He was right. He'd been observing Fox for less than a minute when the boy's eyes opened and he turned toward Brett.

"What you lookin' at, man?" he'd demanded. "I got a bug crawlin' on me or somethin'?"

It was only the shrill sound of the ringing telephone that stopped Brett from firing back a frustrated, sarcastic reply—one he would later have regretted, he was sure. Pulling himself out of his chair, he hurried, barefoot, across the sunbaked deck to the enclosed patio where a portable phone sat waiting on the redwood picnic table. It was Matthew.

And none too soon! thought Brett when he'd heard his lawyer's voice.

"Brett, I've got Elmore's caseworker, Alexander Phillips, on the line. He wants to talk with you."

By the time the conversation had ended, Brett was more confused than ever. Matthew and Mr. Phillips had managed to get permission for Fox to be returned to the hall immediately, and had assured Brett that he would be allowed to visit the boy whenever he wished. So why didn't Brett feel relieved? Isn't that what he wanted, to know that Fox was safe—*somewhere else*—before Ariane returned home from work?

But the ride from Brett's home to the hall—although less than a forty-minute drive—had seemed like a walk down death row. The only thing Brett couldn't figure out was which of them was the condemned man.

Now, sitting side by side in the smothering silence and oppressive heat of the closed-up car, Brett thought about how easy it would have been for Fox to run off during the time Brett was on the phone. Even after he'd returned to the pool and told Fox that they were going to meet Mr. Phillips back at the hall in about an hour, there had been plenty of time for Fox to break away while Brett was in the house changing clothes. But he hadn't.

"Why?" Brett asked suddenly, turning to look at Fox, who jumped at the sound of Brett's voice. "Why didn't you run off when you had the chance? If you hate it so much here, why did you come back?"

Fox glared at Brett defiantly. "Cuz I told you I would, that's why. Even though I know you ain't really gonna help me. I know it! You gonna drop me off, man, and then you're outta here. History, dude. But that's cool. I told you I'd come back, and here I am."

"But I *will* help you. I promised, remember?" Resisting the temptation to reach out and lay a reassuring hand on Fox's shoulder, he took a deep breath and went on. "I'm proud of you, Fox—for keeping your word and coming back, I mean. It's important for a man to keep his word."

Fox's dark eyes flashed and his voice cracked as he squared his thin shoulders and raised his chin. "You think I don't know that, man? *You think I don't know that?* Well, I do know it! I know a lot more than you think I do, dude. And one thing I *always* do is keep my word, you hear? Always! I ain't no liar, man. Not like some people. Not like my mama and—" He stopped, as his eyes narrowed and his voice dropped almost to a whisper.

"It ain't me needs to worry 'bout keepin' my word, man. It's you. You, with your fancy house and fancy cars and fancy wife. You just like all the rest of 'em. Social workers, teachers, politicians—they all the same. Big talk, big promises, but don't never deliver. They just lookin' out for number one, that's all. And now here you come tellin' me the same stuff I been hearin' all my life, and you 'spect me to believe it, just like that?"

He shook his head slowly, almost imperceptibly, from side to side. "That's why I came back here, dude," he went on, his jaws twitching as he spoke. "That's why I came back. To find out if rich, white has-been football dudes like *you* keep *your* word!"

*

Brett had been surprised at the immaculate, modern facilities he'd found once he and Fox walked into the hall. The staff members were warm and cordial, and Mr. Phillips had gone out of his way to make Fox's return as easy as possible. He'd informed Brett that no one was "locked up" at the hall, that if a child wanted to leave, he or she simply walked away. Their policy was to keep the atmosphere pleasant and homelike enough that no one would *want* to leave. Occasionally, however, someone did. In this case, that someone happened to be Fox.

"I was really disappointed when I got the call that you were missing, Elmore," said Mr. Phillips, his voice soft and his freckled brow wrinkled beneath his bright shock of red-orange hair. He leaned forward on the swivel chair that sat in front of a very old and very cluttered desk, laced his fingers together and rested his elbows on his knees. "And I was worried," he went on. "The streets are a dangerous place to be—especially for someone your age."

Fox didn't answer, his hard, old-man mask securely in place once again. He had plunked down in the corner of the worn, brown Naugahyde couch as soon as Mr. Phillips led them into the tiny, windowless office, stretched his long legs out in front of him, and hadn't moved since. Brett sat silently at the opposite end of the couch, watching—and waiting. For what, he had no idea.

Mr. Phillips tried again. "I have to admit," he said, "one of my biggest concerns was that you might have tried to run off to New York. You and I haven't really had a chance to get to know each other very well since you've been here, Elmore, but the few times we have spoken, you've mentioned your dream of going there someday. And from what I understand from some of the staff members, that seems to be your only topic of conversation with anyone else around here, too."

Fox still didn't answer, but Brett saw his jaws twitch at the mention of New York.

"I was hoping you would have made some friends here by now, Elmore," said Mr. Phillips. "But I understand you're as much a loner as ever, that you don't make any effort to get to know the other kids, that if anyone tries to talk to you, you ignore them—except for telling them about your plans to run off to New York, that is. Now, I understand that it's hard for you to get close to people, Elmore, to trust anyone again, but—"

Fox's head shot up and he glared at Mr. Phillips. "You don't understand nothin', man," he said. "Nothin', you hear? Just nothin'."

For a moment no one spoke. Then Mr. Phillips cleared his throat. "Well, you may be right about that, Elmore. At least, about some things. For instance, I don't understand why you're wearing those old clothes. They certainly weren't issued to you here."

Brett saw Fox's fist clench at his side. "You tryin' to say I stole 'em?" challenged Fox. "You tryin' to say I'm a thief like my daddy? 'Cause I ain't, man! I ain't no thief. I found 'em, that's all."

"Of course you didn't steal them," said Mr. Phillips. "And I certainly didn't mean to imply that you're a thief. I simply wondered what happened to the clothes you were wearing when you left here."

Fox shrugged. "Didn't want 'em no more," he said. "Wanted to get my own." He slumped further down into the couch and folded his arms across his chest. The conversation was obviously over.

Mr. Phillips raised his eyebrows and glanced briefly at Brett, as if to say, *You see what we're up against here?* Brett nodded, sympathizing with Mr. Phillips' futile attempts at communication with Fox, yet wondering if it wouldn't help if the man would just quit calling him Elmore. Still, Brett was relieved to know that Fox's caseworker obviously had the boy's best interests at heart, and that the hall was a much nicer place than he'd expected. It made things a little easier for Brett when it was time for him to turn and walk away from Fox. A little easier . . . but not much.

As he made his way slowly down the hall toward the front door, stopping to sign autographs for a couple of kids who'd recognized him, he told himself he should feel happy that Fox was now in good hands. He told himself that he should feel proud that he had done the right thing—not only for Fox, but for himself and for Ariane. He told himself that he should feel relieved to know that he'd done all he could—more than most people would have, he reminded himself. And he told himself that he had no reason in the world to feel guilty.

But as he climbed into his shiny Porsche and pulled the door shut behind him, he did not feel happy or proud or relieved. He felt guilty—very, very guilty—as if two large, dark, liquid eyes were boring accusingly into his back.

*

Her head pounded and her feet ached as she pushed the automatic door opener and pulled into the garage. Climbing out of her Mercedes and walking over to the side door, she caught the pungent, tantalizing aroma of sauteed onions and garlic even before she had her key in the lock.

As she stepped into the kitchen and out of her shoes, Ariane couldn't help but smile. It had been an exhausting day, and all the way home she had been dreading the thought of cooking. She'd considered stopping somewhere to pick up something, but had been too tired even for that. Calling out for a pizza was about all she had the energy left to do. But home-delivered pizza couldn't hold a candle to Brett's special spaghetti and meatballs. Besides, he was so cute, standing there in his chef's apron, smiling at her as he stirred the spaghetti sauce.

"I made dinner," he announced.

"So I see," she said, walking over to him and tilting her head up for a kiss. "Your timing couldn't have been better."

He raised his eyebrows questioningly. "Long day?"

"Endless." She walked over to the table and plunked down in a chair, smiling at the sight of her apron-clad husband and thinking what a contrast it was to the image of the composed, iron-willed quarterback so familiar to sports fans across the country. "Seemed like one of those days where the only law that got practiced around the office was Murphy's—you know, if anything could go wrong, it did."

Brett smiled back, but didn't answer.

"I'm so glad I don't have school tonight," Ariane continued, leaning over to massage her stockinged feet. "I'm just going to have some of your wonderful spaghetti, take a long hot bath and go to bed."

When Brett still didn't answer, she looked up. His forehead was creased, his eyes troubled. Something was on his mind—and she knew what.

"By the way," she said, trying to sound more casual than she felt, "did you finally get things settled with that Fox kid?"

His smile looked forced. "Yes," he answered. "I called Matthew, and he got in touch with Fox's caseworker. Seems he'd run away from the hall a week or so ago. Anyway, I took him back over there this afternoon. It's . . . all settled."

She stared at him silently. Did he really think she couldn't tell, that she hadn't loved him long enough to know when he was holding something back?

"Are you sure?" she asked, breaking the silence. "Is it really all settled—once and for all?"

Brett's frown deepened. "What do you mean? Of course it's settled. I told you, I took him back to the hall this afternoon."

"I know what you told me," she said. "But that look on your face tells me something else. I know you, Brett Holiday. What is it? What are you thinking? What aren't you telling me?"

Brett wiped his hands on his apron and came and sat down beside Ariane.

"I can't abandon him, Ariane," he said. "I can't just walk away and leave him there—"

"Why not?" she interrupted. "From what I've heard around the office, the hall really isn't such a bad place to be. They take good care of those kids, Brett. They do all they can to help them. Why do you need to get involved? Why can't you just let it go? That boy is not your problem."

"I promised I'd help him," he said, reaching for her hand. "I promised him, babe."

She flinched, but didn't draw away. "Let it go," she pleaded, her voice cracking slightly. "You've got to let it go, can't you see? We have enough to deal with in our own lives right now. We don't need this, too."

Her heart pounded in her ears as she waited, refusing to drop her gaze from Brett's face. She was right, she knew she was. She would have to make him understand. She had to.

"I can't," he said, his eyes sad but his jawline firm, the way she'd seen it so many times before a big game. "Oh, babe, if you could have seen him in the restaurant this morning, the tears in his eyes when he talked about his family. He never knew his father; he was an alcoholic who died in jail. And his mother . . . how she chose her boyfriend over Fox . . . how they took Fox's little sister and the three of them ran off and left him behind. But what really got to me was the look on his face when I took him back to the hall . . . when I left him there. . . ."

His voice trailed off, then he took a deep breath and shook his head. "I'm sorry, sweetheart. I won't bring him here, if that's the way you want it. But I can't just walk away from him. I can't, Ariane. And I won't."

She opened her mouth—to plead, to argue, to threaten, if necessary. But the unlikely image of the usually defiant Fox, speaking of his family with tears in his eyes, stopped her. If she hadn't seen him that first night, sitting at her dinner table and staring at himself in the sparkling china plate, his dirty T-shirt stretched tightly across his not-yet broad shoulders, she wouldn't have believed it. But she knew her husband was telling her the truth.

At the same instant, she realized their lives would never be the same. However tender and nurturing a man her husband was, he was also like a bulldog once he got hold of something. It was one of the reasons she loved him so much. The only problem was she couldn't quite decide if this was something Brett had gotten hold of, or if it had gotten hold of him.

Either way, she knew Brett was in it for the long haul. And, although she wasn't ready to admit it to him, she knew she loved him enough to go through it with him—whatever happened.

Two days later, Brett was back at the hall. He'd tried to stay away, tried not to think of the brash, defensive teenager with the streetwise demeanor of a grown man and the wounded heart of a young boy. But as hard as he'd tried, Brett had been unable to think of anything else.

It was Saturday, and the morning fog hung gray and damp overhead, blotting out the sun and easily matching Brett's mood as he made his way toward the grassy field behind the gymnasium. He'd been told that most of the older kids were "hanging out" back there, and he would probably find Fox among them.

Brett spotted him right away. Although the other kids were gathered together in groups, talking, laughing, tossing a football back and forth, Fox was alone, sitting on the far edge of the field with his back against the chain link fence, his head tilted upward toward the sky. As Brett moved toward him, he was glad to see that Fox wore a relatively new pair of jeans, tennis shoes that appeared to be the right size, and a dark blue wind-breaker, zipped tightly against the morning chill.

"Hey, man!" called a voice to his right. Brett turned. A group of five boys, all about Fox's age, stood staring at him, studying him with unabashed curiosity. The largest boy, a Latino with a spiked crewcut and clad only in jeans and a black T-shirt, stepped toward Brett. The others followed.

"Brett Holiday, right?" said the boy.

Brett nodded. "That's right," he said, grasping the boy's outstretched hand firmly. "How are you guys doing?"

The boys introduced themselves as Brett shook hands with each of them. The boy who had first spoken to Brett identified himself as Ernie. "But I'm thinking of changing my name to 'Guapo,'" he added with a grin. The other boys laughed and hooted at the self-imposed nickname, which Brett recognized as Spanish for "hand-some" or "good looking."

The next three boys were all black—Richard, James, and Nathaniel. Richard and James, explained Nathaniel, were brothers. "But not me," he added quickly. "I'm not their brother, that's for sure!"

"That's 'cause you're their sister!" joked Ernie.

The boys were laughing again—all except Nathaniel, who shook his head from side to side. "You guys are cold, man! Cold! Besides, no sister of theirs could be as good lookin' as me anyway!"

Brett couldn't resist laughing along with them. It was obvious they were used to exchanging good-natured insults. *Ariane claims it's part of the male ritual,* thought Brett. *Maybe she's right.*

The final boy to introduce himself to Brett seemed the most unlikely and out-of-place member of the group. A thin, blond boy with glasses, Anthony was referred to by the rest of the boys as "The Brain."

"He helps us with our homework," explained Ernie, throwing an arm around Anthony's neck in a playful headlock. "And we help him with everything else."

What Anthony's handshake lacked in strength, he made up for with enthusiasm. "I've seen you on TV lots of times," he announced with a grin. "I even went to one of your games once. You guys lost."

Brett smiled and nodded. "That happens sometimes."

"Hey, what are you doin' here, anyway?" asked Nathaniel. "You come to see that Fox kid? He says he knows you."

"Yeah," answered Brett, glancing over in Fox's direction. He was sure Fox was aware of his presence by now, but the boy hadn't moved. *A statue,* thought Brett. *Stone pressed up against the fence.* . . . "Yeah, we've met."

"How?" Nathaniel persisted. "I mean, if you're his friend like he says, you're the only one he's got. That guy don't want to be friends with nobody! All he wants to do is go to New York."

Brett looked down at Nathaniel. His round face was turned up toward Brett expectantly, dark eyes shining with excitement and curiosity. No hard mask to shut out the world with all its pain and disappointments. Just a boy on the edge of becoming a man.

"I guess you could say Fox and I . . . met in his travels, you know?" Brett explained to Nathaniel. "Anyway, I'd better get over there and see how he's doing. If you guys are going to be around for a while, maybe we could throw a few passes later on."

"All right!" exclaimed Nathaniel.

"You got it, man," added Ernie.

Although Fox's head was tilted upward, his eyes were closed. He didn't open them, even when Brett stopped and stood right in front of him. It was obvious to Brett that Fox knew he was there. It was also obvious that, if they were going to talk at all, it would have to be on Fox's level. Brett sat down on the grass next to him.

"Cold out this morning," commented Brett, stuffing his hands into the pockets of his blue and gold Rams sweatshirt.

Fox shrugged. "Don't bother me none," he mumbled.

"I thought you liked sunshine," said Brett.

"Sometimes."

Brett sighed. This wasn't going to be easy. But then, with Fox, he had learned it never was.

"I met some of your friends over there," said Brett.

"Ain't my friends," said Fox.

"So I heard." Brett paused. "Why do you suppose that is?"

Fox shrugged again. "Don't know," he said. "Don't care, neither."

"I think you do," said Brett. "Everybody needs friends."

Slowly, Fox opened his eyes and turned to face Brett. "I don't," he said flatly. "I don't need nobody. And that includes you." He closed his eyes and turned away again.

Brett leaned back against the fence. *Why do I bother? he wondered. Why do I even try? With or without my help, chances are that, sooner or later, Fox will end up just like his father, in jail . . . or worse.*

Wait a minute! he told himself. I'm starting to sound more negative than Fox. I'm giving up before I even get started. And I'm sure not going to be any help to him—or anyone else—with an attitude like that.

"Fox," he said, sitting forward and staring at the boy intently. "Listen to me. I know you've been hurt and disappointed, but you can't let yourself get bitter. You can't just shut people out, don't you see? You'll never get anywhere in life if you do that. You have to trust somebody, let somebody in. How can I help you if you won't let me near you? How can I . . . ?"

No response. But he couldn't stop now. There had to be a way to reach him. Maybe a different tactic.

"You know, Fox, there was a time in my life when I thought I didn't need anyone, either. Maybe it was because I was an only child and I got used to spending time alone, I don't know—"

Fox's eyes opened as he turned his head in Brett's direction. "That's right, dude," he said, his voice low and steady, "you don't know. You don't know nothin' 'bout my life and I don't wanta know nothin' 'bout yours. Maybe you was alone once in a while as a kid, but don't try to make out like you understand 'bout me bein' alone, man. 'Cause you don't. You don't know nothin' and you don't understand nothin', you hear? And there ain't nothin' you can tell me 'bout your life's gonna matter to me. 'Cause in case you hadn't noticed, we be different, dude. Way different."

His eyes closed once again, and Brett suddenly felt invisible. He looked down at his hands, as if to be sure they were still there. The only thing he noticed about them was that they were white.

He felt as if he were standing beside the trash can that night again, trying to decide whether to continue or to stop and find out who was hiding behind it. *The kid told me I was crazy,* he thought. *Why do I keep proving him right?*

He tried to get up, but he knew he'd never make it. *I've come this far,* he decided. *I might as well go for broke.*

Continuing on as if he hadn't heard Fox's interruption, Brett said, "When I got older and started playing football, I found out that, no matter how good I was, I couldn't win the game by myself. Nobody can. I needed the other guys on the team, and they needed me. And when I learned to depend on them and to care about them, it made me a better player because I didn't have to stand alone anymore. I was part of a team, and that gave me strength. That's what life's all about, Fox, don't you see? We need each other. We need . . . each other. . . ."

His voice trailed off and he shook his head. He might as well talk to the fence. He sighed deeply.

"What's going to happen to you, Fox? What kind of life are you going to have? Have you thought about that? You're always talking about not wanting to end up like your dad, but . . ."

He stopped himself quickly when he saw the boy tense. He knew he treaded on thin ice. "Look," he went on. "You'll be thirteen in just a few months and—"

"Big deal!" interrupted Fox, snapping his head around and flashing his dark eyes at Brett. "What you gonna do, man? Give me a party or somethin'?"

Their eyes locked, and Brett felt as if he'd just been challenged to a duel. "I might," he said quietly. "I just might."

"Hey, man, what's this about a party?"

Brett looked up. Ernie and the other boys had gathered around and stared down at him and Fox eagerly. Brett hadn't realized they were there until he heard Ernie's voice, but apparently they'd stood around long enough to hear the word "party."

"Ain't gonna be no party," said Fox. "The football dude's just blowin' smoke, man."

"That right?" said Nathaniel. "Were you just kiddin' about the party, or did you really mean it?"

"Yeah," added Ernie. "You gonna throw a party for Fox, or not?"

Brett looked from the five eager faces above him to the controlled, impassive one at his side. *Third and long,* he thought suddenly. *The game's on the line and it's up to me to call the play.*

"Yeah," he answered, still staring at Fox. "Yeah, I'm going to give him a party. A major party. And you're all invited."

Ernie, Nathaniel, Richard, and James—even "The Brain"—started yelling and hollering and slapping high-fives. Some of the other kids, who had wandered over to see what was going on, were also getting caught up in the excitement. Fox, however, didn't say a word.

"Hey, man," asked Ernie, "where we gonna have this party, at your house?"

Brett looked up, but before he could answer, Nathaniel chimed in. "Who cares where we have it! Just so we have a real band, none of that deejay stuff, right?"

"Are you kidding?" exclaimed Anthony. "A guy as famous as Brett Holiday knows everybody. No way would he have a deejay at his party. In fact, he'll probably have lots of other famous people there, like actors and singers and—"

"All right!" cried Ernie, slapping Anthony on the back. "Now I know why we call you 'The Brain.' You're right, man. Brett could get anybody he wanted to come to that party."

"Yeah? Like who?" asked James.

Ernie thought for a minute, then grinned. "Like Jacqueline St. James," he announced, his eyes shining as he looked down at Fox. "Ain't she the one you're so in love with?" he asked. "The one you're always listenin' to on the radio?"

Fox glared at Ernie. "Never said I was in love with her."

"Well, I am," said Nathaniel. "I mean, have you ever seen her on TV? She is *hot!*"

"So," asked Ernie, looking back at Brett, "what's the story? You gonna get her for the party?"

As Brett looked away from the eager, animated faces staring down at him to Fox's chiseled-in-granite profile, he realized that this was more than just a game that was on the line here—this was the Super Bowl. He breathed a silent prayer.

"Sure," he said, the pounding of his heart echoing in his ears. "Sure, why not? Can't very well have a party for Fox without his favorite singer being there, right?"

The twitch of Fox's jawline was almost imperceptible. But for Brett, it was enough.

*

The warmth of Ariane's body beside him and the soft, steady sound of her breathing had always comforted and soothed Brett. Tonight, however, nothing seemed able to ease his growing restlessness.

Could it be true? he wondered. Was Fox destined to end up like his father, drunk and alone, wasting away in the dark . . . ?

No! Brett clenched his teeth, refusing to accept the inevitability of Fox's heritage. *I'm not going to think like that anymore,* he told himself.

Raising up on his elbow, he peeked over his sleeping wife and glanced at the illuminated dial of the clock on the bed stand beside her. Two-thirty. Only a few more hours and Ariane would be getting up for work. How he envied her ability to fall asleep so quickly, to sleep so soundly, regardless of what might be going on in their personal lives. But then, that's just the way she was. From the instant the alarm summoned her to a new day, Ariane set about the task of living with more energy and enthusiasm than any five men Brett had ever known. But when the day was over, she slept with the undisturbed innocence of a young child.

He closed his eyes and lay back down, but it didn't help. Even with his eyes shut, he couldn't block out the sound of his own voice as he impulsively, rashly, *foolishly* promised to throw a birthday party for Fox *and* to have Jacqueline St. James there besides. Good grief, she was one of the most popular singers around, and he'd never even met her, never spoken to her, and didn't know anyone who had. How could he have allowed himself to get sucked into something like this? And how was he ever going to tell Ariane?

Not that he hadn't tried to tell her. When he got home from the hall shortly after noon on Saturday, he had intended to do so right away, but she wasn't home. By the time she got back, she was cross and edgy from several hours at the mall—a "madhouse," she'd called it—and he'd decided to put off his confession until the time was right. Unfortunately, the time never seemed to be right. And now here it was, the wee hours of Monday morning, and still he hadn't told his wife what he had committed himself to do.

What would she say when he finally did break the news? What would her reaction be? More importantly, what could he say to help her understand how—and why—it had happened? How could he explain to her what he himself didn't fully understand?

How many times he'd gone over it in his mind, one minute reminding himself he'd done what he had to do under the circumstances, the next minute berating himself for making promises he had no idea how he was going to keep.

But what else could I do? he thought. *I mean, my back was against the wall. All those kids staring at me. And Fox. He didn't say anything, but I knew he was testing me. I just hope I don't fail him when it comes down to the wire. I mean, I've committed myself now; I have to try. I have to! But . . . I'm only one man. How much can one man do? How much difference can I possibly make—in Fox's life or in anyone else's?*

Ariane stirred then, turning toward Brett. Instinctively, he reached out and drew her close, until her head rested on his shoulder. Still asleep, she snuggled against him contentedly.

Brett rested his head on hers and breathed the soft, sweet smell of her hair. Life was good with Ariane. Good and right and—

Suddenly, his mind flashed back to a night many years earlier, when he was a young boy camping in the Rockies with his father. Snug and secure in his sleeping bag, he could almost hear the gentle rustling of leaves as the night wind soughed through the Aspen trees overhead. The smell of pinion pines and cedar smoke from the smoldering campfire filled his nostrils as his father, zipped into the sleeping bag beside him, talked Brett to sleep with one of their favorite stories.

Although he'd heard all of his father's stories many times over, that one particular night he seemed to "hear" it for the first time, and he sensed that his father was telling him something that would be important to him someday. But the story had faded from his mind over the years—until now. Now. Now, as he lay beside his wife in his king-sized bed in his beautiful big home in southern California, remembering that long ago night when he lay beside his father in his sleeping bag in the Rocky Mountains of Colorado.

It was a story about fish, he remembered that. Hundreds of fish that had washed up on the shore. And something about an old man—yes, that was it! An old man, standing on the shore all by himself, trying to scoop up the fish and throw them back into the water before they died. And somewhere, standing behind the old man, was a boy, watching him.

A boy watching him. Brett shivered and snuggled closer to Ariane as the words echoed through his mind. What was it that had happened next?

Oh yes, now he remembered. The boy couldn't understand why the old man was wearing himself out at such an obviously impossible task. Finally, he had gone up to the old man and asked him why he bothered, what possible difference his efforts could make, when he knew he could never save more than just a few of the hundreds of fish flopping around helplessly on the sand.

The old man looked down at the gasping, flailing fish in his hands, then held it out in front of him. "You see this fish?" he asked, looking back at the boy. "It makes a difference to him."

As Brett held his sleeping wife close, he realized how right he'd been as he'd listened to that story so many years ago. His father had, indeed, told him something that would be very important to him someday.

Ariane stirred again. "You awake?" she mumbled.

"Afraid so," he whispered. "Sorry if I woke you."

"I don't mind," she answered, kissing his cheek. "I was dreaming about you, anyway."

Brett grinned. "Really? What about?"

Ariane raised herself up on one elbow, then leaned down and kissed him, slowly and very, very passionately. "I'll show you," she said, and kissed him again.

All thoughts of Fox and Jacqueline St. James and birthday parties, along with fish, old men, and watchful boys, faded from Brett's mind, as he returned Ariane's kiss hungrily.

*

It was Ariane's muffled voice, singing in the shower, that first pulled him from a deep, heavy sleep. Rolling over to look at the clock, he groaned. His muscles ached and his head pounded. His eyes felt as though he'd rubbed them with sand.

It was six-thirty. How could the woman sing at six-thirty in the morning, especially after such a lengthy, albeit pleasant, interruption to her sleep?

He shook his head gingerly and pulled himself to a sitting position. Maybe some coffee would help. And some orange juice. Climbing out of bed and sliding into his robe and slippers, he wondered if Ariane had made the coffee and set the automatic timer before she went to bed.

Of course she did, he told himself. *Ariane's too efficient to have forgotten something like that. It's part of her nightly routine.*

He was right. The coffee waited for him by the time he made his way from the bedroom, out to the front porch to pick up the morning paper, and finally into the kitchen. Downing a glass of juice, he poured a glass for Ariane, then filled a mug with steaming black coffee and sat down at the table to read the sports page and wait for his wife.

"You look terrible," she said, walking into the kitchen a few minutes later and planting a kiss on top of his head.

"Thanks a lot," he said. "I'd say the same for you, but I can't. You look terrific—as usual."

Ariane smiled. Dressed in a two-piece cream colored suit, the ends of her long dark hair still damp from the shower, she appeared ready—and anxious—to tackle the day. Brett wished he had just a tenth of her energy and enthusiasm.

Ariane drank her juice without sitting down, then poured herself a cup of coffee and joined Brett at the table. "So, did you finally get some sleep?" she asked, picking up the front page of the paper and scanning the headlines.

"A little," he answered.

Ariane took a sip of coffee. "Reliving last night's victory?" she asked.

Brett raised his eyebrows. "What?"

She grinned mischievously. "I was talking about the Laker game," she explained. "I noticed you were reading the sports section, so I assumed you were recapping the game. I know how much you love to do that when they win."

"True," he agreed. "But I read it when they lose, too. It's just not as much fun then."

"I suppose not," she said. "But then, they obviously don't do that very often, or they wouldn't be heading into the playoffs again." She took a final sip of her coffee and stood up. "Well, gotta run," she said, leaning down and brushing his lips with a quick kiss.

"Already?" asked Brett. "I hoped we'd have a chance to talk before you left."

Ariane glanced at her watch and shook her head. "Sorry, honey. No time. Maybe this evening before I leave for school." She disappeared into the bedroom, then came back to kiss him once more before she hurried, briefcase in hand, for the front door.

Brett sighed as he refilled his coffee cup and looked around at the empty kitchen. He really didn't feel like eating anything yet. Was it too early to start making phone calls?

He went to the drawer nearest the wall phone and pulled out the phone book, grabbed some paper and a pen, and started making a list. He knew, of course, that her phone number wouldn't be in the book, but he had to tap all his resources until he found someone who knew how to get hold of Jacqueline St. James.

By mid-morning, his ear ached from all the time he'd spent on the phone. Although he'd been unable to contact Jacqueline directly, he had finally managed, after repeated calls to her recording company, to track down her agent and her manager. After leaving messages asking her to call him as soon as possible, he'd hung up. Until he heard back from her, there was nothing more that he could do.

Exhausted, he wandered back into the bedroom and flopped down on the bed. He was asleep almost as soon as his head hit the pillow.

CHAPTER **9**

That same day, even as Brett slept, recovering from his restless night and his marathon phone search for Jacqueline St. James, Fox sat, slumped in a hard wooden chair, half listening to the steady drone of Mr. Bower, his balding, bespectacled history teacher. The classroom was almost as stuffy as Mr. Bower, and Fox found it more and more difficult to concentrate on what was being said.

Besides, he thought, *who cares what happened at some ancient battle in World War II? What's that got to do with me, anyway? What's it got to do with anythin'?*

He sighed and shifted his weight, glancing up at the round, institutional style clock on the side wall. Twenty more minutes and then he could get outside for some fresh air before he had to come back and sit and listen to another boring teacher talk about numerators and denominators and common factors. As if anyone was ever going to ask him about those things when he finally made it big in New York! Besides, he already knew all that stuff; he just wasn't about to tell anyone that he understood it—especially the other kids. They'd think he was a jerk for sure.

Out of the corner of his eye, he noticed that Nathaniel, who sat on his left, was obviously as bored as he was. Fox turned his head and looked closer. Nathaniel's eyelids were drooping, and his head nodded occasionally. On the other side of Nathaniel, Ernie sat hunched over his desk, drawing some sort of design on a piece of lined paper.

Fox looked back toward the front of the room. Mr. Bower's mouth was still moving, the same dull, dry monotone escaping from his lips and saturating the heavy air around them with empty, meaningless facts.

How can he be so lame, thought Fox. *Don't he know we ain't payin' attention? Or maybe he knows, but he don't care. After all, it's just a job. Don't make no difference to him if we learn this stuff. Long as he gets paid.*

Bet he don't get paid much, though. Not like that football dude. That's what I can't figure out. Teacher's here 'cause he has to be. Prob'ly too lame to find a job anywhere else. But the football dude, he don't have to come here.

He thought back to Saturday morning when Brett had come to visit. Actually, he'd thought about almost nothing else since. A half-smile played on his lips as he remembered how Brett had been backed into a corner about the party and about having Jacqueline St. James there. Fat chance of that ever happening! But it was kind of funny. . . .

"Elmore!"

Fox jumped, glancing around quickly. The way the other kids were staring at him, Mr. Bower had obviously called his name more than once before Fox had heard him. He cleared his throat.

"Yeah?" Fox answered, jutting out his chin and glaring at the teacher.

"I asked you a question, Elmore," said Mr. Bower. "Do you know the answer?"

Fox shrugged. "Don't even know the question."

Laughter rippled through the room as Mr. Bower frowned. "Well," he said, "I thought maybe you did, since I noticed you were sitting there smiling while I talked. But obviously your mind was on something other than the Battle of the Bulge, and obviously it was quite amusing. Would you care to tell us about it, Elmore?"

"Wouldn't care to tell you nothin'," answered Fox.

The room was quiet again, as Fox waited to be sent to the principal's office. But Mr. Bower just stared at him for a moment, then turned away and began to point to different locations on the large map beside the blackboard. Fox couldn't decide if he was relieved or disappointed.

Least I coulda got outta here, he thought. *Trouble is, just woulda had to listen to some other lame dude tell me how I should "respect the teachers and pay attention in class"* . . . *same stuff they always say, like it was gonna make a difference or somethin'.*

Fox stared at the back of Mr. Bower's shiny head as the teacher described the weather in the area where he now pointed on the map. *Wonder why he don't ever tell us nothin' we can use,* thought Fox. *Like, what it's like in places like New York—and today, not fifty or a hundred years ago.*

He shook his head. They were all the same. Living in their big fancy world and trying to tell you how to live in yours, even though they'd never been there—and for sure didn't want to be! Whether they were in it for the money like Mr. Bower and most of the others at the hall, or whether they were just a bunch of "do-gooders" trying to make themselves feel better about having more than most everybody else, they were still the same. All of them.

Yeah, even you, Mr. football dude, thought Fox. *You ain't no different. I see through you, man. I know you ain't in it for the money, that's for sure. A do-gooder—that's you, all right. All your big talk 'bout life bein' like a team, how we all need each other* . . . *who you need, dude? You need me? For what, man? You lookin' for a cause? Go march for animal rights or somethin'. Maybe they jump all over you and wag their tails when you come pat 'em on the head, but not me, dude! No way am I buyin' your story. You 'spect me to believe you gonna come through with that party? Man, you must think I'm the biggest fool in town.*

Nope, you just blowin' smoke, like I said. Ain't gonna be no party, ain't gonna be no Jacqueline St. James. . . . Fact, I be surprised you ever show up here again at all. Real surprised.

But even as his thoughts faded and he observed, once again, Mr. Bower, who was now drawing some sort of illustration on the blackboard, a faint hope tugged at Fox's heart. He blinked his eyes and clenched his jaw, determined to ignore it. Hope, he knew from experience, brought nothing but disappointment and pain.

*

The music was soft and muted, as were the lights. Ariane sensed that Brett had chosen this elegant, seaside restaurant for more reasons than simply the romantic evening he'd promised. In fact, she'd sensed for a couple of days now that he had something on his mind, something she was sure he would share with her sooner or later. And so she'd waited.

Not that it had been easy. Ariane's natural curiosity had made it difficult to be patient, but she had been married to Brett long enough to know that this was one of those times when she would have to wait for him to broach the subject.

"Like the view?" Brett asked, reaching across the candlelit table to take her hand.

Ariane looked him up and down. "Love it," she teased.

Brett grinned. "I appreciate the compliment," he said, turning to look out the window. "But I was referring to the view out here."

Ariane followed his gaze. The harbor was quiet this time of night, as moored boats and yachts of all sizes bobbed peacefully on the water, the lights from the restaurant shimmering on its dark surface.

"It's beautiful," she said, squeezing Brett's hand. "I'm so glad you talked me into this."

"So am I," agreed Brett. "Although, you have to admit, it wasn't easy."

Ariane laughed huskily as they turned back to face each other. "You know how I am sometimes," she said. "All work and no play."

"Believe me, I know," said Brett. "But one night off from studying isn't going to hurt your professional future. And it will do wonders for us."

"You're right," she said. "I just have to be reminded of that occasionally. Thanks, sweetheart."

The waiter brought their salads then, along with a basket of freshly baked sourdough bread. Brett started to reach for a piece, then hesitated, his brow knitting together in a frown.

"What's wrong?" asked Ariane.

Brett shook his head. "Oh, nothing really. It's just . . ."

"Just what?"

"Well, it's . . ." He sighed. "Just something Fox said when I took him out to breakfast that morning. About praying."

Ariane looked confused. "Praying? What could Fox have to say about praying? I was under the impression that was something new to him."

Brett nodded. "It is," he agreed. "But he pointed out to me that I pray at home, but not in public. He asked me if it was because I didn't like people watching me when I pray. It had never bothered me before, but . . . suddenly I felt like a hypocrite."

Ariane reached across the table and covered his hand with hers. "And it's bothering you again."

He nodded again. "Yes."

"Would you like to pray now, before we eat?"

Brett didn't answer. Instead, he closed his eyes and offered thanks for the food. Ariane was touched. She felt she should say something to reassure him, to thank him or encourage him, but she wasn't sure what.

"Fox seems to be having quite an effect on you," she said softly.

Brett gazed into her eyes for a moment, but he said nothing. Instead, reaching for the bread basket, he offered a piece to Ariane.

"No, thanks," she said, more sure than ever that there was something he wanted to discuss with her, but just as sure that she would still have to wait. "I think I'll just settle for the salad right now. If I fill up on bread, I won't have any room left for dinner when it gets here."

"Guess that means I'll have to eat it all myself," said Brett, shaking his head. "Too bad."

Ariane laughed. "You'd better watch out, Brett Holiday. The way you eat sometimes, you'd think you were getting paid for it. I'm warning you, one of these days—"

"I know, I know," Brett interrupted. "One of these days, I'm going to wake up and be as big as a barn. You've been telling me that ever since we got married, and it hasn't happened yet."

"Yet," she said. "That's the key word—*yet*. But you're not getting any younger, you know. Sooner or later . . ."

Brett winced. "Ouch," he said. "Thanks for the timely reminder." He looked down at the bread in his hand, then back up at Ariane. "How about if I just use half as much butter?"

Ariane laughed again. "You're hopeless, you know that? Hopeless!"

Brett didn't answer. He couldn't. His mouth was already stuffed full of bread.

"So," said Ariane, nibbling at her salad, "what's with Ron these days? I haven't seen him in a while. Have you talked to him since you two went to that Laker game together?"

Brett swallowed the bread and washed it down with a drink of ice water. "Briefly," he said. "I stopped by there about a week ago. You know, the morning I took Fox back to the hall. I had hoped to get Ron to go to breakfast with us, but he turned me down."

"I'm not surprised," said Ariane. "He probably thought you were crazy, hauling that kid around with you like you'd adopted him or something. Exactly what was Ron's reaction to Fox, anyway?"

Brett hesitated. "Well . . . let's just say he was less than enthusiastic. In fact, he was curious to know what you thought about the whole thing."

Ariane felt vindicated. "Good for him," she said. "I'm glad to know someone cares about my feelings in all of this."

Brett set his bread down and looked at Ariane intently. "You know I care about your feelings, sweetheart, in this and in everything that concerns us. It's just that this situation with Fox goes so far beyond our feelings. It's so much more important than just—"

Ariane dropped her fork onto her plate, her composure forgotten. "I can't believe you said that! I can't believe that you're actually sitting here telling me that some kid you hardly know is more important to you than I am."

Brett reached across the table and covered her hand with his. "I didn't say that, babe. And if it sounded that way, I'm sorry. I didn't mean for it to. It's just that . . . I feel responsible for him somehow, Ariane. As if that boy's entire future depends on whether or not I follow through on my commitments to him. I know that sounds crazy, but . . ."

Brett's voice trailed off as Ariane's eyes opened wide. Was this it? The thing she'd been waiting for him to share with her?

She did her best to hold her voice steady. "Just what commitments have you made to him?" she asked, locking her eyes firmly into his. "What commitments are you talking about?"

Brett seemed to grow six inches as he sat up straight and took a deep breath. "I told him I'd give him a birthday party," he said, plunging right in. "He's going to be thirteen in a few months, and he's never had a party before. All the kids were there, wanting to come and waiting to see what I'd say, and . . . well, I said yes. I said I'd give him a party." He paused. "I promised him, sweetheart. I promised all of them."

They stared at each other, neither of them speaking. Finally, Ariane shook her head back and forth slowly, deliberately. "You're crazy, Brett Holiday," she said, her voice barely above a whisper. "Absolutely, positively, certifiably nuts. You find some kid hiding behind a trash can in an alley, bring him home, feed him, give him a place to sleep, let him get away with stealing my grandmother's silver—"

"He brought it back," interrupted Brett.

"That's beside the point," she argued, feeling the fire build within her. "If he hadn't taken it in the first place, he wouldn't have had to return it. What we're talking about here is not your average, everyday, run-of-the-mill kid. Fox is a con-artist, do you hear me? A pro! And from what you told me about his father, he comes from a long line of con-artists and thieves and who knows what else. Not only could he have inherited his father's criminal tendencies, he may very well have inherited his alcoholism, too. But do you let little problems like that stop you? Oh, no! You just jump right in with both feet. I'm telling you, Brett, that kid had you pegged from the beginning. He took one look at you and saw 'Sucker' written all over your face. And you really fell for it, didn't you? Poor, underprivileged kid, never had a break in life, so you're the guy who's going to give it to him, right? And now you're giving him a birthday party. Incredible. Absolutely incredible!"

Brett's face reddened as Ariane talked. She sensed it was more from anger than embarrassment, but she just couldn't stop herself. Those things needed to be said, and she'd said them. Now let the chips fall where they may.

"I don't mind your calling me a sucker," he began. "I've called myself the same thing—and worse—lately. But calling Fox a con-artist, as if the boy had chosen his lifestyle, as if he'd had options, that's unfair, Ariane. Totally unfair. Do you suppose he conned his mother into leaving him? Do you suppose he conned his way into the 'privilege' of living in foster homes and state-run halls? And how about sleeping in back alleys and rummaging through garbage cans for food and clothes? Did he con his way into that, too?"

He paused. Ariane considered saying something in her own defense, but she decided to let him finish. After all, she'd had her say. Now he could have his. She only hoped she wouldn't feel too badly about herself when he was finished.

"Remember the other night when you woke up and found I was already awake? You didn't ask me why I was awake, but I'm going to tell you, anyway. I was thinking about that boy, about the promises I'd made him, about how I was going to tell you. But most of all, I was thinking about a story my dad told me once, years ago, a story about how each one of us—each one, Ariane—can make a difference in this world by being willing to reach out and touch and help others. We can't help everybody, I know that. But we can help some. Maybe just a few. Or even one. But it's a start, don't you see? At least it's a start."

Slowly, silently, Ariane turned her head away from Brett and stared out the window. Neither of them spoke. There was truth in what Brett said. His honesty forced her to consider that she could be wrong. Hot tears stung her eyelids as she finally looked back at him. "Is that it?" she asked. "Or is there more?"

For just a moment, he seemed surprised at the obvious emotion on her face. Then, grabbing his glass and taking a quick sip of water, he went on. "Actually, there is something else," he said. "Fox . . . well, his favorite singer is Jacqueline St. James, and I . . . I promised to get her to come to the party."

Ariane didn't move. She didn't speak. She couldn't. She was amazed to discover that she was trying to decide if her husband was completely insane, or just plain wonderful.

Both, she decided. *Definitely both.* She reached over and took his hand in hers, raising it to her lips. "I love you" was all she said.

*

"Hey, check out this car!" exclaimed Nathaniel, climbing into the back seat behind Ernie and Anthony. "This yours, Brett?"

"No way," answered Fox, sitting in the front seat beside Brett. "This here's his wife's car, man. Brett has a Porsche. A red one."

It was the first time Brett had heard anything in Fox's voice to indicate that he was even slightly proud of his relationship with, and subsequent "inside" knowledge of, Brett. And it was obvious in the boys' treatment of Fox that knowing Brett had upped his status around the hall. Of course, Brett realized that it was because he was Brett Holiday, the famous quarterback, and not Brett Holiday, a nice guy. But at least it was a start.

"I love Porsches," said Ernie. "I'm going to get me one someday. How come you didn't bring it?"

"We wouldn't exactly have fit," explained Anthony. "Besides, this Mercedes is nice, too."

Brett smiled to himself, remembering Ariane's reaction the night before when he'd asked to trade cars with her for the day.

"Sure," she'd answered. "No problem. But why?"

He'd braced himself. "I, uh . . . I need the extra room so I can take Fox and some of the other kids to the Laker game tomorrow."

Expecting the worst, he'd waited. But she'd only sighed and shook her head, as if resigning herself to the fact that her husband had lost his mind and there was nothing she could do about it. And now, here he was, exactly one week after his first visit to Fox at the hall, taking four boys he hardly knew to a Laker game in his wife's car.

Not that it had been any problem getting permission to take the boys. The only problem had been when Brett stopped by the hall the day before to tell Fox about his plans.

"Don't know if I wanna go," he'd said. "But if I do, I ain't gonna ask nobody else."

"Why not?" Brett had persisted. "I've got five tickets. Why waste them? I'm sure you can find three other guys who'd want to come along."

Fox had just shrugged. "You wanna ask 'em, fine. But I ain't gonna do it."

So Brett had stopped by the administration office before leaving to make the necessary arrangements.

"Which boys do you want to take?" the heavyset, white-haired woman behind the desk had asked.

"I don't know," answered Brett. "The only other kids I've really talked to much are Ernie and Nathaniel and . . ."

His voice trailed off as he searched his memory for the other boys' names.

The lady smiled, deepening the laugh lines around her eyes. "You must be thinking of James and Richard and Anthony, commonly known as 'The Brain.'"

Brett smiled back and nodded. "That's them. But I only have enough tickets to take three of them."

"Actually, that works out quite well," the woman explained. "As you may know, James and Richard are brothers, and they have some relatives living nearby. Arrangements have already been made for them to spend time with their family this Saturday. So it sounds like it will work out perfectly."

Brett had been relieved, and prayed that having the boys together for the day would open Fox up and help him begin to develop some friendships with the other kids. Or, if that was too much to hope for, that Fox would at least make an effort to get along with everyone. So far, now that they were actually in the car, things seemed to be going reasonably well.

After making sure all seat belts were buckled—although it was obviously an unpopular request—Brett started the car and backed out of the parking space. The three boys in the back seat seemed determined to out-talk each other, interspersing their nonstop chatter with playful insults and laughter. Brett didn't mind the noise; he only wished Fox would join in.

"So," said Brett, taking advantage of the first brief lull in conversation, "any of you boys ever been to a Laker game before?"

"I seen 'em on TV," answered Nathaniel. "Lotsa times."

"That's not what the man asked," said Ernie. "He wants to know, have we ever been there before. This is my first time, man. Always wanted to go, though."

"Me, too," added Nathaniel. "*Always* wanted to."

"I think I went once," said Anthony. "I mean, I kinda remember something about it. I wasn't very old, so I'm not sure. It was when I was still living with my . . . with some people."

Brett glanced in the rearview mirror at Anthony, who was seated directly behind him. He'd heard traces of pain in the boy's voice, but Anthony saw Brett looking at him in the mirror and smiled back.

"So it will really be like my first time there," Anthony added.

Brett nodded. "Well, I'm just glad you could all come. Not much fun going to a game by yourself, you know."

"You mean, your wife don't go with you?" asked Nathaniel.

"Hey, man, what's wrong with you?" asked Ernie. "Women don't go to basketball games."

"Sure they do," said Nathaniel. "Don't you ever watch the games on TV? There's women all over the place."

"Yeah, but that don't mean his wife goes," said Ernie.

"She goes when she can," Brett explained. "But she's real busy with her job and school and—"

"Your wife goes to school?" asked Nathaniel. "How old is she, anyway?"

Brett laughed. "What's that got to do with it? You're never too old to learn, you know."

"I hate school," said Nathaniel. "I'll never go when I get older. I only go now 'cause they make me."

"I love it," said Anthony. "Reading especially."

"That's why you're 'The Brain,'" said Ernie. "It's okay for you, man. But not for me. I got other things to do with my life."

"Like what?" asked Brett.

"Like workin'," answered Ernie. "I'm gonna get me a real good job and make lots of money and live in a great big house and drive a car like this—or better, even. You just watch me!"

"What kind of a job are you planning to get?" Brett asked.

Ernie shrugged. "Don't know. Just somethin' that pays lots of money."

"You mean, like a doctor or lawyer or something like that," said Brett.

Nathaniel erupted into a fit of laughter. "Yeah, right," he exclaimed. "Or maybe a dealer, like his brother!"

Brett saw the warning look that passed from Ernie to Nathaniel. Nathaniel's laughter ceased.

"Yeah," said Ernie, looking away from Nathaniel. "Somethin' like that, I guess."

"All those jobs require a college education," said Brett, ignoring Nathaniel's disturbing comment. "Lots of years of study and hard work. In fact, that's what my wife is going to school for right now. She's going to be a lawyer soon."

"No kidding!" said Nathaniel. "Man, then you'll really be rich!"

"They already rich," said Fox. "I been to their house, remember?"

The three boys seemed surprised, as if they'd forgotten Fox was in the car with them. But their momentary surprise was soon replaced with a tinge of respect.

"What's it like?" asked Nathaniel. "They got a swimming pool?"

"Course they do," said Fox. "Rich people always have swimmin' pools. Don't you know nothin'?"

"I never knew nobody that had a swimming pool before," said Nathaniel.

"That's 'cause you never knew nobody that was rich," said Ernie.

"Neither did you," said Nathaniel.

"So what?" said Ernie, glancing up at Brett. "I do now. We all do."

"That's right," Nathaniel agreed. "Now we all do. Never thought I would, though."

"Me, neither," said Anthony. "And all the times I watched the Rams on TV, I sure never thought I'd meet Brett Holiday—or ride in his car."

"His wife's car," corrected Fox.

"Whatever," said Anthony. "Anyway, I guess that just shows you never know what's going to happen, do you?"

"That's true," said Brett. "Situations and circumstances change all the time. We can't always control that, but we can help steer things in the right direction. You know, like getting a good education, staying out of trouble."

"What if you already been in trouble?" asked Nathaniel. "What if . . . bad things . . . already happened in
your life? What if—"

"It doesn't matter where you've been or what you've
done," interrupted Brett, looking into the rearview mirror once again at all three boys before turning his head
to glance at Fox sitting beside him. "The only thing that
matters is where you go from here."

For once, Fox didn't ignore Brett. He turned toward him and their eyes locked. Fox's jaws were
clenched and he didn't speak, but Brett knew he'd hit a
nerve—and he was pretty sure they were both thinking
the same thing. Was it really possible to break free of
the past, to put it behind you and start over again? Did
Brett really believe what he'd just said to the boys, or
were they just a lot of empty words?

Steering Ariane's sparkling silver Mercedes onto
the street leading to the Forum, he sensed it wouldn't
be long before he'd be forced to answer those questions—once and for all.

CHAPTER 10

T he ringing phone roused him from a deep sleep, and he blinked his eyes groggily. It was morning, he was sure of that, although it seemed later than usual. He must have overslept. But why was the shower running? Why hadn't Ariane left for work already?

As he reached for the phone, he tried to focus on the clock. He was right. It was later than usual. In fact, it was after eight.

"Hello?" he mumbled, closing his eyes once again and lying back on Ariane's pillow as he held the receiver close to his ear.

"Brett? Hey, man, is that you?"

Brett frowned. It was Ron's voice, but what in the world was he doing up so early?

"Yeah, it's me," Brett answered, clearing his throat. "But I sure didn't expect to hear your voice at this hour of the morning."

Ron laughed. "Yeah, well, you'd better put it down on your calendar, 'cause it won't happen again till training season."

"That I can believe," said Brett, stifling a yawn. "So, what's the story? Did I miss something? An earthquake or a tidal wave? A hurricane, maybe?"

"Nah, just one of those weird mornings where, you know, you wake up and can't get back to sleep no matter how hard you try. Maybe I'm just not used to wakin' up to the sound of rain."

Brett listened again. So that was it. Rain. Soft, steady, soothing. That also explained why the room seemed so gray. He should have known, should at least have realized that the water he'd heard couldn't have been Ariane taking a shower. No way was his prompt, dependable wife running late! In all the years they'd been married, Brett couldn't remember Ariane ever being late for work—or anything else, for that matter. Very obviously, she had long since showered and gone to the office, leaving him to snooze comfortably for as long as he wanted.

"What I don't understand," Ron continued, "is why you sound like you got cotton in your brain—not to mention, in your mouth. Don't tell me you were asleep when I called! I thought you usually got up early with Ariane."

Brett yawned again. "Usually," he agreed. "I guess I just overslept today, and my sweet wife decided not to disturb me. Anyway, I'm glad you called. I need to get up and get moving."

"I'm glad to hear that," said Ron. "Because that's exactly why I called. It's not much of a day for jogging or swimming, but we could go over to the gym for a workout. What do you say, should I pick you up?"

"The gym?" Brett hesitated. A workout was probably exactly what he needed, but there was this vague thought nagging at his mind, a need to do something, something he'd decided during the night and promised himself to take care of first thing in the morning, something that had to do with Fox and . . . ah, yes, now he remembered. But it wouldn't take long—fifteen minutes or so—and then he could go to the gym with Ron.

"Sure," said Brett. "Sounds good. But give me about an hour, will you? I got a few things I need to take care of first." He paused. "Uh, by the way, you don't happen to, uh . . . I know this is going to sound like a strange question, but . . . what I need to know is, do you know anyone who might happen to know . . . Jacqueline St. James, somebody who could . . . put me in touch with her?"

"Jacqueline St. James?" Ron laughed. "Right, man. As a matter of fact, I'm having dinner with her brother tonight. Are you crazy? If I just *happened* to know somebody who just *happened* to know Jacqueline St. James, you think I wouldn't have got myself introduced to her by now? I mean, that is one fine lookin' woman, in case you hadn't noticed. Which I'm sure you have, along with just about everybody else in the world—including your wife. So just what reason you got tryin' to meet Jacqueline St. James? Exactly what have you got on your mind?"

"Oh, just wondered," said Brett, then smiled to himself. Ron wouldn't buy that "just wondered" stuff in a million years. Besides, he might as well tell him the whole story—before Ariane did. But not over the phone.

"Well, actually, it's more than just wondering," admitted Brett. "I do have my reasons—legitimate ones, I assure you. But it would take too long to go into them now. I'll fill you in on the way over to the gym," said Brett. "Right now I'd better get moving if I'm going to be ready when you get here."

"Okay," said Ron. "But I gotta tell ya, man, you sure got my curiosity up. I can hardly wait to find out what this is all about. Whatever it is, it's gotta be good."

Yeah, thought Brett, hanging up the phone. *Yeah, it's gotta be.*

Climbing out of bed and walking down the hall to his office, he flipped on the light and sat down in front of the desk next to the TV. Pulling some blank paper out of the top drawer, he cleared a spot on top of the desk and closed his eyes, wondering how to start. How much should he tell her? Should he explain how he'd met Fox, about the boy's background, about how he'd never had a birthday party before? Would she be touched by it, moved in any way? Would she even read the letter, or would it get as far as some secretary's desk and then stop, undelivered and unanswered, just like his phone messages?

He sighed. What difference did it make how far the letter got? All he knew was that he had to send it. Opening his eyes, he picked up a pen and began to write.

✳

With the letter finished, Brett was ready when he heard Ron pull up in front of the house and lean on his horn. Grabbing his gym bag and the letter, he hurried outside, locking the front door behind him. The rain had stopped temporarily, but heavy dark clouds overhead promised more of the same at any moment.

Climbing into Ron's immaculate red Jaguar, he held the letter up in front of him. "Gotta mail this along the way somewhere," he said.

Ron smiled teasingly as he started the engine. "Yeah? What is it, a letter to Jacqueline St. James or something?"

"Actually . . . yes," answered Brett. "That's exactly what it is."

"You're kidding, right?" said Ron, still smiling. When Brett didn't answer, Ron's smile faded and his brown eyes widened slowly. "You're not kidding. You're serious. That's really a letter to Jacqueline St. James. Oh, man, you are crazier than I thought!" He shut the engine off and turned to face Brett. "All right," he said. "We'll mail your letter in a few minutes. But first, I want to know what in the world this is all about."

Brett sighed and shook his head. "It's a long story," he said. "But it has to do with that kid I introduced to you not too long ago. You remember, Fox Richards."

Ron nodded. "Yeah, sure, I remember. The kid you found in an alley. The one who thinks he's gonna make it big in New York, right? But what's he got to do with a famous entertainer like Jacqueline St. James?"

"Well, it seems she's his favorite singer," Brett explained. "And Fox has always wanted to meet her. Also, he's never had a birthday party before and he's going to be thirteen soon, so I—"

"Wait a minute," interrupted Ron. "You're not makin' any sense at all, man. So the kid's gonna be thirteen, so what? I mean, what's that to you? And how do you know all this stuff about him, anyway? Did I miss somethin'? I thought you were just takin' the kid to breakfast that morning. What'd he do? Tell you his life story over French toast, or what?"

"Hardly," said Brett. "In fact, trying to get that kid to talk at all is like pulling teeth. But he did say enough for me to find out a little about his past. He's had a real rough life, Ron. Really rough. Never knew his dad—except what he heard about him from his mom and her boyfriend—all negative, of course. Apparently the guy was an alcoholic who ended up dying in jail while Fox was still a baby. What he was there for I'm not exactly sure. Then his mom took off with her boyfriend and left Fox behind—he was only about four or five then. Been in and out of foster homes and halls ever since. Anyway, when I was over at the hall visiting him the other day—"

"You were over at the hall?" Ron asked, raising his eyebrows. "Why in the world would you wanna be over there?"

Brett looked steadily into Ron's eyes. "Nobody *wants* to be over there. Not that it's all that bad or anything. Actually, it's pretty nice, but . . . if somebody's there—a kid, I mean—it's because they've got nowhere else to go."

Before Ron could say anything, Brett went on. "Anyway, so I was over there talking to him about his birthday . . . well, actually, I was talking to him about something else, but his birthday somehow came up. He asked me if I was going to give him a party. The next thing I knew, half the kids in the place wanted to know where and when and who all was coming, and . . . before I knew it, I'd invited them all and promised I'd have Jacqueline St. James there besides."

For a moment, neither of them spoke, as a few isolated raindrops began to fall from the sky, splashing onto the roof and hood of Ron's car, echoing in the silence that surrounded them.

Finally, Ron shook his head. "Incredible, man," he said. "Absolutely incredible."

"I know," said Brett. "That's exactly what Ariane said. Incredible." He shrugged his shoulders. "But that's what I said I'd do, so . . ." He held the letter up once again. "That's why I've got to mail this."

The rain was coming down steadily now, making a rhythmic drumbeat on the rooftop. Slowly, Ron turned away from Brett, started the car engine once again, then rested his hands on the steering wheel.

"Well," he said, looking back over his shoulder and pulling out into the street, "sounds like you got your work cut out for you, that's for sure. Guess we'd better find a mailbox first thing."

They'd gone only a couple of blocks when Ron pulled over to the curb next to a mailbox. Brett pushed the window button, reached out and dropped the letter into the slot, then pulled his arm back in quickly and closed the window again. Unzipping his gym bag, he took out a towel and dried off his arm.

"Think that'll do it?" asked Ron.

"Do what?" asked Brett.

"Convince Jacqueline St. James to come to the party," answered Ron. "That is what you're trying to accomplish with the letter, right?"

Brett nodded. "Right. I didn't know what else to do. I've called and left messages with her agent and manager, but so far, nothing." He put the towel back in the bag and looked over at Ron. "Unless *you* have any brilliant ideas."

Ron glanced at Brett. "Me? Are you kidding? I told you, if I knew somebody who knew Jacqueline St. James, I would have made her acquaintance *long* ago. Sorry, man, but if you already tried callin' and writin', I don't know what else to suggest." He shook his head, looked over his shoulder again and pulled back into traffic. "You really got yourself in deep on this one, you know it? I mean, throwin' a birthday party for some kid you hardly know. A kid who's spent most of his life in and out of foster homes and halls and back alleys . . . and then promisin' to have one of the most popular singers in the world—someone you don't know *at all*—at the party. You're really somethin', you know that? You are *really* somethin'."

Brett sighed. "Somethin', yeah," he agreed, looking over at Ron. "But the question is, *what?*"

"Well," said Ron, staring out the front window as he stopped for a red light, "maybe you're a successful athlete who got bored during the off-season and decided to do something to make your life more exciting. Or maybe you're someone who enjoys getting himself into painful situations. Or maybe you're secretly in love with Jacqueline St. James and want an excuse to meet her." He turned toward Brett. "Or maybe you're just a nice guy with a big heart and not too much sense. That's my guess, anyway. But what I think doesn't matter. The important thing is do *you* know why you're doin' it? 'Cause if you don't, whether you pull this thing off or not, you're not gonna be doin' *anybody* any favors . . . least of all, that kid."

Brett nodded. He knew his friend was right. His motives had to be greater than simply feeding his own ego or satisfying some need within himself, greater even than fulfilling a young boy's dream for one night. There had to be more.

"And even though I already said that what I think doesn't matter," Ron continued, "I'm going to tell you, anyway."

"I figured you would," said Brett, smiling. "Actually, I was counting on it."

"I think you're doing the right thing," said Ron. "Crazy? Sure. Impossible? Maybe. But the right thing. And that's the bottom line."

"I know," Brett agreed. "Believe me, I know. In fact, it's one of the few times in my life I've been so sure about something, even though, logically, it doesn't make much sense. But in my heart, I know I have to do it."

"Then you have to," said Ron. "And you will."

*

The sun had begun to break through the clouds by the time Brett pulled up in front of the hall. He glanced at his watch. The kids should be out of school by now. He got out of the car and headed for the administration office to find out where he was most likely to locate Fox. That's when he ran into Mr. Phillips.

"Good to see you again, Mr. Holiday," said the red-haired caseworker, pumping Brett's hand. "I understand the basketball outing went well."

"Very well," Brett agreed. "And, please, call me Brett."

Mr. Phillips beamed. "Brett. Well, I'd be honored— if you'll call me Alex, that is. So, I assume you're here to see Elmore?"

Brett nodded. "Yes, I am. I . . ." He paused, then looked the caseworker in the eyes. "Alex, can I ask you something?"

"Of course," answered Alex. "Anything at all."

"I just wondered," said Brett, "why you always refer to Fox as Elmore."

Alex frowned. "Why, because it's his name, I suppose."

"But he hates it," said Brett. "He wants to be called Fox. And if I remember right, when I first heard your name from my lawyer, he called you Alexander Phillips, not Alex. Is there a reason you go by Alex, rather than Alexander?"

Slowly, Alex's frown disappeared and a smile spread across his face. "I get the message," he said. "And from now on, *Fox* it is."

Brett smiled. "Good. Anyway, you're right, I am here to see Fox. And some of the other kids, too. I want to talk to them about the party."

"So there really is going to be a party," said Alex. "I've heard several of the kids talking about it, but I was afraid maybe they were blowing things out of proportion. If what I've heard is true, it sounds like quite a bash."

"It is," said Brett. "And I apologize for not checking with you sooner. I hope it won't be a problem."

Alex shook his head. "I don't see why it should be," he said, "so long as we know the details in plenty of time. You know, when and where, how many people to expect . . . that sort of thing."

"That's why I'm here," Brett explained. "To at least get started on some of those details. I've got a long way to go on firming up dates and all, but I'll get that to you as soon as possible. Meantime, I just want to get some input from the kids and try to get them involved in the planning stage. It's their party, after all."

Once again, Alex's smile lit up his already pleasant face. "I'm glad to hear you say that," he said. "I can see why so many of the kids have come to admire you in such a short time. They sense that you're sincere, that you really care about them. That's important, you know, especially from someone in your position—someone they've seen on TV but never expected to meet in person. With all the negative role models most of these kids have had in their lives, it's encouraging when they have a positive one to look up to for a change."

Brett smiled weakly, his sudden feeling of inadequacy preventing him from responding. Instead, he decided to ask about some of the comments he had heard from the boys on the way to the Forum.

"I, uh, I'm curious," he began. "You know when I took the guys to the game the other day, well . . . some of the things they said . . . Anthony, for instance. He sounded . . . hurt, I guess, when he mentioned some people he used to live with. And Nathaniel said something about Ernie's brother being a dealer. I assume he was talking about drugs?"

Alex's face seemed to sag. "I can't really go into their private lives," he explained. "But it's no secret that most of these kids come from some pretty rough backgrounds. Physical and sexual abuse, gang involvement, drugs. Some of them have actually witnessed members of their own families murdered in gang wars. It's pretty gruesome."

Brett swallowed and nodded. "Thanks," he mumbled, turning on his heel. Alex's words echoed through his mind as he made his way down the long corridor toward the recreation room where he'd been told Fox would most likely be. The sounds of a popular rap group drifted down the hall to meet him, making it difficult for Brett to walk except in time to the rhythmic, repetitive beat. By the time he stepped into the room, he was more than slightly thankful for the house rules concerning "moderate" volumes on TVs and stereos.

Nathaniel was the first to greet him. "Brett!" he cried, jumping up to a sitting position on the couch in the far corner where he'd been sprawled out listening to music. "Hey, Fox didn't tell us you were comin'!"

Fox, who was sitting sideways in a reclining chair near the doorway, his long legs dangling over the arm, looked up at Brett for a moment, then went back to thumbing through a recent issue of *Sports Illustrated.* "That's 'cause I didn't know he was comin'," he said. "He don't have to report to me 'bout what he's doin', you know."

The other chairs scattered throughout the spacious room were vacant except for the one where Anthony sat, hunched over a small wooden desk by the window, obviously lost in his own academic world.

Living up to his name, thought Brett, slapping a high-five with Nathaniel and then walking over to stop directly in front of Anthony. "The Brain" didn't move.

"Anybody home?" Brett asked.

Nothing.

He cleared his throat and tried again. "I said, is anybody home?"

Startled, Anthony jumped and looked up from his book. Brett watched the blue eyes come into focus behind the thick, wire-rimmed glasses, then light up with recognition.

"Brett!" he cried, knocking his book to the floor as he jumped up.

"How ya doin' there, Brain?" he asked. "Looks like you're hitting the books pretty hard. Must be interesting stuff."

"It is," said Anthony, bending over to pick up his book. "History. I love history. Got a big test tomorrow."

"Oh, yeah?" said Brett. "Well, I guess you must be the only one taking it, because you're sure the only one studying for it." He glanced over at Fox, who was still staring down at his magazine, then over at Nathaniel. "That right, Nathaniel? Anthony here, he's the only one taking that history test tomorrow?"

Nathaniel grinned sheepishly. "Nah, me and Fox gotta take it, too. Everybody in Mr. Bower's class gotta take it. It's a big one."

"That's what Anthony just told me," said Brett. "So why aren't you studying? Unless, of course, you already know the subject so well you don't need to."

Nathaniel laughed. "No way!" he said. "I'm just not studying 'cause it's boring."

"Anthony doesn't think so," said Brett. "In fact, he just told me it was pretty interesting stuff. Says he loves history."

Still smiling, Nathaniel shook his head. "Anthony loves anything that comes out of a book. That's why we call him 'The Brain.' All that stuff's easy for him, man."

Brett turned back to Anthony. "That so? All this stuff comes easy to you?"

Anthony looked surprised. "Well . . . some of it." He hesitated, then shrugged his thin shoulders and smiled. "But even when it's not easy, I still like it. I just have to spend more time on it, that's all."

Brett nodded. "That's true. Learning takes time—effort, too." He looked back at Nathaniel. "But then, anything worthwhile usually does, right?"

Nathaniel raised his eyebrows, as if he wasn't quite sure how to answer. "I guess so," he said finally, flashing Brett a crooked smile.

Out of the corner of his eye, Brett noticed Fox looking at him, but as soon as he turned toward him, the boy dropped his eyes once again. *That's all right, kid,* thought Brett. *At least I know you're listening, whether you want to admit it or not.*

"So," said Brett, walking over to the couch and plunking down beside Nathaniel. "Where are the rest of the guys? I thought maybe we ought to all get together and start making some plans for the party. We've got a lot of things to decide, you know."

"You mean, you want *us* to plan it?" asked Nathaniel, his eyes wide with surprise and excitement.

"Why not?" asked Brett. "After all, who's party is it?"

"I thought it was Fox's," said Anthony, walking over to join them. He sat down cross-legged on the floor in front of the couch. "For his birthday, right?"

"That's true," said Brett. "And Fox will definitely be the guest of honor. But the party's for . . . well, for anybody who wants to come, I guess."

"Anybody?" asked Anthony. "You mean, like, any of the kids here? All of them, even?"

"Sure," answered Brett, then smiled. "Well, as long as they're old enough, of course. I understand you have kids of all ages here, including a few babies."

"Oh, man," said Nathaniel, rolling his eyes, "we sure don't want no babies at our party!"

Brett laughed. "Well, we'll leave the cut-off age up to the administration to decide, how's that? Otherwise, the party's open to whoever wants to be there, agreed?"

"Yeah!" cried Nathaniel.

"All right!" added Anthony.

"So, what are you guys waiting for?" asked Brett. "Why don't you two go round up some of the other kids and let's get started on our plans, while I catch up on some things with Fox over here."

As Nathaniel and Anthony raced out of the room, Brett walked over to Fox, turning the stereo down a few notches on the way, then grabbed an empty chair, and pulled it up next to him.

"Hope I wasn't out of line saying the party was open to whoever wanted to come," said Brett. "Guess I should have cleared it with you first, huh?"

Fox shrugged but didn't look up. "Don't make no difference to me who's there and who ain't. Might not even be there myself. Might be in New York by then."

Feeling the irritation rising within, Brett opened his mouth to say something, then thought better of it. "Must be a good magazine," he said instead.

Fox didn't answer.

"What are you reading?"

The boy shrugged again. "Nothin' special. Just lookin' at some pictures, mostly."

"Yeah," agreed Brett. "I know what you mean. There's nothing like *Sports Illustrated* for some good action shots. They got anything about the game we went to the other day?"

Fox shook his head. "Nah. This here's from two or three weeks ago."

"Oh," said Brett. "Well, the new issue's probably out by now. In fact, I think I should be getting my copy in the mail today or tomorrow. I'll save it for you. It's bound to have some highlights from that game, since their win clinched the division title for the Lakers. What do you think? Can they go all the way this time?"

Fox looked up at Brett. "How would I know, man? I look like a sportscaster or somethin'?"

"No," admitted Brett. "You just look like a guy who knows a whole lot more about things than he lets on, that's all."

"Maybe," said Fox, squinting his eyes as he stared at Brett. "And maybe not."

"Either way, you're not telling, right?" said Brett. "Okay, so enough about basketball. How's everything else going? You doing okay in school?"

"What do you care?" asked Fox. "Mr. Bower send you here to see if I'm studyin' for that test, or what?"

Brett shook his head. "No, Fox, Mr. Bower did not send me here. I came because I wanted to see you. I wanted to talk to you and the other kids about the party. But it wouldn't be a bad idea for you to spend a little more time studying and a lot less time daydreaming about going to New York."

Fox threw the magazine on the floor. "Why?" he demanded. "Just what good's it gonna do me to learn 'bout dead people, anyway? New York's alive, dude. It's happenin'. And it's where I'm goin' someday, no matter what *anybody* says . . . not even you."

"I never said you couldn't go to New York," said Brett, his voice low and steady. "I just think you should be a little more prepared before you get there, that's all."

"Prepared for what?" asked Fox.

"Well, for one thing," explained Brett, "what about a job? I mean, you gotta live once you get there, right? You don't want to spend your life scrounging through trash cans in back alleys, do you?"

Brett saw Fox's jaw muscles contract. He was hitting raw nerves again, but he decided to push on. "Once you get to New York," said Brett, "or anywhere, for that matter, you have to eat. You have to have a place to sleep, clothes to wear. Have you thought about that at all? Just what kind of work do you suppose you could get without any training or education? Don't you want a good job someday? A career of some sort?"

"Yeah," said Fox, his lip curled in a sneer. "Yeah. As a matter of fact, I think I'd like to be a famous football dude like you. A rich one, too. What you think of that, man?"

"I think that's a great idea," said Brett, ignoring the boy's sarcasm. "But it doesn't happen overnight, you know. You gotta work hard, Fox. And long. Just like I said earlier. Anything that's worthwhile takes time and effort, whether it's a career or a relationship or whatever. And football's no exception. Nobody's going to just walk up and hand it to you, you know."

Fox smirked. "No kiddin'. They ain't, huh? Well, what a surprise! I mean, all my life, people been walkin' up and handin' me stuff, sayin', 'Hey, Fox, you want this, dude? Here, take it, man. It's yours.' Yeah, all my life, man. All my life!"

Before Brett could answer, Ernie burst into the room. "Hey, Brett," he said, dropping to the floor beside his chair. "Nathaniel told me you were here. Said you wanted to talk about the party."

Brett smiled. "That's right. You got any good ideas?"

Ernie grinned. "I *always* got good ideas. But I guess you mean about the party, right?" He shook his head. "I don't know. I was talkin' to my cousin Carlos—he came to see me the other day, right after you took us to that Lakers game—and I told him about the party. He was jealous, man! Said he wished he lived here at the hall, too. Said we get to do better stuff than he does, even though he lives on the outside with some foster family. Says they're okay and everything, but he's never been to a real basketball game before, and when I told him about Jacqueline St. James—man, he couldn't believe it! He wanted to know if he could come, too. But I told him if we invited him, next thing you know, kids from foster homes and halls all over town would be wantin' to come. I mean, I know you're a major football star and you know all kinds of people and everything, but still, you're only one guy, right?"

"Maybe he is," said Fox suddenly, cutting his eyes from Brett to Ernie, then back again. "But A.C. Green says one guy's all it takes, dude."

Brett frowned, startled by Fox's intrusion into the conversation, puzzled by the words he had spoken. Since when was Fox an expert on anything A.C. Green—or anyone else, for that matter—had to say? Had he read it in *Sports Illustrated*? Heard it on a TV interview? But before he could voice his questions to Fox, Ernie spoke up.

"So how come you know so much about A.C.?" he asked. "I mean, I know we all saw him play at the game the other day, but that don't mean we know what he thinks."

Fox shrugged. "Read it in a book," he said. "Some book 'bout athletes. You know, how they feel 'bout sports and God and helpin' other people . . . stuff like that." He shrugged again. "No big deal, dude. Got it from Mr. Phillips. Mostly I just looked at the pictures."

Brett smiled to himself. He knew the book well. Ariane had given him a copy soon after it was released. Remembering what Alex Phillips had said earlier about a lack of positive role models in these kids' lives, he knew right away why Alex had given the book to Fox. He also knew that Fox had done more than just look at the pictures.

"You mean, A.C.'s picture's in the book?" asked Ernie. "And his story, too?"

"Yeah," said Fox. "Him and lotsa famous people."

"I've read the book," said Brett. "It's called *Winning*. And, come to think of it, I remember the story, too. A.C. was talking about some game they played against one of their division rivals. Seems the Lakers were losing real bad until A.C. got to thinking about how he was always telling people how much difference one person can make. That's when he decided it was time to practice what he preached. He started encouraging his teammates, slapping high-fives with them, and telling them they were going to win. At first they thought he was crazy, but his enthusiasm was contagious, and pretty soon they *all* believed they were going to win."

"And did they?" asked Ernie, wide-eyed.

"Sure did," answered Brett. "Like the man said, one person really can make a difference. . . ."

Brett's voice trailed off as he realized that, although he'd been speaking out loud to Ernie and Fox, he'd really been talking to himself.

"Man, I'd sure like to see that book," said Ernie. "You still got it?"

"I s'pose," said Fox, trying to appear disinterested. "Somewhere."

"That's cool," said Ernie. "Maybe I'll come down to your room later and help you look." Turning his attention back to Brett, he asked, "So, what do I tell my cousin? Can he come to the party or not? And what if other kids from other places want to come?"

Brett looked to Fox for a reaction, but got none. He could hear the sounds of approaching footsteps and excited chatter in the hallway outside. His mind was racing. Other kids from other places? How big was this thing going to get? How much bigger *could* it get?

He sighed. He was already in over his head; what difference could a few more kids make?

"I tell you what," he said, as a flood of eager, animated boys and girls began to pour through the door. "I'll leave that up to all of you to decide. Like I said, it's your party."

CHAPTER 11

There was no doubt about it. Ariane was the most beautiful woman at the party. And Brett was sure he wasn't the only one who had noticed it.

As he watched her from across the room, he was captivated by the gracefulness of her movements, the easy, natural way she tossed her head when she laughed. This was her night, her friends, her colleagues and associates. Radiant in a pale pink silk gown, with all but a few wisps of her dark hair swept up off her neck, she fairly sparkled with energy and enthusiasm.

I love her more now than the day I married her, he thought, sipping the glass of ginger ale he'd been nursing most of the evening. *So why is it I feel . . . threatened by her at times, maybe even a little resentful, as if . . . as if what? As if she doesn't love me anymore? No, I know that's not true. If there's one thing I'm sure of, it's that Ariane loves me. It's just—*

Brett jumped, spilling a few drops of ginger ale onto his dark blue suit pants, as the hardy slap on his shoulder brought him back to the present.

"Brett, hey, it's great to see you again," boomed a voice to his right.

Brett turned. It was Eugene Wesley, the senior partner at the law firm where Ariane worked, grinning from ear to ear and brandishing an almost empty champagne glass in his hand. Having seen Eugene in action at several parties over the years, Brett was relatively sure that it wasn't the first glass of champagne the impeccably dressed, silver-haired gentleman had emptied.

Brett returned the smile. Although he didn't especially care for Eugene, he had to admit the man had always been warm and congenial, and a lot less stuffy than some of the firm's younger law partners. "Good to see you, too," answered Brett, offering his hand to the older man.

Eugene switched his drink to his left hand and grasped Brett's outstretched palm firmly, then nodded his head in Ariane's direction. "Saw you watching that beautiful wife of yours," he said. "I have to admit, she's the best looking woman in the place."

"I was just thinking the same thing," said Brett.

"Smart as a whip, too," Eugene added, turning back to stare at Ariane. She had moved to a small circle of three well dressed men, where she was talking animatedly and obviously holding them all spellbound.

"And capable," Eugene went on. "She's going to make a fine attorney someday, that's for sure. Better than fine, as a matter of fact. I, for one, wouldn't want to be on opposite sides of the courtroom from her. When challenged, I would think she could be a formidable opponent. Remarkable woman. Absolutely remarkable."

Brett nodded. Without a doubt, Eugene Wesley's assessment of Ariane was right on target.

"So," said Eugene, pulling his attention away from Ariane. "What's new in the football world? I imagine you're gearing up for training season. It is just about that time, isn't it?" He paused and frowned, as a slight blush crept up his neck and face. "Oh, I hope I haven't spoken out of turn. You are going to be playing again this year, aren't you? You haven't been replaced entirely by that Nelson kid, certainly. . . ."

His voice trailed off, as Brett breathed deeply in an effort to control his irritation. "No," said Brett. "At least, not as far as I know. I'd like to think I've got a couple of good years left in me, anyway."

"Yes, well . . . I'm sure you do," said Eugene, obviously anxious to change the subject. "After all, it's not as if football is your whole life. There's so much more to who you are." He cleared his throat and shifted nervously from one foot to the other. "So, great party, isn't it? First time I've ever been to Shane's house, but it's really something. A lot nicer than anything I ever had when I was a junior partner, I can tell you that. Ambitious young man, that Shane Stuart. I look for him to go places—in a hurry. Of course, his father was such a successful lawyer that there's no reason to anticipate Shane's doing anything less. Like they say, the apple seldom falls far from the tree, right? Like father, like son, and all that."

Eugene paused and drained the last of his champagne from his glass, then looked at Brett expectantly, as if to say, "Well, your serve."

Brett forced a smile. "I'm sure you're right," he said. "I've heard Ariane mention Shane several times, and she seems to share your opinion of him."

"Well," said Eugene, "I'm glad to hear that. I value your wife's opinion quite highly, as I'm sure you know." Glancing down at his empty glass, he held it out in front of him for Brett to see. "Better go find a refill," he announced, veering off in the direction of the bar. "Wonderful seeing you again," he called over his shoulder.

"Right," muttered Brett, taking another sip of his drink.

It's not as if football is your whole life, Eugene had said. *There's so much more to who you are.*

Brett shook his head. *I know that's true,* he told himself. *But why am I having such a hard time believing it lately? Maybe it's because I'm not sure just what that "so much more" is* .

The apple seldom falls far from the tree . . . like father, like son. That was something else Eugene had said—something Brett did not care to consider at the moment. Still, he couldn't stop his thoughts from drifting back to his last visit to the hall, when he'd talked to the kids about Fox's party. He'd been there for almost two hours, but what stood out most in his mind was Fox's comment about A.C. Green. Brett couldn't get over the fact that he and Fox, as opposite as they obviously were, had been impacted by the same book.

Suddenly he remembered a quote from one of the other athletes in the book—Barry Sanders, the 1988 Heisman Trophy winner. Something about how wonderful it was to achieve success in sports, but that "the real test comes when things get tough and you have to find out who you are away from that sport." *Pretty heavy observation,* thought Brett. *Especially from someone so young.*

He felt her hand on his shoulder at the same time that he noticed the familiar, delicate fragrance of her perfume. He turned his head and looked at Ariane. The warmth of her smile was outdone only by the sparkle in her wide green eyes.

"You ready, sweetheart?" she asked.

Brett nodded. "I am getting kind of tired."

"So am I," she agreed, glancing at her watch. "And it's getting pretty late."

"You don't look tired to me," said Brett, smiling. "You look like you could go another four or five hours."

Ariane tossed her head and laughed. "Not hardly," she said. "Actually, I've been ready to leave for the past half-hour or so, but I didn't want to be rude."

Brett slipped his arm around his wife's tiny waist. "No danger of that," he assured her. "I was watching you. You were charming. Devastatingly so."

"You think so?" she asked, her eyes dancing as she looked up at him.

"I know so," he said, steering her toward the front door.

It took them almost ten minutes to get there, as they stopped several times to say good-night along the way. Rachel Stuart, Shane's wife, was standing near the door, talking with two older women who were also getting ready to leave.

"You're not leaving us, too," said Rachel, turning toward Brett and Ariane with a smile that said, "Please stay," but eyes that said, "Please don't. I'm exhausted and my feet are killing me."

"I'm afraid so," said Ariane, reaching out to hug Rachel. "I've got to get up early tomorrow to get some last minute studying in before I go to work. I won't have time in the evening in between dinner and school."

Rachel shook her head. "I'll never understand how you do it," she said. "A full-time job, school, a home—wherever do you find the time?" She looked up at Brett. "Your wife is an amazing woman," she said. "Absolutely amazing!"

Brett nodded. "More and more so all the time," he agreed.

"Well," Rachel continued, "at least she has you at home to help out now and then. I almost never see Shane anymore. And when I do, he has his nose buried in a briefcase full of papers. Of course, I imagine you were away from home quite a bit more when you still played football. I can hardly wait until Shane reaches the point where he can slow down now and then—maybe even retire, like you. That's a long time from now, though, I'm afraid. Law isn't exactly like sports, where you can retire when you hit middle age."

Before he could respond, Ariane grabbed Brett's hand and squeezed. "We really have to run, Rachel," she said, reaching for the brass door handle. "Thank you so much for inviting us. It was a lovely party."

By the time Brett maneuvered the Porsche onto the freeway, his jaws had unclenched and he had almost managed to convince himself that Rachel Stuart wouldn't know a football from a basketball, so there was no reason in the world to be disturbed over her comments. But he was.

"Don't let her get to you," said Ariane, as if reading his mind. "Rachel doesn't know the first thing about sports."

"I realize that," said Brett, clutching the steering wheel with both hands. "But Eugene Wesley does. And he wasn't sure if I'd be playing again this year or if I'd been replaced by Chuck Nelson."

Ariane reached over and laid her hand on Brett's thigh. "It doesn't matter what Eugene Wesley thinks, either," she said. "All that matters is that *you* know you'll be playing again."

"Do I?" he asked, glancing over at his beautiful, young, successful wife before turning his attention back to the well-lit road in front of him. "Do I really? Or am I just kidding myself? Even if I don't get cut from the team, just how much playing time do you think I'm going to see? Am I supposed to sit there on the bench, hoping that Chuck gets hurt so I can have one last shot at glory? Is that what I've come to, babe?"

Ariane's hand tightened on his thigh. "Pull over," she said.

"What?" he asked, glancing over at her once again, only to find she wore her prosecuting attorney's face.

"Find somewhere to pull over," she said. "We've got to talk. Now."

The look on her face and the tone of her voice convinced him it was useless to argue with her. Besides, deep down, he knew she was right—they needed to talk. Right away. He pulled off the freeway at the next exit.

Driving into a busy restaurant parking lot, he shut off the engine and turned toward Ariane. "All right," he sighed, expecting the worst. "Let's talk."

But the prosecuting attorney's face had softened. The lights in the parking lot weren't bright enough to be sure, but he thought he saw tears glistening in the corners of her eyes.

"I'm worried about you," she said softly. "I'm worried about what's going to happen to you—to us— when your career finally does come to an end. Whether it's this year or the year after or the year after that, it has to end sometime, and you know that. You've always known that. The question is, what happens then?"

It was a question that had haunted Brett for years, one he had tried to ignore, but had found it increasingly hard to do so as his career drew to a close. *The real test comes when things get tough and you have to find out who you are away from that sport.* Young Barry Sanders, at the very onset of his professional career, had acknowledged the question. He knew it was out there—somewhere—waiting to be answered, sooner or later. For Brett, however, the time had come.

"I wish I knew," he whispered. "But I don't, not really. I mean, between your salary and the assets and investments we already have, I know we'll be all right financially. I'm not worried about that. But what am I supposed to do all day long, sit around and wait for you to come home from work? I'd go crazy, you know I would."

Ariane nodded. "I know," she said, smiling crookedly. "And chances are, you'd drive me crazy, too. But . . . aren't you forgetting something?"

Brett frowned. "Like what?"

"Well . . . coaching, for instance," said Ariane.

"I've thought of that," admitted Brett. "A lot. It is a possibility, I suppose. But don't you think every aging athlete thinks the same thing? There's just not room for everybody."

"I didn't mean in the pros," said Ariane. "Or college either, for that matter. I was thinking more of . . . of kids like Fox. I know he's the main reason you keep going back to the hall, but I think those other kids have started getting to you, too. Maybe you could start a sports program for underprivileged kids—locally or nationwide, who knows? But you can't deny it would meet a need—for them *and* for you."

Brett opened his mouth, but he could think of nothing to say. It seemed that every time he thought he'd been married to Ariane long enough to begin to understand her, he was quickly reminded of how very much he still had to learn.

He reached over and took her hands in his. "I don't understand," he said. "I thought you resented the time I spent with Fox. In fact, I thought you resented Fox, *period.*"

"I did," she said. "But it wasn't because of the time you spent with him, or because of his bad attitude, either. I knew his toughness was all part of an act. And it wasn't even because of my great-grandmother's silver." She paused and took a deep breath. "It was because . . . I was afraid. I thought he was going to come between us somehow, cause us more arguments and more dissension than our marriage could handle. But now . . . now I don't think so anymore."

"Why?" asked Brett. "What made you change your mind?"

"You," she said. "I've been watching you, Brett Holiday. You've really gotten caught up in this thing with Fox. The kids, the party, all of it. At first, I thought you were just plain crazy." She smiled. "And I haven't necessarily changed my mind about that part. But I suddenly realized that for the first time in a long time, you were thinking about something besides the end of your career. Fox has pulled you outside yourself, sweetheart, don't you see? How can I resent him or be afraid of him when he's managed to accomplish what I wanted so desperately to do but couldn't?"

She sighed and shook her head. "Besides, you weren't the only one who was so caught up in your own life that you couldn't see anything or anyone else. I was doing the exact same thing. The only difference was you were dwelling on the end of your career, while I was concentrating on the beginning of mine. But Fox . . . well, I guess he just sort of reminded me of why I wanted to become a lawyer in the first place.

"I wanted to help people, sweetheart," she continued. "I thought being a lawyer would give me a chance to do that. But somewhere along the line, I got caught up in the busyness and so-called importance of what I was doing, and I lost sight of what it was really all about."

She raised his hand to her lips and kissed it softly. "So you see, Fox has opened my eyes, too. And that's why I've decided to help you with the party—in any way I can."

As Brett stretched across the front seat and gathered his wife into his arms, oblivious to the amused smiles of a young couple leaving the restaurant, he felt a renewed sense of wonder and hope that he hadn't known in a very long time.

CHAPTER **12**

Brett couldn't decide if it was the bright yellow sun overhead or the afterglow of his renewed romance with his wife that flooded him with such warmth and peace. Either way, he felt more content than he had in months.

Sprawled peacefully in the reclining lounge chair, he peeked out from under his sun visor at the sparkling water in front of him. It was almost noon. He'd spent most of the morning beside the pool, making calls on the portable phone, adding and crossing out phone numbers on the scratch pad he'd brought outside with him from his office. Although he hadn't actually talked to Jacqueline St. James, he had at least gotten through to her manager, Hiram Goebel, who had assured Brett that both his phone messages and his letter had been passed along to her.

"She's considering your request," Mr. Goebel had said.

What's that supposed to mean? Brett had wondered, but decided not to ask.

"We do have a couple of concerns, however," Mr. Goebel had continued. "For instance, what sort of budget do you have for this . . . birthday party, is it?"

Brett smiled wryly. He knew enough about agents and managers to know why "we" were concerned. "Yes, it's a birthday party," he'd answered. "And we don't. Have a budget, I mean. Well, not exactly, anyway. I suppose I'll just cover any necessary expenses myself."

"I see," said Mr. Goebel. "And will there be other celebrities in attendance besides Miss St. James?"

Brett paused. He'd been so caught up with getting Jacqueline to agree to come, he hadn't even thought of inviting other celebrities. But why not? The way the party was growing already, he might as well go for broke.

"I'm working on that," Brett hedged. "Nothing definite yet, though."

"I see," Mr. Goebel repeated. "Well, as I said, Miss St. James is considering your request."

Brett sighed and hung up the phone. It was too nice a day to let anything get him down. After all, at least he knew that Jacqueline was aware of the party and was "considering" whether or not to accept the invitation. Besides, Mr. Goebel's question about other celebrities attending the party had given Brett a lot to think about.

Which is exactly what he'd done. For almost an hour after hanging up the phone, Brett had lazed in the late morning sunshine, making mental notes of possible stars and entertainers who might be willing to come to the party. Beyond that, he hadn't moved. Now, however, with the sun almost directly overhead, the cool blue water looked more and more inviting.

Pulling himself up from the lounge chair, he removed his sun visor and stepped to the side of the pool, then sat down on the edge and dangled his legs over the side. It felt even better than he'd expected. Brett lowered himself slowly into the water, flinching only slightly as it covered his stomach and chest. Taking a deep breath, he leaned forward and put his face in the water, pushing off from the side and gliding effortlessly toward the middle of the pool as his strong arms carried him forward with graceful, practiced strokes.

Back and forth he swam, not pushing himself as he usually did, but rolling over onto his back to rest whenever he felt winded. By the time he pulled himself, dripping and refreshed, from the pool, he felt ready to tackle the telephone once again.

It was much easier to get hold of Alex Phillips at the hall than it had been to reach Jacqueline's agent or manager. Alex's warm voice on the other end of the line was a welcome change, as well.

"Brett, what a nice surprise! How are you?"

Brett smiled as he wiped his face and hair with a towel. "I'm doing great, Alex," he said, lying back down in the lounge chair. "Just sitting out here by the pool, soaking up some rays."

"I'm jealous," said Alex. "I've been cooped up inside so long I've forgotten what the sun feels like."

"Sounds like you need some time off," said Brett. "When's the last time you had a vacation?"

"Now there's something else I'd forgotten about," answered Alex. "But now that you've reminded me. . . ."

Brett chuckled. "Just one thing before you pack your suitcase," he said. "The last time I talked to the kids about the party, someone asked about inviting kids from other halls or foster homes. What do you think about that? Can that be worked out?"

"I can't imagine that would be a problem," answered Alex. "Within reason, of course. I tell you what. I'll check with the 'powers that be' and get right back to you, okay?"

"I'd appreciate it," said Brett. "Thanks. Oh, and send me a postcard from Tahiti!"

He hung up and fitted the sun visor over his eyes once again, ready to drift off for a short nap, when the phone rang.

Too soon to be Alex calling back, he thought. *Maybe it's Ariane calling from work on her lunch hour.* But the somewhat shaky female voice that responded to his "hello" was definitely not Ariane's.

"Is this Brett Holiday?"

"Yes, it is," answered Brett.

"I . . ." She paused, then took a deep breath and went on. "My name is Diane Holland. I'm a secretary at the Martin-Goebel Agency. I believe you spoke with my boss, Mr. Goebel, earlier this morning?"

"Oh, yes, I did," said Brett, springing to attention as he leaned forward in the lounge chair. "Have you got some news for me from Miss St. James?"

"I'm sorry, I don't," said Diane. "But . . . well, I just wanted to let you know that . . . well, the next time she comes in, I'll . . . I mean, if I get a chance, you know . . . I'll mention the party somehow. Remind her, or something."

"That's awfully nice of you," said Brett. "I appreciate it."

"Well," continued Diane, "it's just that . . . you know, I think what you're doing for those kids is really nice and . . . well, besides, I . . ." Her voice dropped slightly. "I'm one of your biggest fans, Mr. Holiday. I've watched you play for a long, long time."

Brett grimaced. A long, *long* time. Oh well, at least she hadn't said she'd watched him since she was a little girl! He supposed he should be grateful for that.

"It's nice to know I've still got some faithful fans out there," he said. "You made my day, Diane."

"You made mine, too," she said. "I sure never thought I'd actually get to talk to you on the phone."

"But you must talk to a lot of celebrities in your line of work," said Brett.

"Not like you, Mr. Holiday," she said. "We hardly ever represent athletes."

Brett smiled. "Well, I tell you what. Since you made my day and I made yours, plus you're going to put in a good word for me with Miss St. James—"

"I'm going to try," interrupted Diane.

"Right," said Brett. "So anyway, why don't you just call me Brett? This 'Mr. Holiday' stuff makes me feel ancient."

"Oh, I'm sorry, Mr.—I mean, Brett," stammered Diane. "I . . . I didn't mean to make you feel old, really, it's just . . . well, if I hear anything—anything at all—about Jacqueline, I'll let you know, okay?"

"I'd appreciate that," answered Brett. "In fact, I'd appreciate it if you could do one more thing for me, Diane."

"What's that?" she asked.

"Do you suppose," he asked, hoping he sounded more casual than he felt, "that you could let me have Miss St. James' home phone number?"

"Oh, Mr. Holiday, I—"

"Brett," he interrupted.

"Yes, Brett, well, I . . . you see, it's just that . . ." Her voice trailed off and Brett held his breath. Finally, he heard her sigh.

"All right," she said softly. "I'll give it to you. But only because of who you are and what you're doing for these kids. If anyone ever found out, it could mean my job, you know."

"No one will find out," he assured her, grabbing the scratch pad and pen he'd been using earlier. "You have my word."

He scribbled the numbers on the paper as she recited them to him. "Thank you, Diane," he said, setting the scratch pad down beside him. "You're a lifesaver; I owe you one. How about a couple of front row tickets on the twenty-yard line, once the season gets started?"

"You're kidding!" she exclaimed. "That would be incredible. My husband won't believe it! Oh, thank you, Brett. Thank you so much!"

"No, thank *you*," said Brett. "You really have made my day."

This time, when he hung up the phone, he leaned back, closed his eyes under his sun visor, and grinned. He might be getting old, but there were still a few faithful fans out there who recognized his name.

*

He'd just stepped out of the shower when the phone rang again. Wrapping a towel around his waist, Brett hurried into the bedroom and grabbed the receiver from the nightstand beside the bed. It was Alex.

"Hey, Alex," said Brett. "Seems you always catch me when I'm wet."

"Don't tell me you're still lazing around by the pool," said Alex.

Brett laughed. "I probably would be except I got hungry, so I decided to come in and take a shower and then fix myself some lunch. So, what's up? You calling from Tahiti, or are you still stuck in the office trying to track down some news for me about the party?"

"I'm afraid Tahiti's still on my to-do list," said Alex. "But I did find out about the party. Nothing official, of course. You know, everything has to go through channels—red tape and all that. But, basically, I can tell you it's a go. Just so we know ahead of time about how many kids to expect. Also, so we can clear any outside invitations with foster families and other halls."

"Thanks, Alex, that's great," said Brett. "One less thing to worry about, anyway."

"So what other things are you worried about?" asked Alex. "Anything I can help with?"

"Well . . ." Brett hesitated. "Actually, yes. You know, here we are inviting all these kids and everything, and I don't even know when or where the party's going to be yet. The date, of course, will depend on . . . Miss St. James' . . . availability. But . . ."

"You're wondering where to have the party," said Alex. "To be truthful, I had just assumed you would want to have it here. We have an auditorium, you know."

"Do you think we could?" asked Brett. "I mean, if it were just a few kids, we could have it here at my place, but the way this thing is growing. . . . What do you think? Will the auditorium be big enough?"

"Hmmm," said Alex. "I hadn't thought of that. With extra kids coming, it might be a bit crowded, but . . . well, unless you have an alternative. . . ."

"None," said Brett. "At least, none that I've thought of. I could work on it, though, see what I come up with."

"All right," said Alex. "Meantime, consider the offer of the auditorium open if you need it."

"Thanks," said Brett, sitting down on the edge of the bed with a sigh. "Now all I have to do is concentrate on lining up some celebrities to be there."

"You mean there will be others besides Jacqueline?" asked Alex. "This is getting better all the time. To be perfectly honest, I was so excited about seeing her that I hadn't even thought about other celebrities. Do you have anyone in particular in mind?"

"Actually, I've been drawing up sort of a mental list while I was out by the pool today," said Brett. "I'm afraid that's as far as I got with it, though."

"Well, I'm sure you'll work it all out perfectly," said Alex. "We have complete confidence in you, Brett. Oh, I know at first some of the kids were a little skeptical about Jacqueline St. James coming—Fox, especially—but now, everyone here is so excited about it, nobody talks about anything else. I know *I'm* certainly looking forward to seeing her there."

Brett's smile was a little weaker this time. "So am I," he said, running a hand through his damp, curly hair. "Believe me, Alex, so am I."

∗

Ariane had gotten off early and hurried home. Stepping into the kitchen, she called Brett's name.

"In here," came the answer, drifting down the hall from his office. She walked in and found him studying one of his more recent game clips.

"You're early," he said, hitting the power button on the remote control and glancing at his watch before looking up at her. "It's only four-thirty. I didn't expect you for over an hour yet. What's the occasion?"

She bent down to kiss him, then smiled and sat down, facing him, on the arm of his reclining chair. "You," she answered, her green eyes twinkling. "I missed you, so I thought I'd come home and spend some time with you before I let you take me out to dinner."

Brett smiled back. "A likely story," he said. "But a nice one. Now, what's the real reason?"

Ariane laughed, as Brett reached up and brushed back a lock of hair from her face. Then she caught Brett's hand in her own and pressed his palm against her lips. It felt warm and strong.

"It really was because of you," she said, still holding his hand. "I mean, things were slow this afternoon and I've been putting in a lot of overtime lately—as you well know—so taking off early was no problem. But, basically, I came home because you've been on my mind all day."

"You mean, usually I'm not?" he teased. "What else could you possibly find to think of besides me, anyway?"

She smiled and lowered their still-clasped hands to her lap. "I've been thinking about the party," she said, "and about your commitment to Fox and the other kids—and about getting Jacqueline St. James to come. Are you making any progress with that?"

Brett sighed. "Some," he admitted. "I did manage to get her home number—not that it did any good. She didn't answer, and the woman who did wouldn't put me through."

Ariane nodded. "It'll work out," she said, squeezing his hand. "I promise."

"It sure makes it a lot easier, having your support in all this," said Brett.

Ariane nodded again. "I know." She leaned over and kissed him on top of the head. "So," she said, glancing over at the TV, "what were you watching when I came in? Old game films?"

Brett shrugged and smiled sheepishly. "Yep," he admitted. "Even with this stuff going on with Fox and the party and all, I can't forget that training camp's right around the corner."

"Of course you can't," said Ariane, reaching out to touch his cheek. "And you shouldn't. You need to get focused on it and pour your energy into it so you can do your very best—and you will, sweetheart, I know you will. But at least now it's not so all-consuming that you feel like your entire life hinges on the outcome of the season. I feel so much better about where you are now—or at least, where you're going. Which, of course, makes me feel much better about us and where we're going, too. Even if we haven't quite figured out where that is yet."

Their eyes locked and Brett shook his head slowly in amazement. "You're really something, you know that?" he said. "How'd I ever get you, anyway?"

Ariane grinned. "I guess you were just in the right place at the right time."

"No doubt about that," agreed Brett. "In fact, it was destiny, you know. *Our* destiny."

She winked playfully and squeezed his hand again. "If you say so," she said, standing up. "And speaking of destinies, I believe I'll go take a shower while you decide where you're going to take me to dinner."

Brett got up and followed her down the hall to their bedroom. "What are you in the mood for?" he asked. "Chinese, Italian, seafood?"

"Anything," she said, sliding out of her shoes. "So long as I don't have to dress up. I'm feeling casual tonight."

Brett grinned. "I know a great hot dog place downtown."

"Not that casual," Ariane said quickly, flipping on the closet light. She pulled a bright pink sundress from her rack of clothes. "This casual," she said, holding it up in front of her.

Brett's disappointment was obviously feigned. "No hot dogs?" he asked, pouting slightly.

"No hot dogs," she answered. "You want hot dogs, you find someone else to eat them with, someone whose tastes run a little more in that direction." She smiled. "In fact, if you're bound and determined to eat that kind of stuff, why don't you take Fox there the next time you two are out on the town?"

"Not a bad idea," said Brett. "I just might do that. Soon, as a matter of fact. Very soon."

Ariane laid her sundress on the bed. "You miss him, don't you?" she said.

Brett sat down next to Ariane's dress.

"You're right, I do," he said, raising his eyebrows in surprise. "But I didn't realize it until just now."

He held his arms out to her and she came and sat down on his lap. "It's all happening so fast," he said. "A little over a month ago, I didn't even know this kid. And now . . ." He paused. "What do you suppose would have happened to him if I hadn't found him in that alley? If I hadn't stopped to talk to him or invited him home for dinner? If—"

She placed a finger over his lips. "Don't think about it," she said. "It doesn't matter what might have happened. What matters is you *did* find him, you *did* stop, you *did* bring him home. You're doing all you can, Brett. More, I'm sure, than anyone's ever done for him before—more than he ever expected, from you or from anyone else."

Brett nodded as she took her finger away from his lips. "I suppose you're right," he said. "It's just that . . . I keep wondering if it's enough. I mean, even if I do pull this thing off with the party and Jacqueline St. James, will it be enough? When it's all said and done, will it make any lasting difference in his life? Can anything offset the bad start he's had? An alcoholic father who died in jail, a mother who deserted him, a string of foster homes and halls. Not to mention the fact that, in spite of a lot of changes for the better, he's still a young black kid growing up in a predominantly white society." He shook his head. "It seems so overwhelming sometimes."

Ariane sighed. "I know," she said. "I've wondered the same thing. And statistics are definitely not in his favor—not just socially or economically, but medically, too. Even though Fox never knew his father, doctors have found that heredity plays a bigger role than they'd ever imagined, especially when it comes to alcoholism. . . ."

Her voice trailed off as Brett's arms tightened around her. "Sometimes I wonder if I'm just tilting at windmills," he whispered, "if I'm fighting a battle that can never be won. Do you really think there's any hope at all for Fox's future?"

She smiled, remembering something Brett had once told Fox and the other boys when they were talking about pasts and futures. "It doesn't matter where you've been or what you've done," she reminded him. "The only thing that matters is where you go from here. Remember when you said that?"

Brett gazed into her eyes. "I remember," he said, smiling. "But I'd forgotten I told you about it. I just hope those kids remember—and that they believed me."

He reached up and gently pulled Ariane's head down until it rested on his shoulder. "I just hope I believe myself," he added.

Ariane smiled. "You do," she whispered. "If you didn't, why in the world would you be working so hard to put this party together?"

She lifted her head and looked into his blue eyes. "And believe me, it's going to be one great party," she said, realizing for the first time, even as she said the words, that it was true.

CHAPTER 13

How did I let him talk me into this? Brett asked himself, as he grabbed his worn Nikes and hurried down the hallway to answer the front doorbell. *About all I ever get from jogging with Ron is a wounded ego and a reminder of my advancing age. I'll have to remember to let him do the talking and save myself for the long haul.*

He pulled the door open, then grinned in spite of himself. Standing on the porch, broad-shouldered and bare-chested except for his ever-present gold chain, stood Ron Daniels—all 6'6", 220 muscular pounds of him—dressed in florescent green running shorts.

"You ready?" asked Ron.

"For what?" joked Brett. "I thought we were going jogging. You look like you're headed to some masquerade party or something. Those things got batteries?"

"Very funny," said Ron, his dimples deepening with his smile. "And, no, there's no batteries. It wouldn't be a bad idea if you had some, though—anything to brighten up those old blue and gold things."

Brett looked down at his Rams shorts. "What's wrong with these?" he asked. "I wear them all the time."

"I noticed," said Ron. "Not exactly original, you know."

"They're comfortable," said Brett. "They're me."

Ron shook his head and grinned. "So you're comfortable, and I'm cool, right? So put on your comfortable shoes and let's get outta here, man. We got some serious runnin' to do."

Brett stepped outside and pulled the door shut behind him. Sitting down on the edge of the porch, he slipped into his shoes, while Ron stretched first one leg out behind him and then the other.

"I'm ready," said Brett, standing up to join his friend, wondering why he was never so aware of the difference in their height and age as when they jogged together.

They took off slowly, pacing themselves as they headed down the street into the late evening sun. The days were longer now, warmer too—a sure sign that training camp was just around the corner, Brett realized. He picked up his pace.

"So what's the hurry?" asked Ron, matching him stride for stride. "Ariane waitin' for you at home?"

Brett shook his head. *No wasted words,* he reminded himself. *Save your breath. Conserve your energy.* "School," he said, hoping to end the conversation as he concentrated on his breathing.

"That's what I thought," said Ron. "So I guess we can run all night if we want to, right?"

We? thought Brett. *You, maybe, but–*

"Hey, I been meanin' to ask you about the party," said Ron as they rounded the corner and headed toward a group of teenage girls sprawled out on a well-kept lawn to their right. The girls whispered and giggled as they ran by.

"Hear anything from Jacqueline St. James yet?" Ron continued. "Any response to your letter?"

"Not really," said Brett.

"What's that supposed to mean?" asked Ron. "Did she contact you or not?"

"Well . . . no," said Brett, spacing his conversation between breaths. "I did manage to track down her home phone number, but I haven't been able to reach her directly. I'm still working on that."

"Give it up, man," said Ron. "If you haven't gotten in touch with her by now, you're not goin' to."

"Her manager says she's considering it," said Brett.

"Oh, yeah, right," laughed Ron. "I've heard that one before!"

It wasn't just Ron's words that were getting on Brett's nerves, but the fact that Ron wasn't even breathing hard when he spoke them. Brett had been right—he should never have agreed to go jogging with Ron. Should have insisted they swim instead. At least there he could hold his own against his younger teammate. And there would have been a lot less opportunity for conversation.

"So what are you gonna do if you can't get her to come?" asked Ron. "You still gonna have the party?"

"Of course we're still going to have the party," said Brett, forcing himself to take slow, deep breaths. "And we're going to get Jacqueline to come, too."

"Who's 'we'?" asked Ron. "You find somebody crazy enough to help you with this project of yours?"

"Ariane," answered Brett, turning to look at his friend. "She's really gotten behind me and supported me on this, Ron. It makes all the difference."

Ron raised his eyebrows. "You're kidding," he said. "You got Ariane hooked into this thing, too? How'd you ever manage that?"

Brett wiped the sweat from his forehead as it dripped down into his eyes. "Charm," he answered with a grin. "Nothing but charm."

Ron was still laughing when a basketball rolled across the sidewalk in front of them. Bending down to retrieve it, Ron turned toward the driveway where two young boys stood watching them. He fired the ball at the hoop over the garage door, swishing it expertly through the net. Brett pulled up, relieved to take a break.

"Wow!" exclaimed the younger of the two boys. "How'd you do that? Are you a basketball player?"

"No way!" said the other boy. "Don't you know nothin'? They're football players. Rams. Brett Holiday and Ron Daniels, right?"

"That's right," said Ron, as he and Brett shook the boys' hands. "And who are you?"

"I'm Kyle Addison," said the older boy. "This is my little brother, Jeff."

Brett looked from Kyle to Jeff. The resemblance was obvious—blond crewcuts, bright blue eyes, flushed cheeks. Kyle, however, seemed outgoing and self-assured, while Jeff stood beside his big brother, looking up at Brett and Ron, awestruck. Brett guessed Kyle to be about Fox's age.

"Hey, could we get your autographs?" asked Kyle. "Nobody will believe we saw you otherwise. Could we?"

Brett looked over at Ron and shrugged. "Sure," he said. "Why not?"

"All right!" cried Kyle, turning to Jeff. "Run in the house and get something to write on," he ordered. "Hurry!"

Jeff hesitated for a moment, then turned and ran into the house.

"Wanna shoot some hoops while we're waitin'?" asked Ron.

"You're on!" shouted Kyle, grabbing the ball and racing toward the garage door for a lay-up. The ball rolled off the rim and bounced toward Brett, who tossed it effortlessly through the net just as Jeff came running back outside.

Brett and Ron jotted personal notes to each of the boys, then took off running once again. Brett was glad

for the slight respite. His breathing had slowed somewhat, and he had hopes of continuing the remainder of
their run in silence. Ron, however, apparently had other
ideas.

"So," he said, "now that I know both you and Ariane
are crazy, what about me? What can I do to help with
this insane plan of yours?"

Brett looked over at his friend. Ron was smiling,
but Brett sensed that his offer was a serious one. If only
he could think of something for Ron to do! But what?
What could anyone do at this point?

"Well," said Brett, returning Ron's smile, "I suppose, since you're single, you could find some way to get
yourself introduced to Jacqueline and then try some of
your well-polished charm on her. After all, it worked for
me on Ariane. And, besides, what have we got to lose?"

Ron's dark eyes sparkled. "Now that's the best idea
I've heard in a long time," he said, nodding as he ran. "I
just may have to take you up on that. If I can just figure
out how. . . ."

*

Brett poured himself a cup of coffee, picked up the
morning paper from the kitchen table, and went to look
for Ariane.

He'd been surprised when he rolled over in bed and
found her gone, especially when he looked at the clock
and realized it was only a few minutes after seven.
Saturday was Ariane's one morning to sleep in, and she
seldom got up before nine.

Opening the sliding glass door, he stepped out onto
the enclosed patio. Ariane was sprawled in a padded
lounge chair, sipping her coffee and looking up at him.

"Good morning," she said. "Hope I didn't wake
you."

Brett shook his head and plunked down on the
bench beside the redwood picnic table.

"Nope," he said. "But I was really surprised to find you up so soon. You got something going on this morning that I don't know about?"

"Nothing," she said. "Absolutely nothing. In fact, I had planned to stay in bed and sleep until I couldn't keep my eyes closed anymore. But wouldn't you know it? Six-thirty sharp, I'm wide awake. I tried to go back to sleep, but finally gave up and decided to sit outside and have some coffee. It's warm out here already, but it's peaceful, too, isn't it?"

"It sure is," agreed Brett. "And beautiful. Like you."

Brett had always believed that no matter how lovely she looked all dressed up, Ariane never looked better than when her face was flushed from sleep and her dark hair flowed, long and uncombed, down her shoulders and back. And it hadn't escaped his attention that she was wearing his favorite peach-colored robe.

"You don't look so bad yourself," she said, smiling as she took a sip of her coffee. "For somebody who just rolled out of bed, that is."

Brett looked down at his faded jeans, which was about all he'd bothered to slip on when he climbed out of bed. His hair was uncombed and he knew he needed a shave, but if his wife thought he looked good, who was he to argue?

He looked at Ariane and winked. "It's good to know you can still recognize a good-looking man when you see one," he said, setting his coffee cup and newspaper down on the picnic table. "So, no plans for today, huh?"

"None," she said. "I was thinking about kidnapping you and driving over to the beach for lunch or something, but then I remembered you had that charity lunch thing downtown."

Brett raised his eyebrows. "I do? Today? I thought that was next week. Are you sure?"

"I double-checked," said Ariane. "It's today at noon. Is that a problem? Did you have something else in mind?"

Brett frowned. "Actually, yes. Well, nothing I can't change, but . . ." He sighed and shook his head. "I should have checked my calendar first," he said. "Should never have promised Fox without checking. Now I'll have to call and cancel. I hate doing that to him, I really do, but . . ."

"What were you two planning to do?" asked Ariane.

"Oh, nothing in particular," said Brett. "Just spend the day together, I guess. You know, go to a show, eat some hot dogs—since nobody else around here will do that with me. That kind of stuff."

Ariane smiled. "So, what about me? Will I do for a substitute? I'm not doing anything today, and that way you wouldn't have to call and disappoint him. What do you think? Would he want to go with me?"

Brett's eyes opened wide. "You're kidding, right? You'd do that for me?"

"Of course I would," said Ariane. "For you and for Fox . . . and for me, too. With the exception of the hot dogs, your plans with Fox sound a lot better than anything I had in mind. If you think he could stand going out for something other than junk food, I'd be happy to fill in for you . . . if you think he wouldn't mind too much."

Brett stood up and moved toward Ariane, reaching down to pull her up from her chair. Ariane set her coffee cup on the ground beside her, then took Brett's hands and let him lift her out of the chair and into his arms. Holding her close, he buried his face in her soft, sweet-smelling hair.

"How could he mind?" he murmured. "How could anyone mind spending the day with someone as beautiful and wonderful as you?"

"I'll bet you say that to all the women in your life," she joked, tilting her head up and kissing the stubble on his chin.

Brett smiled as he gazed down into Ariane's shining green eyes. He knew there could never be any other woman in his life, for what woman alive could compare to the one he already had?

*

Fox eyed her suspiciously as he chewed his spinach salad with hot bacon dressing. He had to admit, it wasn't as bad as he'd expected it to be, but he'd sure hate to have to live on the stuff. The football dude's wife sure seemed to be enjoying it, though. In fact, the way her eyes lit up when the waiter set the salad down in front of her, you'd have thought it was a large pizza with everything. Which is exactly what Fox wished it was.

Woulda been, thought Fox. *Woulda been a nice big fat pizza, or maybe chili dogs and fries, if the football dude hadn't copped out on me and sent his uppity lawyer-wife instead. Wonder what he had to do to talk her into this? I jus' wish somebody'd tol' me she was comin' 'stead of him. Least then I coulda got outta goin' with her. Coulda played sick or somethin'. But I was already out there, dressed and waitin', when she showed. Now I'm stuck! And if this is her idea of a good lunch, I know I'm gonna hate the movie she wants to take me to.*

"A penny for your thoughts," said Ariane.

Fox blinked. "Huh?"

"I was just wondering what you were thinking about," said Ariane. "You looked like you were a thousand miles away."

I wish I was, thought Fox, then shrugged. "Oh, I was just . . . enjoyin' this here spinach salad." He smirked. "It's real good," he said. "*Real* good."

Ariane smiled. "I didn't used to like it, either," she said. "Actually, when I was your age I preferred things like pizza and hot dogs and tacos. But that was before I found out what was in that kind of food and what it does to you over a period of time. You only have one body, you know, and you owe it to yourself to take care of it."

Fox didn't answer. He looked down at his plate and took another bite of salad, then wondered if he'd ever known anybody who'd heard of spinach salad before. He wondered if his father would still be alive today if somebody had fed him spinach salad in jail. He wondered if Ariane had any idea how hard it was to take care of your body when you had to spend most of the day digging through trash cans looking for something to eat.

"I have an idea," said Ariane suddenly.

Fox lifted his head and eyed her warily. He was willing to bet he wouldn't like this idea any better than the spinach salad.

"If you're still hungry when we get through here," said Ariane, "we can stop on the way to the movies and have some frozen yogurt. I know a charming little place not far from here, and their yogurt is scrumptious. What do you say?"

Charming and scrumptious? thought Fox, taking a gulp of lemon-flavored ice water in an effort not to laugh out loud. *I wonder if that frozen yogurt stuff is as charming and scrumptious as this here salad? Don't this woman ever eat no regular food? Man, I don't see how the football dude can stand it! His fault, though. You marry somebody goes 'round sayin' stuff like charming and scrumptious, you gotta know you in for trouble.*

He set his glass down. "Sure," he said. "Why not?"

This time, though, Fox was pleasantly surprised. He decided he wouldn't go so far as to call the place charming or the yogurt scrumptious, but he had to admit the dessert was pretty good.

"Well?" she asked, "what do you think? Do you like it?"

She was watching him closely, her big green eyes following his every move. It gave him the creeps.

"It's okay," he said.

"You picked a good one," said Ariane. "That chocolate-raspberry swirl is a very popular flavor."

Popular with who? Fox wondered. *Nobody I know ever eats it—or any other kind of yogurt, either.*

"So," said Ariane, "what would you like to do next? Do you want to go straight to the movie, or is there something else you'd like to do first? We never did decide which movie we wanted to see, did we?"

What's this "we" stuff? thought Fox. *If we have to find a movie we both like, we might as well hang it up right now!*

"I don't know," he said. "I—"

"Ariane!" cried a voice behind Fox.

Ariane looked up and smiled. "Rachel," she said, as a thin woman with lots of blond hair piled on top of her head came and stood beside their table. "What a nice surprise. How are you?"

"I'm fine, thank you," said Rachel, bending down to kiss Ariane's cheek. "I was just walking by when I looked in the window and saw you sitting here with. . . ." She turned toward Fox, then back to Ariane. "With . . . your friend," she finished.

Ariane smiled. "Yes," she said, nodding in Fox's direction. "This is Fox Richards. Fox, this is Rachel Stuart. Rachel's husband, Shane, is a lawyer with the firm where I work."

Fox was glad the skinny lady with all the hair didn't try to shake his hand. He was also glad—and surprised— that Ariane had called him Fox, instead of Elmore. Score one for the football dude's wife.

"How nice to meet you," said Rachel, directing a half-smile toward Fox, then turning back to Ariane.

Right, thought Fox. *Prob'ly made your day. Mine, too.*

"Would you care to join us?" Ariane asked Rachel.

"Oh no, I couldn't," said Rachel, glancing at her watch. "I'm due for an appointment at the beauty shop next door. I just wanted to pop in and make sure it was you. I couldn't quite tell from . . . outside."

Rachel smiled nervously, her eyes darting from Ariane to Fox and back again. Fox thought she looked like she'd spent her whole life eating scrumptious things like spinach salad and yogurt. He wondered if her smile wouldn't be so tight if she ate a hot dog once in a while. He wondered how long it would take the people at the beauty shop to take all that hair down off her head—and what they'd do with it when they did.

"Well, I suppose I should get going," said Rachel, her voice trailing off. "Besides, I'm sure you two have plans. . . ."

"We were just discussing that," said Ariane. "But we hadn't quite decided yet. We have the whole afternoon. Any suggestions?"

Rachel raised her eyebrows. "Oh, well, I . . ." She paused. "How about a museum," she suggested. "Or an art gallery?"

Fox groaned silently. The day was definitely going from bad to worse.

"What a fantastic idea," said Ariane. "We just might do that." She smiled at Fox, then turned back to Rachel. "Oh, by the way," she said. "Thank you again for the wonderful party the other night. Brett and I really enjoyed it."

This time the skinny lady's smile seemed to thaw a little. "I'm so glad," she said. "Shane thrives on parties, you know. And there's nowhere he'd rather have them than at our house."

"And why not?" asked Ariane. "You have a lovely home. And you're such a gracious hostess."

Rachel's smile widened even more. "You're a dear for saying so," she said. "We'll have to get together again soon. But for now, I really must run." She turned toward Fox. "Good-bye, . . . Fox," she said. "Delightful to have met you."

Delightful, thought Fox, watching her as she headed for the door. *Delightful and charming and scrumptious.* He ate another bite of yogurt, wondering what the football dude's wife would do if he jumped up and ran out the door—for the hall, for New York, for *anywhere* that would get him out of spending the rest of the day inside some building looking at stuff that had been dead for years and pictures that nobody except people who ate spinach salad could understand.

"Nice lady, don't you think?" asked Ariane, stirring her yogurt with a plastic spoon.

Fox shrugged. "Don't know," he said. "Couldn't tell. She a lawyer, too?"

Ariane looked surprised. "Rachel? A lawyer? Not hardly! Her husband is, like I said, and he loves it. But not Rachel. In fact, she told me once that she couldn't imagine why I was working so hard at trying to become one myself—or why I was working at all, actually."

Fox put his spoon down and studied Ariane. "Can't figure that one out, either," he said. "I mean, it ain't like you need the bread or anythin'. The football dude, he takes good care of you, don't he?"

Ariane smiled. "My husband makes plenty of money, yes. And, of course, he would give me anything I asked for. But I'm not a puppy, Fox. I don't need to be taken care of. I need to be me. Being Brett's wife is part of who I am, but becoming a lawyer is also part of me. It's something I've dreamed about for years—long before I met or married Brett. And when I married him, I brought my dream with me. If I gave it up, I'd be cheating myself, and Brett, too, because I'd no longer be the woman he fell in love with. Does that make any sense?"

The part about the puppy does, thought Fox. *I know jus' how it feels when people look at you like they gonna pat you on the head.*

"Yeah," he said, nodding. "Yeah, it makes a lot of sense. But . . ." He hesitated.

"But what?" she asked.

"What about . . . kids?" he asked. "Don't you want none?"

Ariane's face changed. Fox was sure he saw pain in her eyes before she answered.

"Yes," she said. "Of course I want children. But we've decided to wait until my career is established. You can understand that, can't you?"

Fox wasn't sure he understood much at all about kids or careers, but he figured it didn't really matter anyway. He shrugged. "Yeah, sure," he answered.

Ariane smiled again. "I'm glad," she said. "Because I really do love children, and I—we, Brett and I—want them. But I guess I'm just not ready yet to give up my dream of becoming a lawyer first. Everybody needs dreams, Fox. And everybody deserves a chance to make those dreams come true. And nobody should try to take them away from you." Her voice got softer then. "That's one of the reasons I love my husband so much. I know he wants children—and he'll be a wonderful father someday—but he's willing to wait so I can chase my dream for a while first. It's the greatest gift you can give anyone, you know—helping them to fulfill their dreams. Brett's good at that."

Fox's eyes locked into Ariane's, but this time it didn't give him the creeps. This time he sensed that she was willing him a very special gift. He wasn't quite sure what it was yet, but he knew he wanted it.

"Well," said Ariane, pulling her eyes away from his and glancing down at his yogurt dish. "Are you about ready? Did you decide what you wanted to do? A movie or . . ." She raised her eyebrows and shrugged her shoulders. "It's up to you."

Fox shoveled the last spoon of yogurt into his mouth. "Nah," he said, swallowing. "I been to movies before—lots of 'em. Ain't never been to no art gallery, though. Not too many museums, either."

He tried not to smile, but he couldn't help it when he saw her eyes light up with surprise and excitement. Museums and art galleries still sounded like a boring way to spend the afternoon, but he figured if he'd made it through the spinach salad, he could handle this too.

Besides, maybe the lawyer-lady wasn't quite as bad as he'd thought. . . .

CHAPTER 14

I sure hope that's the last one of those charity things for a *while*, thought Brett, hitting the garage door opener as he pulled into his driveway. *They're always for a good cause, but they seem to go on forever.*

He was surprised, as he eased his Porsche into the empty garage, to see that Ariane wasn't back yet. *Must be a good sign*, he told himself, climbing out of the car. *But I can hardly wait for her to get home and tell me how it went.*

He thought about surprising Ariane by fixing dinner, but decided against it since he had no idea what time she would get back. Instead, he rummaged around in the pantry until he found a half-empty bag of onion-flavored chips, poured himself a tall glass of soda, then headed for his office and his favorite chair.

Sinking down into the worn, brown Naugahyde recliner, he sighed. *What a way to spend a Saturday afternoon*, he thought, grabbing a handful of chips. *Of course, I could go outside and swim a few laps. Or go down to the gym, or . . .* He picked up the remote control and punched the power switch. *Or, I can just sit here with my mind in neutral and do absolutely nothing.*

He smiled. Easy choice. Even though he knew Ariane would disapprove. With the exception of sports events or an occasional educational or spiritual program, TV was anathema to Ariane—ranking right up there next to junk food. *Oh well,* he thought, shoveling another handful of chips into his mouth, *these will be long gone before she gets back, anyway.*

He found a baseball game on the sports channel, but it was already the top of the ninth, and the game ended before Brett had polished off his chips and soda. Flipping from one channel to another, he decided maybe Ariane was right. Sometimes there just wasn't anything worth watching.

Shutting off the TV, he reached over to the lamp table beside him and picked up the latest copy of *Sports Illustrated*. When it had arrived a couple of days earlier, Brett was intrigued when he noticed an article about an up-and-coming, if somewhat controversial, tennis player. Until now, however, he hadn't gotten around to reading it. This seemed like the perfect time.

Brett had seen the kid play on TV several times and, he had to admit, he was good. Real good. Maybe even great. But he'd never been impressed with his brash, swaggering personality. Before he'd gotten halfway through the article, Brett was even more sure that he did not care for this cocky young man who so obviously thought of himself as a cut above the other players and, therefore, not bound by the rules that applied to everyone else in the game. Just when Brett had come to the point of thinking the kid had said all he possibly could to irritate Brett, the interviewer asked the young athlete what he thought of one of the all-time greats of tennis, someone Brett had admired for years.

"Yesterday's news," the boy had answered. "He's nothing but yesterday's news."

Brett tossed the magazine toward the TV, where it bounced off the screen and landed on the floor. *Yesterday's news,* he thought. *Who does this smart-aleck kid think he is, anyway? Where does he think the game of tennis would be today if it weren't for the people he refers to as "yesterday's news"? People like Arthur Ashe and Billie Jean King and Bobby Riggs. . . . Who does he think is responsible for all the fame and fortune he's raking in today? At least those "yesterday's news" guys earned their stripes through talent and hard work. This one, all he wants to do is attract attention to himself, and maybe even give tennis a bad name at the same time. What I can't believe is how fast the fans fall for it! How can they forget the heroes they've been cheering for all these years, just because somebody newer and younger comes along and makes a lot of noise? How can they forget? How can they be so fickle? How . . . ?*

*

"Brett!" called Ariane, bursting into the kitchen from the back door. "Honey, where are you?"

When he didn't answer, she hurried through the kitchen and living room, down the hallway and into his den. Sure enough, there he was—sound asleep in his recliner, with a half-empty soda glass and a discarded potato chip bag on the table beside him.

Ariane smiled and shook her head. *Guess I'll never get him to give up junk food,* she thought, bending over to pick up the sports magazine on the floor in front of the TV. *But I suppose I should be glad that at least he wasn't sitting here staring at some mindless TV program.*

She laid the magazine down on the table, then sat on the arm of Brett's chair. "Honey," she said softly, laying her hand on his shoulder. "Sweetheart, I'm home."

Brett's eyes opened slowly.

"Hi," she said, bending down to kiss his forehead. "Sorry to wake you, but I was so anxious to tell you about my day with Fox. You want to hear it?"

His smile was halfhearted. "Sure," he said. "Of course I do, babe. How'd it go?"

"It was wonderful," she said. "Really wonderful. Well, maybe not at first. I mean, it took a little time for us to feel comfortable together, but it happened, Brett. I'm sure of it. He . . . softened a little, or something. I don't even know exactly what it was that brought him around, but . . . well, it was sometime during the yogurt, that much I know. We'd already finished our spinach salad and—"

Brett arched his eyebrows. "You took Fox out for spinach salad? And he actually ate it?"

Ariane nodded. "Sure. Why not?"

Brett shrugged and shook his head. "Oh, nothing," he said. "I was just remembering Fox's reaction to a Denver omelette. Anyway, sorry I interrupted you. Go ahead. What happened after the spinach salad?"

"Well, I had a feeling he was still hungry," said Ariane, "so we stopped in at that quaint little yogurt shop by the theater downtown . . . you know which one I mean, don't you?"

Brett nodded.

"Anyway," Ariane continued, "we were sitting there having yogurt—still polite and somewhat strained, you know—and then Rachel Stuart stopped in for a minute on her way to the beauty shop next door. She didn't stay long or anything, but soon after she left, I began to notice a slight difference in Fox."

Ariane smiled. "You know what he asked me?" she said. "First, he asked me if Rachel was a lawyer. Then, he asked me why I wanted to be one. He couldn't understand why I would want to work when I already had you to take care of me."

Brett didn't return her smile. "What did you tell him?" he asked.

She shrugged. "The truth," she said. "That being a lawyer was a dream of mine long before I met you, and that marrying you didn't change that. I also told him that, even though you obviously could and would take care of me if I wanted you to, I wasn't a puppy that needed to be taken care of. I wanted him to understand that it was important to me to be able to take care of myself, to fulfill my dreams so I could find out who I really was, over and above being Mrs. Brett Holiday. And I wanted him to know that you supported me in all that. I think he understood—part of it, anyway—because right after that, he suggested we go to an art gallery or a museum instead of a movie. What do you think of that?"

Brett's eyebrows shot up again. "You're kidding. Fox did that? Are you sure it was his idea? You didn't influence him or anything?"

"Well, Rachel had suggested it at first, but I could tell from his expression that he wasn't too hot on the idea," explained Ariane. "So I wasn't going to mention it again. But when we finished our yogurt and I asked him what he wanted to do, he said he'd been to lots of movies in his life, but very few museums or art galleries."

"And?" asked Brett. "What was his reaction when you got there? Did he have a good time?"

Ariane smiled again. "Well, I don't know if touring art galleries and museums has become his favorite form of entertainment yet, but I'd say we at least made some progress in expanding his horizons a bit. And somehow I know it was tied in to our discussion about dreams, even if I'm not sure exactly how." She bent down to kiss him again, this time on his lips. "I feel good about it," she said. "It was a wonderful day."

She paused a moment, wondering whether to broach the subject, then decided to plunge in. "There was something else," she said. "Something Fox asked about."

Brett raised his eyebrows questioningly.

"Children," said Ariane. "He wanted to know if we were going to have children."

"What did you tell him?"

"I told him we were," she answered, "when my career is established."

"And?" asked Brett. "What was his reaction?"

"I'm not sure," Ariane admitted. "I couldn't really tell." She paused again. "What I really want to know is how *you* feel. Do you resent that we've waited so long? Do you mind waiting a little longer?"

Brett studied her before answering. "Sometimes," he answered. "Sometimes I wish we didn't have to wait so long. But most of the time, I know it's for the best. You do still want them eventually, don't you?"

Ariane felt her heart skip a beat, and she was surprised at the passion that rose up inside her as she answered. "Definitely," she said. "In fact, more and more so lately." She smiled. "Must be my biological clock ticking."

Brett flinched. "Yeah, I suppose," he said.

Ariane eyed him curiously. "What was that for?" she asked. "Did I push the wrong button?"

Brett shook his head. "It's nothing," he said. "Really."

It was obvious the subject was closed. "So," said Ariane, trying to redirect the conversation, "what about you? How did your day go?"

"Oh, okay. Nothing special," said Brett. "Definitely not as productive or enjoyable as yours, I'm sure. The charity thing was . . . nice. Well, you know how charity things are. Anyway, that's basically all I did."

Ariane reached over to the table and picked up the potato chip bag. "Except plunk down here and eat garbage and then go to sleep," she teased. "Not a very healthful way to spend your afternoon, you know."

"I know," said Brett. "And I knew you'd mention it to me."

"Only because I love you," she said. "And I want you to take care of yourself so I can keep you around for a long, long time. Like forever." She kissed him once again. "Maybe even longer."

Brett returned her kiss, but Ariane knew him well enough to know that it was an automatic kiss, not a responsive one. "All right," she said. "What's going on? What's the problem?"

Brett looked mildly surprised. "What problem?" he asked. "What makes you think there's a problem?"

"I'm your wife, remember?" she said, sliding down off the arm of the chair into his lap. "And I know you better than you know you. So you might as well give up and tell me, because I'm not getting up until you do."

Brett rolled his eyes and groaned. "Not that!" he said. "Not your full hundred pounds right here on my lap! I'll never survive."

Ariane grinned. "Don't try to kid your way out of this, Brett Holiday. I mean it. Tell me what's wrong or I won't let you help me fix dinner tonight—or wash the dishes, either."

"You drive a hard bargain, lady," said Brett, reaching up to run his fingers through her hair. "I guess there's no use trying to get out of it, is there?"

"None," she said.

He gazed at her for a moment, then reached over and picked up the issue of *Sports Illustrated* from the table. "Have you seen this?" he asked, flipping the pages open to the article on the tennis player.

"Sure," said Ariane. "You know how much I love tennis. I read everything I can find about it."

"That's what I thought," he said. "So, what did you think?"

"I think he's young and talented," said Ariane. "And I think he still has a lot of growing up to do. Why?"

"What about his comment about 'yesterday's news'?" asked Brett. "Didn't that bother you?"

"I'm not sure I even remember it," said Ariane. "Where was it?"

Brett pointed it out to her, and she reread that section.

"Well, like I said," repeated Ariane, "the kid has a lot of growing up to do. And a lot to learn. But what's the big deal?"

Brett frowned. "What's the big deal? You didn't think that was a cheap shot?"

"I think it was an ignorant remark," said Ariane. "But I doubt it caused any permanent damage to anyone's psyche. You just consider the source, right?"

"I suppose," said Brett. "But sometimes it's not so easy."

Neither of them spoke for a moment, as Ariane studied her husband's blue eyes. She scolded herself for not having seen the pain sooner, for not realizing what he was *really* trying to say to her. And then she pulled him close, cradling his head against her shoulder.

"I'm sorry," she said. "I didn't realize. But he wasn't talking about you, sweetheart. You are not yesterday's news—and you never will be—anymore than the Fearsome Foursome or Bart Starr or Johnny Unitas. Don't you see? You're a football player, just like I'm a law student. Those are our dreams. That's part of who we are—an important part. But it's not everything, Brett. There are a lot more dreams out there just waiting for us. Always. Don't you see? You're just making the transition, that's all. From one dream to another. And this dream could turn out to be even more exciting than any you've had before."

Slowly, Brett lifted his head, as Ariane felt his hand on the back of her neck, turning her toward him. This time his kiss was not automatic.

"I love you," he said.

"I know," she answered, reaching up to stroke his cheek. "I know."

*

The remainder of the weekend had been a quiet one, uneventful except for the intimate, unspoken interchange that can occur only between two people who are secure enough in their love for each other to be comfortable in silence. But now it was Monday, and Ariane had gone off to work, leaving Brett to sip his coffee and read the morning paper by himself.

Talk of football trades and contract negotiations had begun to infiltrate the sports section once again. Where two days earlier this would have made Brett uncomfortable, today he felt an inexplicable peace about the situation—not only because of his renewed commitment to double up on his physical workouts before training season officially began, but because the importance of his career had suddenly paled in light of something bigger and more exciting waiting just around the corner. He only wished he knew what that something was. But whatever it was, he was finally confident that it would all work out for the best.

Even as that sense of peaceful anticipation pervaded the air around him, however, his thoughts were interrupted by the ringing doorbell.

Brett glanced at his watch. Eight-thirty. Who in the world would be coming to his door at this hour? He laid the paper down and walked into the living room to answer the door.

Pulling it open, he stopped, blinked in surprise, then checked his watch once again. Maybe he'd looked at it wrong. Nope. Eight-thirty sharp. But it couldn't be. . . .

"Hey, man," said Ron, wearing a blue and gold Rams jersey, faded jeans, his gold chain, and a smile. "You ready, or what?"

Brett blinked again. Had he forgotten something? Did they have plans for today? And why were those other guys here—especially Chuck?

For there, standing on the porch behind Ron, were three other Rams players—Dave Dobson and Kevin Briscoe, two defensive linemen, and Chuck Nelson, the hotshot quarterback who was slowly but surely pushing Brett out of a job. They, too, were dressed in Rams jerseys, all of them smiling eagerly, as if wherever it was they were going had to be the greatest place on earth.

"I don't know what you're talking about," said Brett. "What's going on?"

"Why don't you invite us in and we'll tell you?" asked Ron, still smiling.

Brett stepped back as his four teammates came in. Although they were all taller than Brett, Dave and Kevin were the ones whose size was most noticeable. Brett figured they each weighed close to three hundred pounds.

"There's coffee in the kitchen," offered Brett, leading the way as the others followed. "Help yourself," he said, setting out extra cups. "And then tell me what in the world is going on here."

By the time they'd all poured themselves a cup of coffee and settled down at the kitchen table, Brett had begun to wonder if this was some sort of practical joke—especially since they all seemed so happy and excited. Whatever it was, he sure wanted to be in on it.

"Nice place you got here," said Dave, looking around appreciatively. "I'm gonna have to settle down and get married myself one of these days, if this is what I got to look forward to." He grinned. "Not that my place ain't nice, you understand. But it sure ain't this neat."

Brett smiled. "That's all thanks to my beautiful wife—and, of course, the help of a weekly housekeeper," he said. "But with or without a housekeeper, the word 'messy' is definitely not in Ariane's vocabulary."

"Maybe I can get her to come over and talk to my wife," said Kevin. "Shelly's beautiful and sweet—and a wonderful mother—but neat? No way. Never heard of it." He grinned. "Even the maid is starting to complain."

They all laughed—even Brett, remembering how much trouble he'd had talking his perfectionist wife into getting household help. It wasn't as if they couldn't afford it, he'd argued, and as busy as Ariane was with school and her job, she could certainly use it. But every time Brett had brought up the subject, Ariane had balked. What stranger, she had asked, could ever come into their home and clean it the way it was supposed to be cleaned? Finally, however, she had given into his arguments—and her full schedule—and had consented to the housekeeper. She still insisted on occasion, however, that the housekeeper didn't do as good a job as she did herself.

"Personally, I'm in no hurry to get married," said Chuck, interrupting Brett's thoughts. "I enjoy living alone. I can be as neat or as messy as I want. And besides, I love doing my own cooking. That's another one of my talents."

Figures, thought Brett. *I wonder if he does windows, too.*

"Well, you guys can forget finding a wife like Brett's," said Ron. "I know the woman, and I'm tellin' ya, there's nobody else like her anywhere. Believe me, I been lookin'! Besides, I already got first dibs on her when she finally wises up and gets rid of this old guy here."

Everyone was laughing again—everyone except Brett, who barely managed to force a smile. This small talk was beginning to get on his nerves. He looked from Ron to Dave to Kevin to Chuck, then back to Ron again. He didn't know any of the others nearly as well as he did Ron, but he knew without a doubt that they were up to something.

"Well?" said Brett, trying to hide the impatience in his voice with a touch of humor. "Are you guys going to let me in on your little secret, or am I going to have to call the coach to find out the game plan? I mean, have we got a date with the president or something?"

Kevin, with his sandy blond hair and blue eyes, flushed a bright red as he burst out laughing once again. Dave and Chuck, both black and younger even than Kevin and Ron, joined in. Ron, however, was making an obvious attempt at keeping a straight face.

"You're really very perceptive, ya know that, man?" said Ron. "Well, not that you're completely right. We're not going to see the president, but . . . we are going to see someone special."

"Who?" asked Brett.

The others stopped laughing and watched Brett closely.

"Why don't you just come with us and find out," suggested Ron, taking Brett by the elbow and steering him toward the front door.

"Wait a minute," said Brett, pulling his arm away and looking Ron in the eye. "I'm not going anywhere with you guys until you tell me who it is we're going to see."

Ron grinned, his dark eyes sparkling as he glanced from Brett to the others and then back again.

"We'll just see about that," he said, as Brett felt himself being commandeered from behind by too many big bodies to resist. Still protesting, he resigned himself to his trip into the unknown, as he half-walked and was half-carried, out the front door to Kevin's van, which waited on the street in front of Brett's house.

CHAPTER 15

Insisting on doing so under his own power, Brett climbed into the back of Kevin's van and slid across the seat to make room for Chuck and Dave. Picking up a small, stuffed rabbit from the seat near the window, he decided to make the best of his kidnapping. He tried to smile at Chuck as he sat down next to him, but he couldn't help but notice that even sitting down, Chuck was a couple of inches taller than he.

"Nice rabbit," said Chuck, grinning at the stuffed animal in Brett's hand.

"Yeah," said Brett, trying even harder to force a smile. "It's my favorite. I take it everywhere with me."

Kevin, who had just turned on the ignition, glanced in the rearview mirror at Brett, then burst out laughing. "Sorry about that," he said. "It's Korin's. Must have gotten left in here yesterday when Shelly took the kids to town. I'm surprised that's all you found. Like I told you, Shelly's not known for being neat, and she and the kids practically live in this thing during the week. I only drive it when I need the extra room."

Brett set the rabbit down on the seat beside him. "I didn't think this was your usual mode of transportation," he said, glancing out the window as he tried to get a feel for where they were going. "Don't you have a Mercedes?"

"I did," answered Kevin. "But I traded it in on a Ferrari when I got this van for Shelly. She insisted she needed all this room when Matthew was born."

"How old are your kids now, anyway?" asked Ron, who was sitting on the passenger side next to Kevin. "I don't think I've seen them since . . . when? That Super Bowl party we had?"

Kevin nodded. "Probably so," he agreed. "Matt was only a couple of months old at the time. We haven't really gotten together much since then, I guess."

"Not till now," said Dave, grinning with anticipation. "And somethin' tells me, today is gonna be even better than the Super Bowl!"

"Better than watching it, maybe," said Chuck. "But not better than playing in it!"

Brett shook his head. "You guys are terrible," he said. "I can't believe I let you talk me into going with you without even knowing who it is we're going to see!"

"You had no choice," Ron reminded him. "And you still don't. So just sit back and enjoy."

Brett sighed. He knew Ron was right. He had no choice, so he might as well enjoy the ride. He thought it a bit ironic, however, that he had to do so sitting next to his competition. And yet, he had to admit, Chuck seemed to be doing his best to be pleasant. And he'd certainly been right when he'd said there wasn't anything to compare with actually playing in the Super Bowl. It had been quite a while since the Rams had made it to the Super Bowl—slightly over ten years, as a matter of fact. Brett would never forget it. It had been only his second year with the Rams—his first as starting quarterback—and, even though they'd lost, Brett had played a brilliant game. All the newspapers had said so. The TV commentators had said so. The players and coaches had said so. And Brett's career had been off and running.

"Speaking of Super Bowls," said Chuck, turning toward Brett and snapping him out of his reverie, "I'll never forget the one you quarterbacked. I was just starting high school—my first year. I was so excited about going out for the team. Of course, being a scrawny freshman, I didn't see much playing time, but it was so great just getting a chance to put on the uniform and run out there on the field with the rest of the guys before the game. You were my hero then, you know. It was only your second year with the pros, but I knew you were going to make it big. And the way you played that day—man!" He shook his head in amazement, his dark eyes shining. "I thought sure you were going to pull it off with that last-second Hail-Mary pass. You would have, too, if they hadn't called the play back for offsides."

Brett's eyes opened wide. Was he hearing right? Was Chuck Nelson really praising his quarterbacking ability and telling him he was his hero? Did he really mean it, or was this his way of reminding Brett that his glory days were behind him, while Chuck's were still out there waiting for him just around the bend?

"I remember that game, too," said Dave. "I wasn't a Rams fan then, but I have to admit, when I saw you play, Brett, I was impressed. Sure never thought I'd end up playin' with you after all these years, though."

"Man!" exclaimed Ron from the front seat, turning around to face them. "What's with this 'all these years ago' stuff? You guys sound like you're plannin' a retirement party back there or somethin'. Or maybe a funeral!" He looked at Brett and laughed. "I knew you were old," he said. "But I didn't realize *how* old! I mean, when your own teammates start tellin' you how they watched you when they were kids, you *know* your days are numbered!"

"Not *that* numbered!" said Chuck, surprising Brett with the force of his statement. "I watched you throw last season," he said to Brett. "And there's no way your career is over! I've seen the firepower in your arm. And your knee's better now, right?"

"Right," agreed Brett, nodding as he watched Chuck intently. This was the last person he had expected to come to his defense. For the first time, Brett wondered if there might be more to this hotshot new quarterback than he'd realized.

"That's good," Chuck went on. "We need our team healthy—all of us—if we're going to make it to the Super Bowl this year. Only this time, we're going to win! Especially with you up front, because you've got the experience I don't. And whether you start or I do, you're still our leader, you know. I've always felt that way, and I know the other guys do, too. That's what being a team is all about, right? Knowing who your leader is, and then pulling together for the same goal." Chuck smiled. "Like I said, you've been my hero for a long time, Brett, and I'm really proud to be on your team."

"I appreciate that," said Brett, his smile coming easily this time. There was no denying the sincerity in Chuck's voice—or in his eyes. And there was no denying the renewed assurance Brett felt in his heart—the assurance that this would be a winning season, no matter what.

*

Brett stared out the van window as they pulled up and parked in front of a sprawling white Tudor-style mansion, which sat back off the street, surrounded by a huge wrought iron fence. He couldn't imagine any one person living in a place that size. In fact, as they piled out of the van and gathered in front of the locked gate, he almost expected a tour guide to appear and ask for their admission tickets.

"So this is it?" he asked, looking directly at Ron. "This is where we're going?"

"This is it," said Ron. "Jacqueline St. James's place. Not bad, huh?"

Brett's mouth dropped open in disbelief. "This is Jacqueline's house? We have an appointment to see Jacqueline St. James?"

Ron looked at the other guys, then back to Brett. "Well, not exactly," he admitted. "See, I read in the entertainment section of the paper yesterday that she was back in town from her latest tour. So I figured if we just came over here early enough, we could catch her at home."

Brett's eyes opened wide. "You mean, she has no idea we're coming? You haven't even called and made an appointment or anything? We're just showing up on her doorstep?"

Ron shrugged. "Sure, why not? Admit it, man, you tried everything else, right? Phone calls, letters, whatever. And you got nowhere." He paused and grinned. "Besides, it was your idea, you know."

Brett frowned. "My idea?"

"Absolutely," said Ron. "Don't you remember? When I asked you how I could help, you told me to find some way to get myself introduced to Jacqueline and then use my charm to persuade her to come to your party. So, I'm just followin' through on your suggestion. You can't have any objection to that, right?"

Brett was sure he must have several objections, but for the life of him, he couldn't think of what they were. He just stood there, staring, waiting for someone to do something.

"So, now what?" asked Dave, breaking the silence as he turned toward Ron. "How do we get in this place?"

Ron raised his eyebrows in surprise. "What are you lookin' at me for? All I did was get us down here." He gestured toward Brett and grinned. "This here's the guy who's so hot to meet Jacqueline St. James. Let him come up with a plan!"

All eyes turned toward Brett. "Me?" said Brett. "Why me? I mean, sure, I'm the one who really needs to talk to her, but you guys are the ones who dragged me down here. Obviously you want to meet her just as much as I do."

"That's true," admitted Chuck, his dark eyes twinkling. "But not necessarily for the same reason!"

They all laughed, except Brett. "Come on, you guys," he said. "Now that you've got me involved in your crazy scheme, we have to get serious. What good's it going to do us to come all the way down here if we can't get past the front gate?"

"Brett's right," said Kevin. "We really do need to come up with a plan."

Dave looked the fence up and down. "Doesn't look all that high to me," he said. "I could climb it with one hand tied behind my back."

"Sure," said Ron. "And have the cops haulin' us off to jail in two minutes flat."

"Or get our legs chewed off by a bunch of guard dogs," added Kevin. "Sorry, but I'm not taking those kind of chances, not even to meet Jacqueline St. James."

"Why not try ringin' the buzzer?" suggested Chuck casually, pointing toward the inside of the cement pillar next to the locked gate. "That's probably what it's there for, don't you think? And it looks like there's a built-in intercom right next to it."

A smile played on Chuck's lips as he watched Kevin, Dave, and Ron walk over to examine the intercom.

Brett grinned and clapped Chuck on the back. "You're going to make a great quarterback," he said.

Chuck shrugged. "I've got a great teacher."

Ron pushed the buzzer, and immediately a crisp female voice responded, "Yes?"

"Uhhh . . ." Ron hesitated and looked around. When no one offered any suggestions, he turned back to the intercom. "Uh, I . . . I mean, we . . . want to see Jacqueline . . . I mean, Miss St. James," he said.

The voice on the intercom changed from crisp to frigid. "Do you have an appointment?" she asked.

They all looked at each other again.

"Uh, no," said Ron, "but—"

"Miss St. James does not see anyone except by appointment," said the voice.

Ron turned to Brett. "You're our leader, remember? What now?"

Brett hesitated for a moment, then stepped in front of Ron and leaned close to the intercom. "Excuse me," he said. "My name is Brett Holiday, and I've been trying for weeks to get an appointment with Miss St. James. It's really urgent that I get a chance to speak with her and—"

"I'm sorry, Mr. Holiday," interrupted the voice. "Miss St. James does not see anyone without an appointment."

"So how do I get an appointment?" asked Brett. "I've tried everything. I've called her agent, her manager, her secretary—I don't know what else to do. Like I told you, it's urgent that I speak to her as soon as possible. You see, there's this kid—his name is Fox—and he's never had a birthday party before, so I promised him that—"

"I'm sure I have no idea what you're talking about," said the voice, interrupting him once again. "And as I have explained to you repeatedly, Mr. Holiday, Miss St. James sees no one without an appointment. You will simply have to come back when you have one."

"But—"

"Good day, Mr. Holiday," said the voice.

The intercom clicked off and Brett's shoulders slumped. *So close,* he thought. *So close, and yet . . .*

He turned back toward the others. "She's here," he said, shaking his head slowly. "I'm sure of it, or that woman wouldn't have asked if I had an appointment. But what good is it, knowing she's here, if—"

"Mr. Holiday? Brett Holiday?"

Brett whirled around. The voice had come from the intercom, but it was a different voice this time—softer, richer, and definitely warmer.

"Yes," he said. "Yes, this is Brett Holiday."

"Mr. Holiday," said the voice, "this is Jacqueline St. James. I overheard you speaking with my maid, and I understand you need to see me."

"Yes, I do," said Brett, feeling the excitement rising within as his teammates gathered closely around him. "Actually, I've been trying to reach you for quite some time," he explained, his words coming quickly now. "I've been calling you and writing you letters and . . . Miss St. James, I really need to talk to you. It's about a birthday party for a young friend of mine. His name is Fox and he's never had a party before, and he's one of your biggest fans and—"

"Yes, I know," said Jacqueline. "I'm aware of the situation. My manager's secretary, Diane, filled me in when I stopped by the office yesterday. Apparently she spoke with you on the phone a few days ago."

Of course! Mr. Goebel's secretary. The one who'd made Brett's day by telling him what a big fan she was. The one who'd given him Jacqueline's phone number. The one who'd promised to try to talk to Jacqueline about the party. Obviously, this Diane was a woman who followed through on her promises. Brett felt a twinge of guilt when he remembered that he had forgotten his promise—to get tickets to a Rams game for Diane and her husband. He resolved to get those tickets before the day was over. He also resolved that they would be for the best seats available in the entire stadium.

"Yes," said Brett. "And I really appreciate her mentioning it to you. Like I said, it's really important that I talk with you about this and—"

"Well, then," interrupted Jacqueline, "why don't you come on up, Mr. Holiday? If this party is as important as both you and Diane seem to think it is, maybe we'd better discuss it right now."

Brett's eyes opened wide, and he turned to look at his teammates. They were grinning and nodding excitedly.

"Great!" said Brett, turning back toward the intercom. "I mean, fine. Now would be fine. But . . . I . . . have some friends with me. Four of them. Well, actually, they're teammates—friends, too, but . . . what I mean is . . . we're all Rams. Football players."

Brett could almost hear Jacqueline smile over the intercom. "Yes, I understand that," she said. "Please, come on in. All of you."

A buzzer sounded as the intercom switched off and the long wrought iron gate began to swing open.

"You want me to get the van so we can drive up?" asked Kevin.

"No way," said Ron, stepping onto the long, circular, oak-lined driveway that led up to the house. "Let's just walk up. This place is fantastic. I don't wanna miss any of it."

"You're right," said Brett, as they began to make their way past the immaculately manicured lawns, flower beds, and shrubs toward the spacious porch that stretched across the front of Jacqueline's home. "This place is fantastic. Of course, someone like Jacqueline St. James isn't exactly going to live in a two-bedroom apartment somewhere, but . . . I don't know, it's just hard for me to picture someone as young as her living here all by herself."

"Besides that," added Dave, "can you imagine what this place musta cost? We're not exactly on welfare or anything, but the kind of money these superstars make, man!" He whistled and shook his head in amazement.

"I think I read somewhere that she bought this place a couple of years ago when she moved out on her own," said Kevin. "Before that, she was supposed to have been living with her parents in the house she bought for them. I'll bet it's real nice, too."

"Undoubtedly," said Chuck. "How old do you think she is, anyway?"

"Twenty-one," said Ron. He grinned and winked. "I checked."

"Twenty-one!" exclaimed Dave. "Man, I knew she was young but . . ." He shook his head. "I don't know, I guess I thought she was more like twenty-five or so, just 'cause she's been around so long. I know I been listenin' to her sing for at least six or seven years—maybe more."

"Yeah, but don't forget," said Ron, "she was one of those child stars. Hit it big when she was a kid, and just kept on gettin' better."

"Better at singing?" teased Kevin. "Or better looking?"

"Both," said Ron.

"I'll agree with that," added Chuck. "I just wonder if she looks as good in person as she does on TV."

"Well, I'd say we're about to find out," said Dave, as they all stepped up onto the porch.

Brett reached for the heavy brass door knocker, but before he could lift it, the door opened, and Brett knew the answer to Chuck's question. Jacqueline St. James did not look as good in person as she did on TV—she looked better. And a lot more real, decided Brett, as this wealthy young superstar stood in the doorway, smiling warmly and wearing a pale pink sweat suit and tennis shoes. Her long black hair, which she usually wore in elaborate styles that Brett thought made her head look too big for her small, sleek body, was pulled back in a loose ponytail. A few frizzy tendrils had escaped the band that held her thick hair in place, curling around her face and accentuating the softness of her flawless brown skin. But it was her eyes, Brett decided, her huge, coal-black eyes and her finely chiseled cheekbones that made her beauty absolutely breathtaking.

Which is exactly what it must have been because, for several seconds, these fearless heroes of the gridiron stood speechless, transfixed as they stared at the lovely young woman standing before them.

And then she laughed—a joyous, melodic laugh that immediately relaxed them so they could begin breathing normally once again.

"Forgive me," said Jacqueline, her dark eyes moving from one to the other of the five men standing on her porch. "I didn't mean to laugh. It's just that . . . , well, I suppose I expected you all to be so . . . so big and menacing." She smiled again and offered her hand to Brett. "Instead, you looked so . . . sweet . . . vulnerable almost. I guess you just caught me off-guard."

"I'm afraid that's the way you affected us, too," said Brett, surprised at the strength of her grip as he shook her hand. "We're just . . . thankful that you agreed to see us. I was beginning to think I'd never get a chance to talk with you."

"Well, I'm glad it worked out," she said. "And I assume that you are Brett Holiday. I wasn't sure at first. I'm afraid I'm not much of a sports fan. When Diane mentioned your name to me yesterday, it rang a bell, but a very faint one. She filled me in on all the details of your illustrious career, however. Quite impressive." She turned toward Ron, who had edged up as close toward Brett as he could. "And you are . . . ?"

"Oh, I'm sorry," said Brett. "I forgot to introduce you to these other guys. This is Ron Daniels. He's a wide receiver—and a real flirt, so be careful. These two big guys over here are Dave Dobson and Kevin Briscoe, a couple of our best defensive linemen. And this is Chuck Nelson, the hottest new quarterback to hit the league since . . . , well, since I came on the scene, I guess."

Jacqueline laughed again, as she shook hands with each of them. "I don't know what any of that means," she said. "But I'm very pleased to meet all of you."

She turned back to Brett. "So," she said, gesturing toward the open front door, "shall we get started?"

"The sooner the better," said Brett. "I know you must be anxious to get back to whatever it was you were doing before we showed up."

"Actually, I was just getting ready to go into my gym for my morning workout," explained Jacqueline, looking down at her sweat suit. "But it can wait. Come on in."

They followed her through the front door, then on past a plushly carpeted staircase near the entryway, and down a long, oak-paneled hallway. "Let's go into my office and sit down," she said, opening the door at the end of the hallway. "I'm anxious to hear all about this birthday party you're planning. It must be for someone very, very special."

*

Ariane hadn't even gotten her key into the lock when the back door jerked open and there stood Brett, grinning from ear to ear.

"What's with you?" she asked. "You look like you just got nominated to the Hall of Fame or won the Super Bowl single-handedly!"

"Even better," he said, taking her elbow and ushering her into the kitchen. "Well, almost, anyway." He put his arms around her and pulled her close, kissed the top of her nose, then stood looking down at her, his blue eyes dancing.

"I thought you'd never get here," he said.

"This is the same time I always get home," she reminded him. "What's the matter, are you starved to death?"

He grinned. "No. Although I am taking you out to dinner later—unless you have school tonight. You don't have school, do you? Tell me you don't have school."

"I don't have school," she said, frowning at him. "For heaven's sake, Brett, you know when I go to school.

What in the world has got you so excited that you can't even remember my schedule?"

"You'll never believe it," he said. "You will *never* believe it."

"Try me," she said, pushing him away as she kicked off her shoes. "But, first, let me go put my shoes and purse and briefcase away. Then we can sit down and talk."

Before she could bend over to pick up her shoes, he stopped her. "Forget the shoes," he said, taking the purse and briefcase from her and dropping them on the floor beside her shoes. "And the rest of this stuff, too. We'll just leave them right here while we go talk."

"Brett," she protested, "it will only take a minute to put them away. You know how I am about—"

"I know exactly how you are," he interrupted, scooping her up into his arms and carrying her into the living room. "You think the world will come to an end if everything isn't neat and clean at all times. It won't, you know. I promise."

She opened her mouth to protest again, but thought better of it as Brett eased himself down onto the plush white couch with her still in his arms. As he lowered his lips to hers, she decided her shoes and purse and briefcase—and everything else—could wait, for a few minutes anyway.

"All right, I give up," she said, relaxing in his arms. "What is it that I will never believe?"

"Jacqueline St. James," he said, sitting up straight and gazing down at her expectantly.

"What?"

"I saw her today at her house."

Ariane sat up on his lap, her arms still around his neck, and looked him directly in the face.

"What are you talking about?" she asked, feeling her husband's excitement beginning to take hold of her as well. "What do you mean, you saw her? How? Did you ask her about the party? What did she say? What? Tell me!"

The faint lines around Brett's eyes crinkled slightly as he laughed. "Well, now I've got your attention, don't I? Okay, I promise to tell you the entire story—play by play—over dinner. But for right now, I'm just going to tell you this. We talked about the party and she agreed to check her calendar and get back to me. Isn't that great?"

Ariane's heart sank. "Oh, Brett, that's the oldest brush-off in the book. Don't you see? She didn't want to come out and say no, so she was trying to let you down easy."

Brett shook his head. "I don't think so, babe," he said. "I really don't. She just isn't that kind of person. I mean, if she had absolutely no intention of even considering the party, she would have said so, I'm sure of it."

"How?" Ariane argued. "How can you be so sure? You just met her today. How can you tell what kind of person she is in just one short meeting?" She shook her head and gently laid her hand against his cheek. "Oh, sweetheart, I just don't want you to get your hopes up and then—"

She jumped when the phone rang, then reached over to the chrome and glass end table beside them and picked up the receiver.

"Hello?" she said.

"Is Mr. Holiday in, please?" asked a warm female voice. "This is Jacqueline St. James calling."

Ariane caught her breath. "Yes. Yes, he is. Just a moment." She handed the phone to Brett, then watched him closely as the look on his face changed from puzzled to excited to ecstatic.

"You can?" he said, his eyes growing wider and wider. "You will? Oh, that's great! That is really great! What? You're kidding! Are you serious? Jacqueline, that is incredible! Absolutely incredible! I mean, I just don't know what to say, except . . . thank you. I can't tell you

what this is going to mean to those kids! And to me, too.
Yes, of course, I'll get back to you with the details just
as soon as I can. And, Jacqueline? I . . . thanks . . . I mean,
I . . . I don't know what else to say. It's . . . much more
than I'd even hoped for."

"I can't believe it," he said, as he hung up the phone
and turned back toward Ariane, his face glowing with
happiness. "I absolutely cannot believe it! She's actually
going to do it! She's going to sing at Fox's party. And,
babe," he added, planting a quick kiss on her lips, "that's
not all. She's going to invite some of her celebrity
friends. *And*—wait till you hear this—she's offered to let
us have the party at her house!"

"You're kidding," exclaimed Ariane. "At her house?
Honey, that's fantastic, but . . . what's her house like?
You never did tell me. Will there be enough room?"

Brett's grin spread across his face again. "Is there
enough room in the Astrodome?" He laughed. "I tell
you what," he said. "Why don't you go back into the
kitchen and grab your shoes and purse—leave the briefcase here, though—and let's go out to dinner and cele-
brate. And while we're eating, I'll tell you all about her
place—which, believe me, is no tiny vine-covered cot-
tage—and then we'll start making plans for the greatest
party this town has seen in years!"

CHAPTER 16

It was one of those rare, golden mornings when Brett knew he was exactly where he was supposed to be. Not a trace of coastal fog lingered in the summer sky. Not a breath of sea breeze disturbed the crisp, salty air. Only the soothing, reassuring sound of waves crashing to shore, rushing up onto the shiny wet sand to lap at his faithful, worn Nikes, then slowly, reluctantly, retreating into the depths as time and again, Brett managed to outrun them.

He had left home before Ariane had gone off to work, explaining to her that he wanted to get his run in before the heat and sunbathers invaded the beauty that only a deserted, early-morning beach can offer. He hadn't been disappointed. Even as he'd pulled into the parking lot next to the picnic grounds, he'd noticed that the only other people in sight were two fishermen, leaning over the railings with their backs to each other, on opposite sides of the pier. Brett had watched them as he got out of his car. As he did his stretching exercises, he wondered if the two men would ever turn and acknowledge each other's presence. By the time he headed for the sand to begin his run, he'd decided they probably wouldn't. In fact, the only time he'd seen either of them move was to reel in his line, then cast it out into the ocean once again.

That's us, he thought, still breathing easily as he jogged along at a comfortable pace. *That's the way we go through life—most of the time, anyway. Ignoring each other, doing our own thing, pretending like the guy right behind us isn't really there.*

His running shoes splashed rhythmically through the wet, loosely packed sand, leaving fading footprints in his wake as slowly, steadily, he quickened his stride.

Until somebody comes along and forces you to turn around, he reminded himself, grinning slightly as the beads of sweat that had formed on his forehead began to drip down his face. *Who'd have ever thought I'd find that somebody in a back alley hiding behind trash cans?*

Brett adjusted his breathing to fit his pace, pleased at the improvement he saw in his physical condition and stamina since increasing his workouts. His added investment had begun to pay dividends.

Not just physically, either, he thought. *Since I met Fox—since I've been forced to give a little more of myself—everything else seems to be improving, too. I know for a fact that my marriage is better. And not just because of Ariane's support—although I sure am glad I have it! But now that I'm not so wrapped up in "me" all the time, I can look at our marriage—and at my wife—more objectively.*

I can't believe I was actually thinking of her as a threat. He reached up and wiped the moisture from his eyes. *To what, I'm not sure. My manhood, I suppose—which doesn't say a whole lot for my manhood! I guess the bottom line was that I was tying my whole identity into my career. With it ending and Ariane's just starting, it seemed like the only identity I had left was "ex-football player" and "successful attorney's husband." No wonder I felt so insecure!*

In the distance he spotted a lone figure moving toward him—male or female, he couldn't tell yet. But another jogger, he was sure of it. Besides, who else would be at the beach at this hour?

*"It's a wonderful thing to achieve success in your chosen sport. But the real test comes when things get tough and you have to find out who you are away from that sport."**

Now, where had that thought come from? He knew he'd heard it somewhere before, but where? Who . . . ?

And then he remembered. Barry Sanders. The 1988 Heissman Trophy winner. One of the athletes featured in the book that had made such an obvious impression on Fox.

Drafted by the Detroit Lions at the age of twenty, offered more money than most people ever dream of seeing in a lifetime, this young athlete had the maturity and presence of mind to realize that, as wonderful as his sports career might be, it could also end in a bone-shattering second. And then what? Would it all be gone—everything? Or would he have enough sense of who Barry Sanders was *over and above his sport* that he could move on with confidence to the next phase of his life?

That's the key, thought Brett, his eyes fixed on the approaching jogger, who he now realized was a young woman about Ariane's age. *Knowing who you are, and then living within the freedom of that knowledge. Learning and growing and . . .*

He nodded and smiled as the young woman jogged past him, her long brown hair pulled back in a swaying ponytail, her face flushed but determined, her green shorts and tank top clinging to her well-toned, sweat-soaked body. With her eyes riveted straight ahead, she did not acknowledge Brett's smile—nor even his presence.

Now there's a woman who's focused, thought Brett. *But on what, I wonder? Has she thought beyond her immediate*

---

*Rosey Grier and Kathi Mills, *Winning* (Ventura: Regal, 1990).

goal—today's five miles, maybe ten? Does she really know where she's headed? Or is she like I was, focusing so intently on my immediate goal that I lost perspective on everything else?

Brett reached the jetty that marked the halfway point of his run, then turned around and headed back toward the pier. Once again wiping away the sweat that now streamed steadily down his face, he began to wish for a cool ocean breeze. The still, windless morning, which had seemed so peaceful when he'd first started jogging, had steadily grown hotter with every step he ran. He also noticed that a few other people had arrived, too—a handful of surfers in black wetsuits riding the waves into shore, a middle-aged couple walking hand-in-hand along the promenade above the sand.

Brett smiled. *I suppose that will be me and Ariane in a few years,* he thought. *But I wonder what else we'll be doing with our lives then, what we'll be talking about while we walk, what our goals and dreams will be?*

Not that it really matters, he reminded himself. *The important thing is we'll be dreaming those dreams together. And the only limits to those dreams will be the ones we put on them ourselves. After all, if a chance meeting in a back alley can lead to all the things that have happened in our lives lately, then anything is possible. Absolutely anything!*

He was breathing hard now, approaching the pier, when he noticed the two fishermen once again. Only this time they didn't stand with their backs to each other. The smaller—and judging from the slow, labored way he moved, the older of the two— appeared to gather up his pole and bucket and tackle box, ready to call it a day and head on home. It was obvious, however, that he had trouble managing it all as he began to trudge his way back along the length of the pier.

That's when the other fisherman responded. Staring for a brief instant at the figure of the struggling, overburdened man who, for the past several hours had been his silent companion, the younger man grabbed his gear and hurried to catch up. It wasn't long before the two of them shared the load, talking and walking together, as hungry sea gulls followed them, swooping and screeching above their heads.

Brett slowed his run to a walking pace. *Swapping fish stories, no doubt,* thought Brett, his heart pounding in his ears as he took long, slow gulps of sea air. *Well, why not? It's as good a way as any to start a friendship.*

He grinned. *After all, Fox and I started off in an even more unlikely place. Me, out for a jog; Fox, rummaging through trash cans. Makes you wonder. . . .*

His mind flashed back to a phrase he hadn't thought of in years, one his father had used a lot: "divine appointments." "I don't believe in accidents," he would tell Brett. "God's not a God of accidents. He puts us together with certain people in a certain place at a certain time for a reason. Sometimes, for several reasons. You'd do well, son, to find out what those reasons are. More often than not, there's a lot more to it than what you see on the surface. Look deeper—past the obvious. Then, let God work. His reasons are always better than ours anyway."

Brett stopped in his tracks, squinting his eyes against the sun as he studied the two departing fishermen. Was it only the old man who had needed and received help? Only the young man who had given it? Or had the giver been the one with the deeper need? In giving, had he truly been the one to receive?

Fox. The name seemed to echo in his soul. *Our meeting was no accident, was it?* he thought. *And the reasons for that meeting go a lot deeper than my helping you, don't they? In fact, all this time I thought I was the giver, but it was you, wasn't it? It was you all along. . . .*

The fishermen were gone now. Brett looked away from where he'd last seen them and turned his gaze toward the parking lot. His bright red Porsche sat gleaming in the sun. Perched on its hood was a lone sea gull, waiting for him. Brett wiped the sweat from his face one last time and headed for home.

CHAPTER 17

He lay in bed watching her as she moved gracefully around the bedroom getting ready for work. The morning sunlight filtered through the peach-colored drapes, casting a faint highlight to her otherwise dark hair. As she struggled with the zipper on her bright pink dress, she turned and caught him staring at her. Her eyebrows raised in surprise.

"How long have you been awake?" asked Ariane, smiling as she walked over and sat down on the edge of the bed beside him.

"Not long," said Brett, returning her smile. "Just a few minutes."

"So why didn't you say something?" she asked, bending down to kiss him. "I didn't realize you were watching me."

His smile widened. "I know. That's why I didn't say anything. I just wanted to lie here and watch you and think about how beautiful you are."

"Well, now that I know you're awake, you can help me with this zipper," she said, turning her back toward him. "But just remember, Brett Holiday, I have to be at work in exactly thirty minutes."

Brett sighed as he lifted her slightly damp hair out of the way and carefully pulled the zipper up to the back of her neck. "All work and no play," he teased. "How's a guy supposed to have any fun around this place, anyway?"

She laughed as she turned back to face him. "Oh, so now I'm no fun, huh? Just a minute ago you were telling me how beautiful I was."

"Oh, you're still beautiful," he said. "Just no fun, that's all."

Ariane laughed again and jumped up from the bed and headed for the walk-in closet. "Well, I don't know how to tell you this, sweetheart," she called to him, "but you don't have any more time for fun this morning than I do. Didn't you tell me Ron was coming by to pick you up so you guys could go over to the gym and work out?"

Brett winced and glanced at the clock beside the bed. Seven-thirty. She was right. Ron had said he'd be there at eight.

"Besides," said Ariane, appearing at the closet door with a pair of white pumps in her hand, "isn't this the day you planned to go visit Fox?"

"It sure is," said Brett, sitting up and swinging his legs over the side of the bed. "In fact, as soon as Ron and I finish working out, I'd better get right back here and get ready to head over to the hall. I told Fox I'd come by before lunch."

"So what have you two got planned for the day?" asked Ariane, grabbing her purse and briefcase from the closet and coming back over to sit beside Brett. "I mean, is everything set in cement, or are you flexible?"

Brett looked at her curiously. "Why?" he asked. "What do you have in mind?"

"Oh, nothing special," she said. "I just thought that, maybe, well . . . maybe you two could come and pick me up and we could all have lunch together. What do you think? Would Fox mind?"

Brett grinned. "Now how could anyone mind having lunch with you?"

Ariane grinned back at him. "Oh, I don't know," she said, her green eyes sparkling. "Just a few minutes ago you said I wasn't any fun, remember?"

He laughed and pulled her close. "I lied," he said, burying his face in her hair. "You're lots of fun. More fun than anything or anybody!"

She lifted her head and kissed him. "You'd better say that if you know what's good for you," she teased, then pulled away and stood up in front of him.

"I've got to go," she said. "Do you want to come by the office and pick me up, or should I meet you somewhere?"

He looked up at her. "We'll come and get you," he said. "About one-thirty?"

Ariane nodded. "Perfect," she said, heading for the bedroom door, her purse slung over her shoulder and her briefcase in hand. She stopped at the doorway and looked back at him.

"Just one thing," she said. "I get to pick the restaurant."

Brett groaned. "Don't tell me," he said. "Spinach salad again."

"Really, Brett," she said, shaking her head. "Haven't you got any imagination? I was thinking of something a little more . . . *fun*. You know, like chili dogs or something."

Without another word, she turned and walked out the door, as Brett burst into laughter. *If I live to be a hundred, I will never figure that woman out,* he thought, shaking his head. *But it sure will be fun trying.*

*

The offices were bigger than any he'd ever seen before and a whole lot nicer. He was sure the doors were real wood, and when he walked on the rug, he felt as if he were stepping on clouds. The lady at the front desk appeared to have had her face starched, even when she smiled at them.

Rich dudes, he thought. *Ain't nobody but rich dudes workin' in a place like this. Man, if I worked here I'd have so much bread—*

"Ariane's office is down at the end of the hall," said Brett, interrupting his thoughts. Fox looked back at him.

"Straight ahead," said Brett, nodding toward the hallway in front of them.

Even the hallway smelled rich. Sounded that way, too. Quiet. He guessed rich people never got excited or made any noise. He wondered what would happen if he laughed or sneezed. Just thinking about it made him want to. But he didn't.

He peeked into a couple of open doors as he passed by, but all he could see were huge, glass-topped desks and brown leather chairs—empty ones.

Maybe that's why it's so quiet 'round here, he thought. *Nobody really works here 'cept the football dude's wife and the stiff lady out front.*

"Right here," said Brett, reaching in front of Fox to open the last door on the right at the end of the hallway. Fox stepped inside.

Two desks—much smaller than the ones he'd seen when he peeked through the open doors as he came down the hallway—stood side by side along the right wall of the tiny, windowless room. They were piled high with papers and folders and books and telephones, but the chairs that sat in front of them were both empty.

I was right, he thought. *Nobody else does work here.*

To his left stood a row of five metal file cabinets, with a water cooler jammed in between the last cabinet and the far wall. In the very back of the room sat Ariane.

Neat, thought Fox. *Her desk is neat, jus' like her house. Not like those other two desks. How's she 'spect to get any work done with her desk so neat like that?*

Then she smiled at them, that special smile she had that made her green eyes dance—and that almost made Fox forget that women couldn't be trusted. His lips smiled back at her, even though his head was telling them not to.

"Hey, you two," she said, getting up from her chair (which squeaked when she moved and was definitely not leather) and coming around in front of her desk to greet them. "I'm so glad you're here! I've been looking forward to this all morning."

She reached up and kissed Brett, then turned to Fox and hesitated. Fox wasn't sure what she expected from him, so he stuck his hand out. When she took it, he was surprised at how cool it felt. He wasn't sure why, but he suddenly remembered the sheets on the guest bed that very first night at their house.

"How are you, Fox?" asked Ariane.

"I'm okay," he said.

"Okay, nothing," said Brett. "Look at him. The man is starved! And so am I. Let's go eat."

Ariane glanced at her watch. "Actually, you're a few minutes early, you know," she said, looking back up at Brett. "Bev and Mike aren't due back until one-thirty, and I really shouldn't leave until they get here. Do you guys think you can make it until then?"

Brett rolled his eyes. "Do we have a choice?" he asked, turning toward Fox.

"No problem for me," said Fox. He just hoped they couldn't hear his stomach growling.

"Oh yeah, right," said Brett. "I saw your face light up when we were coming up the elevator, and I told you that Ariane wanted to go out for chili dogs. You going to stand there and tell me your mouth's not watering already?"

Fox grinned. "Yeah, well, maybe a little," he admitted. "But I can wait."

"You hear that?" said Ariane, standing with her hands on her hips as she smiled up at her husband. "If Fox can handle the wait, I should think that you can, too."

"That's cuz I got more practice waitin' than him," said Fox, surprising himself with his words, as if they'd slipped out of his mouth before he'd had time to think about them.

He looked at Brett and Ariane. They were staring at him as if they were as surprised by what he'd said as he was.

Ariane's eyes got real soft then. So did her voice. "What did you mean by that, Fox?" she asked.

Fox shrugged. "Don't know," he said. "Nothin' really. Just said it, that's all."

For a moment no one spoke, and Fox was beginning to wish that he and Brett had gone out to lunch alone, or that Brett hadn't come at all and he'd just stayed in his room at the hall, or that he'd never met Brett in that alley, or—

"So," said Ariane, raising her voice slightly, "isn't it wonderful that Jacqueline St. James has offered to let us have your party at her house? Have you told the rest of the kids? Were they excited?"

"Yeah, I guess so," said Fox, shrugging once again, glad Ariane had changed the subject, but refusing to get his hopes up over somebody else's promises—no matter whose they were. He'd believe all this party stuff when he saw it.

"A lot can happen between now and then," he continued. "She might change her mind." *Or you might,* he thought, glancing over at Brett.

"I don't think so," said Brett, shaking his head. "I mean, I only met her that once, although I've spoken to her on the phone a few times since, but she strikes me as a lady who keeps her word."

Fox looked back at Ariane. "Maybe," he said. "Maybe she is, and maybe she ain't. We'll see."

The look in Ariane's eyes made him flinch. Could she see inside of him, know what he was thinking and feeling? Fox decided she would make a good lawyer someday.

"So, when you gonna finish school and get yourself a real office?" he asked, pulling his eyes away from Ariane's and pointing at her desk. "And a real desk," he added, "like in them offices down the hall?"

Ariane smiled. "I hope by this time next year," she said. "I'm really getting anxious. It's been a long, hard pull."

Their eyes met once again. Fox nodded. "Yeah," he said, glancing at Brett, then back at Ariane. "He tol' me you been goin' to school for a lotta years. You must want this lawyer thing real bad."

"I want it real bad," said Ariane.

"I know," said Fox. "You tol' me. That dream you had 'fore you two met."

Ariane nodded.

"My mama had a dream once," said Fox, his mind suddenly reaching back to grasp a wisp of a long-ago memory. His mama, holding him on her lap, rocking him back and forth as she told him stories about when she was a little girl in New York. "Wanted to be a dancer," he said, "on Broadway."

He could almost hear her voice now, crooning softly in his little-boy ears as he fell asleep to dream dreams of his own, dreams of New York and—

He shook his head. "Stupid dream," he said. "Dancers gotta be pretty. Talented, too. Mama wasn't. Even the boyfriend tol' her that. Guess that's why she gave up."

"You should never give up on your dreams, Fox," said Ariane, her eyes softening again. "Especially not because of what somebody else says. You have dreams, don't you?"

Before Fox could answer, the door opened behind him. A short hispanic man with a mustache and a plump blonde woman burst in, talking and laughing and carrying diet soda cans. Fox breathed a sigh of relief.

Must be that Mike and Bev she was talkin' 'bout, he thought. *Maybe now we can get outta here and forget 'bout all this dream stuff and go have some real food.*

*

He had put the last of the dinner dishes into the dishwasher when she came up behind him and slipped her arms around his waist, laying her head against his back.

"All done?" she asked.

Brett nodded. "Yep. Just finished."

"Good," said Ariane. "Because I just finished studying, and since I don't have school tonight, that means we have the whole evening together."

Brett wiped his hands on the dish towel, then turned and took Ariane in his arms. "Best offer I've had all day," he said. "What did you have in mind? Would you like to go out? See a movie or something?"

She pulled back and looked up at him. "No," she said. "I'd like to curl up on the couch with you and just talk."

He raised his eyebrows. "About anything in particular?"

"Oh, you know," she said. "World affairs, life and death, that sort of thing."

Brett grinned. "Well, that's a relief! I was afraid it was going to be something heavy, like what shade of lipstick you should wear to work tomorrow."

Ariane laughed. "Oh no, anything that serious I'll take care of all by myself."

"Good," said Brett, turning her toward the living room. "Then, in that case, let's not waste any time. We don't have entire evenings to ourselves like this very often."

"I know," she said. "And once training camp opens, our time together will really be scarce."

"It won't be long, will it?" he said, settling into the corner of the couch as she snuggled up next to him. "Football season's just around the corner now."

"Mmmm," she agreed, as he slid his arm around her shoulders and she leaned her head against his chest. "And that's not all that's just around the corner. Fox's party will be here before we know it. Everything moving ahead according to schedule? Do you need my help on anything?"

"Now that you mention it," said Brett, "there is one thing . . . if you think you have the time, that is."

"I'll make the time," she said. "What is it?"

"Well, I talked to Jacqueline on the phone this morning, and she asked about decorations and catering, that sort of thing," explained Brett. "I told her I wasn't much of an expert on any of that stuff, but that you were great at it, especially the decorating part. You know, I told her how you decorated our whole house and everything. So, anyway, she suggested you come by sometime and maybe the two of you could sort of plan things together."

Ariane sat up and looked at Brett. "Are you sure?" she said, her eyes opening wide. "You don't think she'd mind?"

Brett smiled. "I know she wouldn't," he said. "It was her idea. Besides, it'll give you two a chance to get to know each other before the party. You'll like her, I promise."

"I'm sure I will," said Ariane. "From what you've told me about her, she sounds like a very warm, caring person. But do you think she'll like me?"

Brett pulled her close and kissed her softly. "How could she help it?" he asked, gazing down into her eyes. "What's not to like?"

"A totally unbiased opinion on your part, no doubt," she teased.

"Totally."

"I just hope you're right," she said.

"Aren't I always?" he asked.

Ariane rolled her eyes and laughed as she leaned back against his chest. "I'll plead the Fifth on that one," she said.

Brett smiled. "Wise woman."

For just a moment, Brett closed his eyes and laid his head back on the couch. The only sound he could hear was his own breathing, as he gently stroked Ariane's hair. Then she sat up again, and Brett opened his eyes.

"What's the matter?" he asked.

"I just remembered something," she said. "While you were out jogging before dinner, Diane called. You know, the secretary down at Jacqueline's manager's office? Anyway, she wanted me to be sure and thank you for the tickets you sent for her and her husband. She sounded really excited. Grateful, too."

Brett smiled. "Not half as grateful as I am for the part she played in getting me in to see Jacqueline. She's been one of the crucial pieces in pulling this whole thing together, you know, along with a lot of other people—you included."

Ariane smiled back at him. "Thanks, sweetheart. But none of it would be happening if it weren't for you. Your time, your effort, your commitment." She reached up and touched his cheek. "I'm really proud of you."

He took her hand and laid it against his lips, kissing it softly. "I can't tell you how much it means to me to hear you say that," he said. "I know you've said it before, but this is different. This is . . ." He paused, then shrugged. "I don't know exactly. But it has something to do with what you were talking about once, about dreams, remember? How we always have new dreams waiting for us in the future. . . ."

His voice trailed off, and Ariane nodded. "And it all started with a young boy who's afraid to even talk about his dreams," she said. "Afraid of dreams and beaten down by reality. Until he met you, what was left for him?"

Brett swallowed the lump in his throat. He just couldn't bring himself to voice the nagging question that, even now, echoed in his mind: Once the party was over, what would be left for Fox then?

He closed his eyes and pulled Ariane close. If there was an answer to that question, he hoped they would find it together.

CHAPTER 18

Brett nodded and waved at the now-familiar faces as he came through the front entrance to the hall. His visits were so regular these days, he rarely had to check in.

School had been out for almost an hour and he was sure he would find Fox down in the recreation room, thumbing through a magazine and listening to music, keeping to himself as usual. The only occupants of the room, however, were two preteen girls who broke into giggles as soon as Brett asked if they knew where Fox might be.

"Playing basketball," squeaked the short, chubby blonde girl, slapping her hand over her mouth as she erupted into giggles once more.

Her companion was a petite Oriental girl with long straight hair and braces on her teeth. "He always plays basketball after school," she said between giggles. "He used to come in here," she added, glancing over at her friend, whose giggles immediately increased in volume and intensity.

Brett had the feeling that Ariane wouldn't have considered their behavior the least bit strange and would easily have figured out by now what it was that had struck them as so funny. But he didn't have a clue.

"All right," he joked, "I give up. What'd I do, forget to comb my hair this morning, or what?"

Apparently this was more than the blonde girl could handle because she collapsed on the couch in a renewed fit of laughter as the other girl tried to explain.

"No, it's not that," she gasped. "It's just, it's just . . ." But she couldn't finish. Instead, she threw herself down on the couch next to her friend, shaking her head and laughing while Brett stood there totally perplexed.

"Hey, Brett," called a voice from behind him. Brett turned, relieved to see Nathaniel's familiar, smiling face.

"What're you doin' here?" asked Nathaniel. "How come you're hangin' out with these here girls?"

Brett shrugged. "Actually, I came down here looking for Fox." He winked and nodded toward the girls, whose laughter had subsided only slightly. "I found these young ladies instead. We've been having a very deep and serious discussion."

Nathaniel rolled his eyes. "Oh, yeah, right," he said. "Those two have never been serious in their lives. All they ever do is laugh—at everything!"

"I noticed," said Brett, grinning. "And I'm glad to know it's everything they laugh at. I was beginning to think it was just me."

Nathaniel shook his head. "No way," he said. "Julie and Cindy, they do this all the time."

"Julie and Cindy," said Brett, turning back toward the girls. "Well, it's nice to know you, Julie and Cindy. I'm Brett Holiday, a friend of Fox's—"

At the mention of Fox's name, the girls experienced yet another attack of giggles. Brett looked at Nathaniel and raised his eyebrows. "What?" he asked. "What is it? What did I say?"

"*Fox,*" said Nathaniel disgustedly. "That's all you have to say, just *Fox.* They hear his name and they lose it, everytime."

"Fox?" asked Brett. "You mean, they think his name is funny?"

Nathaniel sighed impatiently. "Don't ya get it?" he said. "They like him. That's why he don't come down here after school no more. None of us do. 'Cause they're always here, waitin' for Fox. So we go shoot hoops instead." He shook his head again. "Girls."

Brett smiled. He'd been right. Ariane would have figured it out right away. He peeked over at Julie and Cindy. Still giggling, they hid their faces behind their hands. Apparently having a crush on someone was just too embarrassing to do anything but laugh.

Well, well, he thought. *Fox has admirers. I wonder what he thinks of all this. I'll have to be sure to ask him.*

"So, Nathaniel," said Brett. "You want to walk outside with me and find Fox or you want to stay here with the girls?"

Nathaniel's eyes opened wide. "No way," he said. "I ain't stayin' here with them! I was just walkin' by and heard your voice. That's the only reason I even came in."

"Well, if you're sure," said Brett.

"I'm sure," exclaimed Nathaniel. "Positive!"

"Okay," said Brett, turning to wave at the girls. "Good-bye, Julie and Cindy. Nice meeting you both."

His only answer was more muffled giggles.

Brett and Nathaniel made their way out the recreation room door and walked, side by side, down the corridor toward the back entrance that led to the school rooms and to the adjoining gymnasium. Nathaniel talked nonstop all the way, discussing details about the upcoming party—what he was going to wear, what he thought Jacqueline St. James would wear, what kind of food and music there would be, how late the party would last. As Brett listened, glancing down occasionally at Nathaniel's animated, upturned face, he realized how much he cared about these kids. Fox, of course, but the rest of the kids, too. How would he ever have explained it to them if he hadn't been able to get Jacqueline to come? Thankfully, that was no longer a problem. All that was left to do now was tie a few last-minute details together.

He pushed the heavy gymnasium door open and heard the sounds of a bouncing basketball, tennis shoes squeaking on the wooden floor, and grunts and yells from the handful of sweaty boys beneath the basket. Brett was pleased to see that Fox was right in the middle of it all, rather than sitting on the sidelines alone, watching. It was a good sign. Ernie was the first to notice them.

"Hey, man, look who's here," he announced, grabbing the ball out of the air as it sailed past him, then tucking it under his arm. "You come to challenge us to a game?"

Brett grinned as he and Nathaniel walked toward the basket where the boys had gathered. "I might," he said, "if you think you could handle it."

Ernie hooted and laughed, and the rest of the boys joined in. Except Fox. He just looked up at Brett from under hooded eyes and shook his head. "No chance, dude," he said. "We too good for you, man. We been practicin'."

"So I see," said Brett. "But I have to admit, I'm real surprised. I mean, here you are down in the gym playing basketball when you could be up there in the recreation room with . . . " He turned to Nathaniel and raised his eyebrows. "Julie and Cindy, was it?"

Nathaniel laughed. "Yeah," he said. "That's their names, all right. Julie and Cindy."

Brett turned back to Fox. "Didn't I tell you that you wouldn't have to go clear to New York to find good-looking chicks? See? I was right. You got 'em right here, right down the hallway!" He raised an eyebrow at Fox. "Not only that, I understand they're crazy about you."

The boys laughed again, and Brett could see Fox try to suppress a grin. "You are really cold, man," he said. "*Really* cold."

"He ain't cold," said Ernie, slapping Fox on the back. "Just truthful, that's all!"

He's come so far . . . but then, so have I, thought Brett, watching Fox as he gave Ernie a playful shove, then grabbed the ball out from under his arm and fired it at Brett. Brett caught it mid-chest and bounce-passed it across the court to a tall boy he hadn't seen before. The boy lunged for the ball, pivoted, drove for the basket, and made a perfect lay-up. The game was on.

As Brett moved into action, he knew it didn't make any difference how the final score ended up. He already felt like he'd won.

*

"How did it go with Fox today?" asked Ariane, her head nestled on Brett's shoulder as they lay in bed in the dark. His eyes were closed, but he tried desperately to stay awake. He could tell his wife was in the mood to talk, and he knew how annoyed she got with him when he fell asleep in the middle of a conversation. But it was tough. The basketball game had gone on for what seemed like hours. The boys had beaten him soundly, and now, relaxed and content with Ariane next to him, he was fading fast.

"Mmm, fine," he mumbled. "It went fine."

"That's it?" she asked. "Fine? Gee, sweetheart, you're so articulate, did you know that? Maybe after I get my degree you can help me write some of my presentations to the jury."

"Mmm."

She reached up and laid her hand against his face, gently prying open one eye. "Wake up and talk to me, Brett Holiday," she said. "I feel like talking tonight."

Brett sighed. "I know," he said. "I can tell. Okay, I'll try, but only for five minutes. That's the best I can do, just five minutes."

She began to run her fingers through his hair. "If that's all I can get, I'll take it," she said. "So talk fast. What happened with Fox? Did you ask him about Saturday? Is he coming over?"

"Yeah," answered Brett. "I told him I'd pick him up mid-morning or so. Why? Did you have something special in mind to do that day?"

Ariane's hand stopped for a moment. "In a way, yes, but . . . well, it wasn't really just Saturday I was thinking about. It's . . . well, I thought maybe we could get permission for Fox to stay over for the whole weekend. You know, go to church together Sunday morning, maybe brunch afterward, or . . ."

Her voice trailed off as Brett reached up and took her hand, pressing it against his face. "You're really something, lawyer-lady. You are really something." He kissed her fingertips. "I'll check on it first thing tomorrow."

They both jumped when the phone rang, startled by the intrusion on their private time together. "I wonder who that could be," said Brett, dropping Ariane's hand as he raised up on his elbow and reached across her to grab the receiver on the nightstand. He lifted it to his ear and peered at the illuminated alarm clock. Ten-thirty. Not really too late for a phone call, but still . . .

"Hello?" he said.

"Hello, is this Brett Holiday?" asked a vaguely familiar male voice.

"Yes," answered Brett, an uneasy feeling rising within him.

"Brett, this is Bryan Ludlow," explained the voice. "I interviewed you at the end of last season, remember?"

As he listened to the reporter's voice, Brett put it all together. Sure, he remembered now. The sports reporter from the newspaper. The aggressive one. The one he hadn't liked very much, even though he had to admit the guy had done a good job on the article. Yeah, he remembered. But what was he calling about this time? And why at this hour? As if in answer to Brett's unspoken question, Bryan continued his explanation.

"I'm sorry to be calling you at home like this, especially so late and all, but you know how we reporters are when we get a line on a hot story. And from what I heard, you've got a party planned that could turn out to be one of the hottest stories I've run across in a long time."

Brett's tone was guarded. "Just what is it you've heard, Bryan?" he asked.

"Well, that you're planning a party for a bunch of homeless kids," answered Bryan. "And that you've teamed up with Jacqueline St. James to do it, not to mention a lot of other celebrities who are going to be in attendance. Am I on target so far?"

"Basically," answered Brett, undecided as to how much to tell the guy at this point.

"Basically?" repeated Bryan. "That's all you're going to tell me? Come on, Brett, elaborate a little. Fill in the blanks. We want this to be an accurate story, don't we? For the kids' sake, I mean."

Brett couldn't help but smile. Suddenly now he and Bryan had become a team, a "we," working together for a common good. But he had to hand it to the guy, he knew how to make a point.

"You're right," said Brett, deciding to capitalize on their implied teammate status. "And I should have realized that, sooner or later, this party would attract some major publicity. I guess it's up to you and me to make sure that publicity is not only accurate, but favorable, right?"

Brett could almost see Bryan's satisfied smile over the phone. "You can count on me," he said. "So, what's the scoop?"

Brett opened his mouth, then stopped, as the memory of Fox, laughing and interacting with the rest of the kids on the basketball court, flashed through his mind.

So far, thought Brett. *Fox has come so far. And he's finally starting to trust me. All the kids are. No way am I going to let them down now.*

"I tell you what, Bryan," he said. "It's a little late to get into it now. Why don't we meet somewhere tomorrow and we can talk about it then."

"Sure," said Bryan. "How about in the morning? I'll buy you breakfast."

Brett smiled. "If there's one thing I don't turn down, it's a free breakfast," he said. "But I've got some things I need to do first. Maybe I could drop by your office in the afternoon instead. Around four or so?"

"Great," said Bryan. "I'll be expecting you."

"What was that all about?" asked Ariane as he hung up the phone.

"A reporter," he said, lying back down beside her and pulling her into his arms. "He got a lead on the party and wanted the details for a story."

"Sounds like you decided to give them to him," she said, settling her head onto his shoulder once more.

"I don't really have a choice," he said, kissing the top of her head. "I mean, he's the kind of guy who'll get the story one way or the other, so I'd just as soon he got it the right way. Besides, I have a feeling he's only the first of many reporters we're going to hear from, now that word is obviously out about the party."

"So that's why you agreed to meet with him," said Ariane. "But why did you put him off until afternoon? I didn't know you had plans for tomorrow."

"I didn't," he said, "until he called. Now I think I better call Jacqueline first thing in the morning. I want to explain the situation to her and make sure she has no objections to my giving him the story. Then, I need to clear it with the kids. It is their party, after all."

Ariane raised up on her elbow and bent over to kiss Brett. "That's sweet," she said. "I'm proud of you for feeling the need to consult Fox and the other kids first."

"Thanks," he said, faking a yawn. "Well, good night, sweetheart."

"Good night? What do you mean 'good night'?"

"Your five minutes are up," he said, a smile tugging at his lips. "That's all I promised you, remember? I get to go to sleep now."

"Oh, no, you don't," she laughed. "Not a chance!" She leaned down to kiss him again. "Not a chance in the world."

*

She'd been watching them all day—arguing at the park, playing baseball, barbecuing hamburgers out on the patio, sprawled out in the den watching Brett's old film clips. But it wasn't the stiff, awkward shadow-box arguing they had danced around each other with in the beginning. It was more of a good-natured sparring match, a comfortable interchange of ideas between close friends—or family. The sort of family interaction Ariane had always dreamed of having with her father, the sort of family interaction that should take place naturally between a father and child.

A father and child. Family interaction. The realization of her thoughts shook her a bit. Not that the idea hadn't nagged at her on more than one occasion lately, but she'd always been able to shove it aside before. After all, some things were so far-fetched they weren't even worth considering. Today, though, Ariane had to admit that she was having a much more difficult time keeping her mind from drifting toward thoughts of the future. And that Fox always seemed to be a major part of those thoughts was more than slightly unsettling.

Leaving Brett and Fox in the den, absorbed in football films, she sighed as she walked down the hallway. It really had been a wonderful day; she just hoped she hadn't made a big mistake suggesting to Brett that they have Fox stay over for church and brunch the next morning. Not that Brett had given her any indication that he, too, had begun to think of Fox as part of their future. And surely it was the farthest possible thing from Fox's mind! But was it fair to any of them to spend so much time together, to encourage such a close relationship when there was obviously no chance that anything permanent would ever come of it?

She walked into the kitchen and opened the freezer. It had been only a couple of hours since they'd finished their barbecue, but she had a strong hunch that the two armchair quarterbacks were already getting hungry again.

Pulling out a quart of fudge ripple ice cream, she smiled. The fact that she stocked up on junk food whenever Fox came was just one more reason Brett loved having him over. One reason, but definitely not the main one.

I wonder what the main reason really is, she mused, pulling down a couple of bowls from the cupboard. *And I wonder if Brett's figured it out yet? Maybe he has and he just doesn't want to admit it—to me or to himself. Everytime he talks about Fox, though, I see it in his eyes. Like the other day when he came home from the hall after he'd told the kids about the reporter wanting a story about the party. He was so relieved to find out how much they trusted his judgment, what complete confidence they had in him to say and do the right thing. But nothing compared to the look on his face when he told me about Fox's response.*

"He just stood there grinning at me," Brett had told her. "And then he said, 'What you askin' me for? You the football dude. You call the plays, man.'"

Ariane almost laughed out loud as she remembered how silly Brett had sounded trying to talk like Fox. But she had to admit, both she and Brett seemed to be learning a lot from this brash young man who had so recently disrupted their once orderly lives.

Especially me, she admitted. *Me, the original perfectionist. Since Fox has come into our lives, I find myself indulging in junk food, sitting in front of the TV with them—the next thing you know I'll be turning into a total slob and leaving things lying around on the floor!* She smiled to herself. *Whatever would James think?*

James. Why did thoughts of Fox seem to turn her mind toward her father? You couldn't find two more completely different people, she reminded herself. James was neat, cultured, precise. Fox was real and honest and . . .

She caught herself, shocked to realize that she thought of Fox as honest. The one who had stolen her great-grandmother's silver. She closed her eyes and sighed. The one who had stolen her heart.

It was true. Why not admit it? Fox had stolen her heart—and she didn't mind one bit. Since Fox had come along, she felt softer, warmer, more real than she had ever allowed herself to feel before. It was as if his reality had torn down the facade she had built up to impress her father. Suddenly, she realized it didn't matter anymore whether or not she impressed James. She would always love him because he was her father, but she no longer needed to prove herself to him. She was free—and she had a boy Brett had found in an alley to thank for it. No wonder she had begun to think of him as family!

Family. Was it possible that Fox had begun to think of them as his family? Was it possible for him to move past the memory of a mother who had deserted him and a father he had never known? She shivered. Every time she thought about Fox's father, all the warm feelings that she had begun to associate with Fox died within her. In their place, a hard, cold knot seemed to form way down deep in the pit of her stomach, sucking the air out of her lungs, deflating her like a balloon. As she dished the ice cream into the bowls, she felt as if someone had robbed her of her joy—again. That someone, she decided, was a father—no longer her own father, the cool, proper, polite James who had held her at arm's length all her life—but the tired, beaten down alcoholic father who had died in a jail cell, all alone.

That's not fair, she told herself. *It wasn't his fault. Anymore than it's Fox's mother's fault, or even the boyfriend's, or . . .*

She shook her head. Trying to find someone to blame for Fox's situation was pointless. It was too late to change the past. All they could hope for was to help him find a brighter future.

"Hey, we wondered where you'd disappeared to," said Brett, walking up behind her and placing his hands on her waist as he peeked over her shoulder at the two bowls of ice cream on the counter in front of her.

He kissed the top of her head. "I should have known," he said. "You're always one step ahead of us, aren't you? What do you have, built-in radar or something that tells you when we're hungry?"

She turned and smiled up at him. "I figure it's a pretty safe bet that you're hungry ninety-nine percent of the time, and the other one percent, you'll eat whatever's put in front of you anyway, right?"

Brett laughed. "You got me on that one," he admitted. "Unless it's some of your bean sprouts or some other disgustingly healthy thing."

"Like spinach salad or yogurt?" asked a voice behind them.

Brett turned and Ariane looked past him to where Fox stood beside the table, watching them and grinning. His dark eyes danced with mischief, and Ariane couldn't help remembering the first time she had seen him standing in her kitchen doorway, dirty, defiant, and dressed in clothes that didn't fit him and should have been burned long ago. Now, clad in a purple and gold Lakers shirt and a new pair of blue jeans, it was hard for her to believe that their smiling, pleasant guest was the same boy who had so abruptly invaded their existence only a few months earlier. What was even harder to believe was how quickly his smile could melt the cold knot in the pit of her stomach, restoring her warm feelings once again.

"Don't worry," she said, laughing as she turned and grabbed the two bowls of ice cream from the counter. "I'm fresh out of spinach salad." She held the ice cream out to Brett and Fox. "Will this do instead?"

Brett took his bowl, then looked over at Fox and winked. "Not bad for a lawyer-lady," he said.

Fox walked over and eyed the ice cream before taking the bowl from Ariane's outstretched hand. "I don't know, dude," he said, shrugging his thin shoulders as he glanced over at Brett. "It ain't exactly my favorite kind." When he looked back at Ariane, she could tell he was swallowing a grin. "But I s'pose it'll do."

Ariane feigned a scowl. "I s'pose it'll have to," she said. "I didn't offer you no choice, *dude.*"

Fox's smile escaped then, and he shook his head back and forth. "You gonna make some kinda lawyer someday," he said. "Some kinda lawyer."

CHAPTER 19

The sun had just begun to set as they turned into the parking lot in front of the hall. It had been a good weekend, and Brett hated to see it end. Although Fox hadn't said anything, Brett was sure he felt the same way.

"Well, here we are," Brett announced, wondering even as he said it why he seemed to make such inane comments when the situation obviously called for so much more.

I suppose that's the reason, he told himself, pulling into an empty space. *To avoid talking about the real issues. At least, that's what Ariane would say. She claims that's why men have such a hard time communicating, because we aren't in touch with our feelings. She's probably right, but what's the point of getting in touch with your feelings if you can't do anything about them?*

The car was still running as Fox grabbed his overnight bag from the floor in front of him. "Thanks," he said, reaching for the door handle. "It was okay, man. Really."

Brett looked at the boy. He was doing it, too—hiding his feelings behind empty words, slipping his protective mask over his face to keep his dark eyes from betraying his emotions. Brett realized it was up to him to break the barrier.

"Wait," he said, shutting off the engine. "What's your rush? You got something going on I don't know about? A hot date with one of those good-looking chicks of yours maybe?"

Fox grinned and shook his head. "You ain't never gonna let me forget that one, huh?"

Brett returned his grin. "Probably not," he admitted. "But only because I don't really think you mind it too much. Am I right . . . , or am I right?"

Fox still grinned as he shrugged his thin shoulders. Brett could tell he wasn't about to commit himself one way or the other.

"So," he said, changing the subject. "I'm glad you thought the weekend was okay. I thought so, too—except maybe it went by a little too fast."

He watched Fox closely and caught the faint twitch of his jawline before he answered. "Yeah, well . . . maybe," he said, not quite looking at Brett.

"I feel like all we did was eat," joked Brett, patting his still-full stomach. "From the time I picked you up yesterday morning until we finished all that pizza a little while ago . . . I'm going to have to work out like crazy all week just to make up for it."

Fox laughed. "Not me, man," he said. "I ain't worried. I eat all the time and I ain't never gonna get fat."

"Don't count on it," said Brett. "Ariane keeps telling me that one of these days I'm going to wake up and weigh five hundred pounds if I don't start eating right. I wouldn't pay any attention to her, except she usually seems to be right about everything else she says."

"Yeah," said Fox, nodding his head. "I know what you mean, dude. She's a real smart lady. But that wouldn't make no difference to me if I was you. I'd rather weigh five hundred pounds any day than live on stuff like spinach salad. Pitiful, man. Pitiful."

Brett laughed. Their warm camaraderie of the weekend had been temporarily restored. But he knew it wasn't going to make their parting any easier.

What's wrong with me? he asked himself. *You'd think we were never going to see each other again. Why is it so much harder to say good-bye this time?*

"Hey, dude, I better get goin'," said Fox. "The guys are prob'ly waitin' for me."

Brett nodded. "I suppose," he said. "And Ariane's probably waiting for me, too. I told her I wouldn't be long."

Fox opened the door. "Yeah, well . . . later, man," he said, climbing out of the car.

"Hey, don't you want me to walk you in?" asked Brett.

"Nah," said Fox. "You better get home, 'fore you get in trouble with your wife."

Brett smiled. "I'll call you," he said, but Fox had already slammed the car door shut. As Brett watched him in the rearview mirror, Fox hurried toward the hall as if there were no place else on earth he'd rather be.

Brett knew better. As he turned the key and his Porsche roared to life, he wondered if going home would ever hold quite the same meaning for him again.

*

The soft strains of violins—"elevator music," as Fox called it—teased Brett's ears as he stepped through the back door from the garage into the kitchen. He knew he would find Ariane waiting for him in the living room, probably sitting on the couch with her eyes closed, relaxing to the sounds of her favorite classical music station.

He was right.

"Hi," she said, as he walked into the living room. Her eyes were still closed. "I heard you come in. Care to join me?"

Although he didn't particularly care for classical music, there was nothing he would rather do at that moment than sit down next to his wife and listen to anything she wanted to hear. He crossed the room and sat down, draping his arm across the back of the couch. For a moment, neither of them spoke. Then she leaned her head against his chest.

"I'm glad you're home," she said. "I missed you."

He kissed the top of her head. "That's always good to know," he said. "Although I really wasn't gone that long."

"Long enough," she answered. "The house seemed so lonely after you and Fox left."

"I know what you mean," he said, closing his eyes and leaning his head back. "I felt the same way after I dropped him off."

"We're getting awfully attached to him, aren't we?" asked Ariane. "Too attached, maybe?"

Brett sighed. "I don't know, sweetheart," he said. "I really don't know."

They were silent again, as he stroked her hair and let the soothing music wash over him in gentle waves. Maybe this elevator music wasn't so bad after all, he decided. Maybe it was just exactly what they both needed right now.

"I'll bet Fox is listening to music, too," said Ariane. "But I'll bet it's not the same kind we're listening to."

Brett chuckled. "Now that's a safe bet, if I ever heard one! Can you imagine those kids trying to rap to the beat of a bunch of violins?"

Ariane giggled. "What beat?" she asked, then shook her head slightly. "No, it would never work. Never."

"Never say never," said Brett, "because the next thing you know, you turn on the TV, and there's some new group rappin' to elevator music."

Ariane laughed again. "I suppose," she said. "But I sure can't imagine it."

"Stranger things have happened," said Brett.

"Like what?"

"Well . . ." Brett hesitated. "Like you falling in love with Fox."

Ariane sat up abruptly and turned toward him, her green eyes open wide. "Love! Who said I was in love with Fox? I never said—"

Brett grinned. "You didn't have to."

The look of surprise faded from her face as a slight blush rose to her cheeks. She dropped her eyes. "You're right," she said. "I guess I've only recently admitted it to myself." She looked back up at him. "But you're right. I do love him, Brett, in spite of . . ."

"In spite of what?"

She shrugged. "I'm not sure," she said. "Everything, I guess. The way he came into our lives, the fact that he stole my family's silver—"

"And brought it back again," interrupted Brett.

Ariane nodded and smiled. "And brought it back again. But most of all, I think it's his background that concerns me. An alcoholic father, a mother who abandoned him. . . ."

Her voice trailed off as Brett reached out and gently laid his hand on her arm. "That's hardly something to hold against him," he said softly. "I mean, he certainly didn't have anything to do with the circumstances of his life."

"I know," Ariane whispered. "And of course I don't hold it against him. But . . . but I can't help wondering how it will affect his future. Can he ever really break free of all that and start over again?"

Brett gazed tenderly into her eyes. "I believe he can," he said. "I have to believe that. Because if it's not true, we'd have to write off everybody who was ever born into those kinds of circumstances. And you and I have both seen too many lives that have been completely changed for the better to buy into that kind of defeatist philosophy."

"That's for sure," Ariane admitted. "In fact, I'd say our own lives are proof of that. Just this weekend, watching you two together, I realized it isn't just you and Fox that have changed through all this; I have too. It's as if . . . as if, in learning to love Fox, I'm learning to love myself more. As if . . . I don't have to work so hard to be perfect." She sighed. "And if I can get rid of some of the excess baggage I've been carrying around all my life, I guess there's no reason to think Fox can't do the same, is there?"

Brett swallowed. His heart felt so full, he wasn't sure if he could speak. Finally, he nodded. "You're right," he said, his voice hoarse. "So I guess the only thing we have left to do now is convince Fox."

Ariane's eyes misted over as she smiled up at him. "Exactly," she said. "And if anybody can do it, you can."

＊

It had been a busy week. With training camp opening in just a few days, Brett had worked out faithfully every morning and evening. The rest of his time had been spent planning and checking and working out last minute details for the party. But no matter how busy he stayed, he could not ignore the argument going on inside of him. By Thursday night, he'd made his decision. With Ariane's wholehearted support, he had called the hall and arranged to pick up Fox for the weekend once again.

He hadn't been sorry. In fact, things had gone so well, they'd stretched the weekend out as long as possible. But now, as Sunday drew to a close and they drove through the gathering darkness toward the hall, the reluctance to say good-bye began to grow once again. Brett, however, was determined to keep things light.

"So," he said, "you got anything big going on this week? Basketball games, history tests?" He glanced over at him and raised an eyebrow. "A date with Julie or Cindy, maybe?"

Fox refused to take the bait. "Nah," he said, looking straight ahead. "Nothin', really. Just school and stuff." He turned and looked at Brett. "Gonna be busy for you, huh? With the party and football and all."

Brett shrugged as he turned his attention back to the road in front of him. "Actually, I haven't got too much left to do for the party. Jacqueline and Ariane made all the arrangements for the food and decorations, that kind of thing. And I've still got a little over a week before I report to training camp. I'll hit the workouts pretty hard, though." He smiled. "Gotta whip myself into shape so I won't lose my job to some young, wet-behind-the-ears kid."

He heard Fox chuckle. "Must be sad to get old, man. Real sad."

"Hey," said Brett. "Who said anything about getting old? I'm not old, just seasoned. There's a difference, you know."

"If you say so," said Fox. "Jus' hope you able to hold up for 'nother year, man. Kinda like to turn on the TV sometime and see you throw one of them Hail-Mary passes you so famous for."

Brett grinned. "You would, huh? Well then, I guess I'll just have to dedicate the first one to you. But no way are you going to be watching it on TV. Ariane told me just the other day how much she was looking forward to taking you to the home games with her."

"No kiddin'?" exclaimed Fox. "She really said that?"

"Sure did," said Brett.

"All right!" said Fox. "Man, that'd be great. I ain't never been to no football game before—no real one, I mean."

As Brett signaled for a right-hand turn, he suddenly realized where they were, and an idea flashed through his mind. Flipping the turn signal to the opposite direction, he quickly checked his side mirror, then pulled into the far left lane.

"Hey, dude, what you doin'?" asked Fox. "This ain't the way we usually go."

"I know," said Brett. "We're taking a detour."

"A detour?" asked Fox. "Why?"

"You'll see," answered Brett. "It'll just take a few minutes."

As he drove, the excitement began to mount in Brett and he wasn't quite sure why. All he knew was that he had to show it to Fox. Now. Tonight. He didn't want him to see it for the first time in broad daylight, packed full of screaming, boisterous fans.

He knew as soon as he pulled up and parked in front of it that he'd made the right decision. This was the time to show it to him. The perfect time.

"The stadium," Fox said, his voice almost a whisper as he peered out the front window. "You brought me to the stadium." He turned to Brett. "Why?"

"To show it to you," Brett answered. "What else? You want to see it or not?"

Fox had the door open and was standing outside next to the car before Brett could say another word.

"Let's go, dude," said Fox.

They made their way into the darkened stadium through one of the few gates open at that hour, down an unlit tunnel and out onto the open field. Brett could almost hear the roar of the crowds as they trotted out to the middle of the grass. Their only lights were the partially smog-obscured stars twinkling faintly in the summer sky overhead.

"So this is it," said Fox, dropping down onto the grass beside Brett.

"This is it," Brett agreed. "This is where I work."

Fox laughed. "Not bad," he said. "Ain't many of us get to work and play at the same time—and get paid all that bread besides."

Brett laughed, too. "You think everybody that works here is a millionaire or something?"

"Maybe not," said Fox. "But even the dudes sellin' peanuts make more'n I do."

"For now," said Brett. "But that won't always be true."

"No?" asked Fox. "Why? What you think I'm gonna be someday, a astronaut? Or maybe president?"

"Maybe," said Brett. "Why not?"

Fox didn't answer. Brett reached out and picked a stem of grass. In the faint starlight he could barely make out the outline of Fox's profile, staring up into the sky. What was he thinking of? What was going on in his mind?

"How many black presidents you know 'bout?" asked Fox. "And how many presidents you s'pose had drunks for daddies?" He turned toward Brett. "How many, man?"

Brett couldn't quite make out the boy's features in the dark, but he could picture them in his mind. He'd come to know that face so well. And yet, what could he do? What could he possibly say that would ease the pain that he knew burned behind the smoldering defiance in those dark eyes?

"Our country hasn't had any black presidents," admitted Brett. "At least, not yet. But that will change." He hesitated, then went on. "And as far as presidents with alcoholic fathers, I don't know. I really couldn't tell you because—"

"'Cause there ain't none," said Fox. "There just flat ain't none. Not one."

"We don't know that," argued Brett. "Just because we've never heard about a president whose father was an alcoholic doesn't mean there never was one."

Fox turned away and looked back up into the sky. Brett began to wonder if coming to the stadium had been such a good idea after all. He was about to suggest they head back when Fox interrupted his thoughts.

"You 'member that time you took us to the Laker game?" he asked, still staring straight ahead. "Me and the rest of the guys?"

"Sure, I remember," said Brett. "Why?"

"You said somethin' that day," said Fox. "Somethin' 'bout how it don't matter where you been, what you done . . . somethin' like that."

As he sat there in the warm, windless night air, Brett felt a chill pass over him. He took a deep breath. "I said it doesn't matter where you've been or what you've done. The only thing that matters is . . ." He paused and cleared his throat. "The only thing that matters is where you go from here."

Even as he spoke, the words seemed to echo through his mind, as if someone else had spoken them, as if he were detached from his body, watching two strangers sitting in the middle of an empty football stadium, talking about things that were almost too sacred to discuss. The echoes of the crowds had long since faded from his ears, as a holy hush drifted down out of the darkness and settled over them like a mantle.

Suddenly, Fox sat up straight and pointed into the sky. "Look!" he cried. "Up there in the sky! Do you see it?"

Brett jerked his head up and followed Fox's pointing finger just in time to see what appeared to be the last of a shooting star streak out of sight. Because of the smog, Brett couldn't be sure, but he felt his heart leap inside him as he remembered the many nights he and his father had watched together for shooting stars over the Rockies, making wishes that he never doubted would come true.

"A shooting star," said Brett. "At least, I think it was. They aren't nearly as clear here as when I was a boy growing up in Colorado, but . . ." His voice trailed off. "I guess it's kind of like presidents with alcoholic fathers. Just because we don't always see them or know about them, it doesn't mean they don't exist, does it?"

Fox didn't respond, but Brett knew he was listening. "I haven't seen a shooting star in a while," Brett went on, "not since . . ." His voice trailed off again as he remembered the night he had come home from the basketball game to find Fox asleep on his front porch, clutching the pillowcase full of Ariane's silver. He thought he'd seen a shooting star that night, too, but he'd been afraid to make a wish. Did he dare make one now?

Yes, he decided. *Yes! Now's the time.*

"Let's make a wish," said Brett, turning toward Fox. "That's what you're supposed to do when you see a shooting star, you know."

"Sure I know," said Fox. "But we ain't even sure we saw one. 'Sides, you s'posed to make a wish when you first see the star, not after it's gone."

"Trust me," said Brett. "I've got a real good feeling about that star."

For a moment, Fox didn't move. Then, slowly, he lifted his face back toward the heavens. "Me, too," was all he said.

Brett closed his eyes and wished harder than he'd ever wished in all his life.

CHAPTER 20

Ariane was curled up in the armchair in the corner of their bedroom, reading, when Brett walked in. Her long dark hair fell over her face as she sat, absorbed in a huge black textbook that looked to Brett as if it weighed almost as much as she did.

"Still studying, huh?" he said, walking across the room to kiss her as she looked up, startled.

"I didn't hear you come in," she said, raising her head for his kiss. "Guess I was too caught up in what I was reading."

"So I noticed," said Brett, grinning as he sat down on the edge of the bed and untied his tennis shoes. "Must be fascinating."

"It is," she agreed. "Want me to read it to you?"

Brett quickly waved away her suggestion. "No thanks," he said. "You've read to me out of your 'fascinating' law books before. I get lost on the first sentence every time, remember?"

Ariane smiled back at him. "I remember," she said, marking the place in her book as she closed it. "So, what happened? You come home by way of Cincinnati or something?"

Brett frowned as he set his shoes on the floor and looked up at her. "Cincinnati? What do you mean?"

"I mean," explained Ariane, "you left to take Fox back almost three hours ago. Unless they've moved the hall in the last couple of days, you must have stopped somewhere else along the way."

"Very observant," he said, smiling. "Can't get much past you, can I?"

"Not a thing," she said. "They don't call me 'lawyer-lady' for nothing, you know."

Brett eyed his wife lovingly. "No, they sure don't," he said. "In fact, I'd say you earned that name the hard way—along with a lot of love and respect."

Ariane's eyes went soft. "Do you think so?" she asked. "Really?"

"Really," he answered, still watching his wife closely, as he wondered how he ever could tell her about the decision he'd come to tonight.

"We stopped at the stadium," he said, "on the way to the hall. We . . . saw a shooting star."

Ariane raised her eyebrows. "Oh? Did you make a wish?"

Brett nodded and took a deep breath. "We . . . I . . . wished that Fox could . . . live with us . . . and be a part of our family." He swallowed. "Our son."

Neither of them moved. The room was so quiet Brett was sure he could hear his heart pounding in his ears. He wondered if Ariane could hear it, too. He wondered how long it would take her to tell him he'd lost his mind. And he wondered if she would be right.

"I love you," she said.

He frowned again. *That's it?* he thought. *She loves me? What's that supposed to mean? She loves me even though I'm crazy, even though . . . ?*

And then he saw the tears forming in her eyes. The next moment he was on his knees in front of her, reaching up to hold her face between his hands as the tears spilled over onto her cheeks.

"I love Fox, too, remember?" she whispered, gazing down at him.

"Then you don't think I'm crazy?" asked Brett.

"Of course you're crazy," she said, smiling between her tears. "So am I. But it doesn't matter, does it?"

Brett shook his head. "No," he said. "No, it doesn't matter at all, even though . . . well, for a long time, just like you, I thought it did. All the problems, I mean. His dad being an alcoholic and dying in prison, his mom deserting him, the string of foster homes . . . not to mention the fact that we just happen to be white and he's black."

Ariane grinned and her green eyes danced. "You noticed," she teased. "Do you think anyone else will?"

Brett shrugged and returned her smile. "Like you said, it doesn't matter, does it? Unless . . . unless, of course, it matters to Fox."

"Do you think it will?" asked Ariane.

"I suppose there's only one way to find out, isn't there?" said Brett.

Ariane nodded. "You're going to have to talk to him," she said. "We both are. About a lot of things." Then she reached up and took his hands in hers, lowering them from her face to her lap, where she held them tightly. The look in her eyes changed from soft to intense. "Brett, doesn't it sometimes seem as if . . . well, as if Fox is already a part of our family? As if he's always been here with us?" She shook her head slightly. "I guess what I'm trying to say is that I think maybe all this was planned a long, long time ago, don't you? As though God was bringing the three of us to this point all along, even before you first set foot in that back alley."

Divine appointments. The memory of his father's words flashed through Brett's mind. "Yes," he said. "I'm sure of it."

She smiled and leaned down to kiss him. "Then it will all work out," she said, putting her arms around him and pulling his head against her chest. "Everything will work out just the way it was meant to."

*

He'd seen a lot of big houses in his life, but he'd never expected to be inside any of them. For sure he'd never expected the owner of one of those houses to be throwing him a birthday party! And if anyone had ever told him that it would be Jacqueline St. James giving that party—no way! Even standing right there in the middle of it all, it was still almost impossible for him to believe.

For me, he thought, *all of this is for me! Bands, movie stars, singers, athletes—and all them presents piled up on that table by the food, they're for me too. Man!* He shook his head as he stood in the open French doorway, looking out onto the patio at the three tables full of salads and chips and dip and cookies and pies and cakes and punch. The smell of barbecued hamburgers, steaks, chicken, ribs, and even hot dogs filled the late afternoon air, as kids continued to arrive by the busload to share in the excitement and festivities of this incredible day.

Fox jumped only slightly when he felt the gentle touch on his shoulder. Turning, he looked into the huge, coal-black eyes of Jacqueline St. James. Even though he'd already been at the party for over an hour and had seen Jacqueline several times, he still couldn't believe she actually stood there next to him with her hand on his shoulder, smiling at him so beautifully he thought his legs would give out underneath him.

"What's our guest of honor doing standing here?" she asked, her voice as sweet as he'd ever heard it on any of her songs. "You should be outside with everybody else, attacking those food tables. That's what they're there for, you know."

He knew he should say something, but when he opened his mouth, nothing came out. He nodded his head instead.

Jacqueline removed her hand from his shoulder and took him by the arm. "Come on," she said, stepping out onto the patio. "No one's ever going to accuse me of letting anyone starve to death in my house—especially not on his birthday! Besides, I'm hungry, too. We can eat together."

Fox swallowed and walked with her to one of the tables, conscious of her arm linked through his. As he noticed some of the other kids watching them together, he knew he'd never felt quite so proud in all his life—or quite so nervous, either.

Sure hope I don't drop food on myself, he thought, scooping out some potato salad onto his plate. *Or my voice don't start crackin' when I talk. Gotta say somethin' sooner or later. Can't jus' sit here an' nod my head like some fool. Man, all the stuff I was gonna ask her 'bout, now that I see her I can't 'member none of it!*

"Are you having a good time?" she asked, as they carried their full plates over to an empty table.

Fox waited until Jacqueline had sat down, then wondered if he should have pulled out her chair for her. *Too late now,* he told himself, sitting down next to her. "Yeah," he answered, watching her closely. "It's great."

Realizing that he was staring, Fox tore his eyes away from her and looked out past the patio to the crowd of kids splashing and jumping into the Olympic-sized pool. "Big, too," he added.

"What's big?" asked Jacqueline, smiling again as he turned back toward her. "The party or the house?"

"Both," said Fox. "Everythin'. The house, the party, the yard, the pool. Jus' everythin'."

"I'm glad you like it," she said. "And I'm glad we finally got to meet. I've heard so much about you from Brett and Ariane."

Fox took a sip of punch. "Yeah?" he asked. "They been talkin' 'bout me, huh?"

"Sure," said Jacqueline, dabbing at her mouth with a napkin. "Why not? They think quite a lot of you, you know."

Fox felt a strange mixture of excitement and fear begin to stir in him, but refused to acknowledge it. "Yeah, well," he said, shrugging to show his indifference, "they okay, I s'pose. For rich dudes, that is."

Jacqueline raised her eyebrows, and Fox realized he had said the wrong thing. He knew he should never have started talking to her, should have kept his mouth shut. How come he was always saying the wrong thing to people? He didn't mean to, but it always seemed to come out that way.

"I, uh . . . I wasn't talkin' 'bout you," he said, feeling his face grow hot. "I was talkin' 'bout, uh . . . ."

Jacqueline smiled reassuringly and laid her hand on his. "It's all right, Fox," she said, her eyes soft as they locked into his. "I understand, really. Sometimes it's hard to understand why some people have so much, while others . . . ."

Her voice trailed off and he nodded. Maybe she did understand. Maybe the football dude and his lawyer wife understood, too. Maybe someday he'd understand—why he'd been born black and poor, why Brett and Ariane were rich and white, why Jacqueline had made it out and his daddy never did, why his mama had chosen the boyfriend over him—

"Hey, what's this?" asked a familiar voice. "A private party or something? I thought everybody was invited!"

Fox looked up at Brett, standing over them with his blue eyes shining and a smile spread across his face. Fox couldn't help but smile back. Whatever he'd thought all his life about rich people—white ones, especially—just didn't hold up when it came to Brett. He was for real. He had to be, or this party would never have happened.

The realization only intensified the feelings of fear and excitement Fox had experienced all day.

Jacqueline's golden laughter brought him back from his thoughts. "Of course everyone's invited," she was saying, pointing to a chair on the other side of the table. "In fact, we saved that chair just for you." She turned to Fox. "Didn't we?"

Fox nodded slowly. "That's right, dude. Jus' for you."

Brett pulled out the chair and flopped down. "So, how's it going so far?" he asked, looking from Fox to Jacqueline and back.

Fox shrugged again, wondering why he just couldn't come out and tell Brett it was the greatest day of his life. "It's okay," he said, swallowing a bite of his hot dog. "Food's all right."

Brett laughed. "Yeah, well, I knew you'd like that part. But what about everything else? I haven't seen you out there dancing or swimming yet. Some of the guys have a real good game of basketball going, too. Aren't you going to join them?"

Fox opened his mouth, but before he could say anything, Jacqueline answered for him.

"Actually," she said, "Fox has been so sweet and attentive to me. He's been sitting here keeping me company, even though I'm sure he'd rather be off doing something else with his friends."

"I doubt that," said Brett, winking at Fox. "I have a feeling he's doing exactly what he wants to be doing, isn't that right, Fox?"

Fox grinned. He might as well admit it. "Yeah," he said. "I s'pose."

"Well, that makes two of us," said Jacqueline. "I've really been looking forward to this party and hoping that we'd get to spend some time together." When she smiled at him again, Fox thought his heart would melt. "Besides," Jacqueline went on, "the party's just begun. We've got plenty of time to swim and dance and—" She paused. "You are saving your first dance for me, aren't you?"

Fox's eyes opened wide as he took another drink of punch. "You mean it?" he said. "You really wanna dance with me?"

"Why not?" asked Jacqueline. "You're the best looking guy at the party."

"Oh, I don't know about that," joked Brett.

"Don't know about what?" asked another voice beside them.

Fox looked up. He didn't recognize the short, balding man in the brown suit standing next to their table. Fox wondered why he was wearing a suit when everyone else was dressed in jeans or shorts. Even Jacqueline and Ariane had come in sundresses and sandals. And why was the guy carrying a notepad in his hands and a camera over his shoulder?

"Bryan," said Brett. "I had a feeling you might show up."

"Wouldn't miss it for anything," he said. He looked over at the last empty chair around their table. "Mind if I join you for a few minutes?"

"Of course not," said Brett. "Help yourself." He looked over at Jacqueline. "Jacqueline, this is Bryan Ludlow, the reporter I told you about. Have you two met?"

"Not in person," said Jacqueline, reaching out to shake Bryan's hand. "But I believe we spoke on the phone."

Bryan nodded. "Yes, we did," he said. "I'm the one who called you about doing a story on the party."

"Yes, of course," said Jacqueline. "I'm glad you could come."

"Well, like I said, I wouldn't have missed it." He sat down between Brett and Jacqueline, then looked across the table at Fox. "And you must be . . ."

"This is Fox," said Brett. "Fox Richards, our guest of honor."

Bryan smiled and reached across the table to shake Fox's hand. "Well, Mr. Richards, it's nice to finally get a chance to meet you. This is quite a birthday party you're having here. You must feel very special."

The man was right. Fox did feel special. But he wasn't too sure he wanted to talk about how he felt to any reporter, even though Brett had already explained to him and the rest of the kids how important it was to get the right kind of publicity for the party. He wanted Jacqueline and Brett to be proud of him, but he was sure that if he talked to this guy, he'd say the wrong thing. So he just nodded and took another bite of his hot dog. He wished they'd all stop looking at him.

"Well," said Bryan, turning from Fox to Jacqueline. "This is quite a place you have here."

"Thank you," she said.

"And quite a turnout," he added, glancing around in all directions. "I'd say, everybody who's anybody is here today. Over half the Ram team, most of the Lakers, singers, entertainers—going to make quite a story, I can tell you that!"

Brett smiled at him. "A favorable one for the kids, right, Bryan?" he asked.

Bryan raised his eyebrows as he looked over at Brett. "What else?" he asked. "We already talked about that, when we agreed for me to get this exclusive, remember?"

"I remember," said Brett. "And I appreciate it, believe me."

"No problem," said Bryan. "I'm a man of my word, just as I'm sure you are."

"He sure is," said Fox, surprised at the words that were coming from his own mouth. "Or we wouldn't be sittin' here talkin'. When this here dude first tol' me he was gonna throw me a party, I thought he was jus' blowin' smoke. But he wasn't. Everythin' he said he was gonna do, he did it, man. Everythin'."

He stopped and looked around the table. Three sets of eyes were fixed on him, and he wondered if he'd opened his big mouth and said the wrong thing again. But when he saw the look on Brett's face, he knew he hadn't. And even if he had, it didn't matter.

Suddenly, the feeling of excitement he'd been fighting all day rose up in him and defeated the fear once and for all. Something wonderful was about to happen, something bigger even than this party.

He could hardly wait.

*

He was tired, but it was the kind of satisfied tired that makes you just want to sit and savor it. And that's what he was doing. All alone in the now-quiet patio, sprawled in a lounge chair as he nursed a final cup of punch, Brett leaned back and closed his eyes, reliving the seemingly nonstop events of the day.

He'd been amazed at the turnout. Although he hadn't been able to get an exact figure, he estimated that there had been at least two hundred kids at the party. And the response of the athletes and entertainers had been even more astounding! He had known that Jacqueline planned to invite several celebrities along with the athletes that he himself had invited, but he'd never dreamed that so many of them would actually come.

He smiled, remembering the looks on the kids' faces as a well-known celebrity would come up and join them in a game of basketball or horseshoes. And when the live entertainment had started—well, he had to admit, even he'd been impressed.

But of all the talented performances of the day, none had surpassed Jacqueline's, particularly her rendition of "Love for a Lifetime." Even as he and Ariane had sat, with Fox between them, listening to Jacqueline sing, his mind had drifted back to the very first time he'd ever heard that song. It was the morning only a few months earlier when he and Fox were in the restaurant, eating Denver omelettes and eyeing each other like two wary jackals. Could it really have been only a few months ago? He'd glanced over at the neat, clean, smiling young man beside him and marveled. As he'd watched him, Jacqueline's words rang in his ears. She was right, and Brett knew it. Love without a commitment was no love at all. There had to be enough to last a lifetime.

The ice tinkled in his glass as he lifted it to his lips, aware suddenly that he was no longer alone. He opened his eyes.

"Hey, dude," said Fox, looking down at him. "What's the matter with you, man? You gettin' so old you can't make it through a party without a nap?" He shook his head, and Brett could see him grinning in the colorful party lights that still surrounded the patio.

Brett smiled. "Nah," he said. "Just saving my energy for the first big game of the season. Won't be long now, you know."

Fox nodded and pulled up a chair. "Yeah, your wife was jus' talkin' to me 'bout that a few minutes ago. We was makin' plans."

Brett raised his eyebrows. "Making plans with my wife behind my back, huh? What's next? You going to start practicing football so you can move in on my job, too?"

Fox shrugged. "Somebody gotta do it, man. Like I said, you gettin' old."

"You are one cold dude," said Brett.

Fox just grinned.

"So," said Brett, "what's my wife up to anyway? You think she's about ready to head home? Everybody else has been gone for almost an hour."

"No tellin'," said Fox. "She's in there with Jacqueline. They talkin' 'bout who was here, what they was wearin' . . . stuff like that."

Brett sighed. "You know what that means, don't you? We might never get out of here."

"You want me to go in there and tell her there's a old person outside needs to go home and get some sleep?" asked Fox.

Brett cut his eyes toward Fox. "Very funny," he said. "Then again, it just might work. I tell you what, if she's not out here in fifteen minutes, let's try it. If I'm going to be accused of getting old, I might as well take advantage of it."

"Yeah, well, I gotta give you one thing," said Fox. "You didn't look too old when you was out there dancin' with your wife."

"Oh, yeah?" said Brett. "Well, thanks for the compliment. And while we're on the subject of dancing, you did a pretty good job yourself, especially when you were out there with Jacqueline. In fact, I'd say you were hot!"

Fox laughed out loud. "Hot, huh? I don't know 'bout that, but I know one thing. I sure never thought I'd be dancin' with somebody like Jacqueline St. James." He shook his head. "Man, she is somethin' else, ain't she?"

"She sure is," said Brett. "In fact, I think you had every guy here jealous from all the attention she was giving you."

"'Specially your friend Ron," said Fox. "You see the way he was watchin' her? Course, I don't think she minded too much. I seen her watchin' him, too. Sorta smilin' and all."

"That bother you?" asked Brett.

Fox looked at him, surprised. "You kiddin', right? Hey man, jus' 'cause I like her singin' don't mean I'm in love with her, like ol' Ernie and the rest of them guys always sayin'. I'm only thirteen, 'member?"

Brett laughed. "Yeah, I remember. I just wasn't sure you did." He paused. "You're not disappointed, are you? I mean, you looked forward to meeting Jacqueline for so long, and now . . ."

Fox didn't answer right away. "Nah," he said finally. "I ain't disappointed. I already done more today than I ever thought I would. It's just . . . see, now I gotta figure out what's next. Can't hang 'round the pit forever. Gettin' too old for that place, man. Been thinkin' 'bout things a lot lately. S'pose it's time to head out for New York."

"New York!" exclaimed Brett, sitting up straight in his chair. "What do you mean, it's time to head out for New York. Are you crazy? You can't just pack up and go off to New York. You can't—"

"I can't what, man?" interrupted Fox, the familiar mask of defiance slipping down over his face again. "What can't I do, huh? Man, I can do anything I want. This here's a free country, 'member? Can't nobody tell me what I can or can't do, you hear? Who you think you are anyway, my daddy or somethin'?"

Brett saw a shudder pass over the boy's body as he spoke those words, but the defiant stare remained. Brett regretted his overreaction to Fox's mention of New York. But he couldn't help it. The thought of Fox running off again, of sleeping on the streets and rummaging through garbage cans, of walking out of his life—it would be like the last few months, the party, all of it, had been for nothing.

"Ariane had an idea once," said Brett, watching Fox closely. The boy's guard came down a little, obviously puzzled by Brett's change of subject.

"She suggested that I consider going into coaching when I retire," Brett went on. "But not at a college or professional level. She was talking about me working with kids like Ernie and Richard and James and . . . well, you know, kids from the hall, places like that. Anyway, I've been thinking about it a lot, and I've decided it's a pretty good idea, but the thing is, I . . . well, I'd need an assistant coach. You know, somebody younger who could help me relate to the kids and—"

"What you really tryin' to say?" asked Fox, his eyes fixed on Brett.

Brett swallowed and took a deep breath. "I'm trying to tell you that I don't want you to go to New York. I don't want you to go anywhere. I'm trying to tell you that I . . . that we . . . Ariane and I . . . have been talking, and we . . . we want you to come and live with us . . . that is, if you want to . . . I mean, if you think . . ."

Fox didn't answer. Brett could see his jaw muscles twitch as he tilted his head and looked up into the sky. Brett waited.

"Been thinkin 'bout lotsa stuff lately," said Fox, his face still turned upward. He paused, and Brett waited. Finally, Fox asked, "You s'pose some wishes really do come true, after all?"

"Sometimes," said Brett. "Yes. Sometimes they do."

They sat in silence for a moment, then Fox said, "You want me to go in the house an' see if your wife's ready to leave yet?"

Brett nodded again. "Sounds like a good idea to me," he said. "Just tell her I think it's time we all went home. The three of us have a lot of things to talk about."

ABOUT THE AUTHORS
===

A former All-Pro defensive tackle with the New York Giants and a member of the Los Angeles Rams' "Fearsome Foursome," **Rosey Grier** retired from professional football in 1968. He has since starred in at least ten movies and has been a guest star in over seventy television roles. A superb singer, Rosey has performed at Carnegie Hall and other prestigious concert halls and cabarets throughout the country. His latest album, *Committed*, was released in 1986 by Word Records.

Shooting Star is Rosey's fifth book, the second co-authored with Kathi Mills. An ordained minister, Rosey is a husband, father, and grandfather, with a heart as big as his 6'6", 300-pound frame. Committed to helping those in need, Rosey is known as a spokesman for the elderly and the inner city youth of America.

An award-winning writer and former newspaper columnist, **Kathi Mills** has published ten books and numerous magazine articles. A frequent speaker at churches, women's groups and writer's conferences, Kathi is a licensed minister and serves on the pastoral care team at her church, South Coast Fellowship of Ventura, California, as a counselor and overseer of small-group ministries. Kathi also serves as chairman of the board of the Employment Aptitude and Placement Agency (EAPA) in Ventura, California. A mother and grandmother, Kathi lives in Santa Paula, California, with her husband, Larry.